TOEFL
托福字彙 中冊

李英松／著

[2500托福字彙]
＋相似詞補充＋詞性連結

輕鬆舉一反三，
有效擴展你的英語字庫！

of pottery.　An ominous view would be threatening.
不祥的 (形容詞)

To speak ruefully means to speak sorrowfully.
悲傷地(副詞)　Dresden is a type of pottery.

task is one which is burdensome.　陶器(名詞，德國陶器)

An epigram is a witty thought.
警語，思想(名詞)　A parody is an imitation.
模仿(名詞)
To be impeccable is to be blameless.
無瑕疵的，完善的 (形容詞)

o sarcasm.
A valid story is sound.

確實的 (形容詞) To affiliate with a group is to join. To mesmerize persons is to hy
結交，聯絡 (不定詞)　迷惑(不定詞)

who is lazy.
An insolent manner is insulting.
fers to unity.　無禮的，侮慢的 (形容詞) 劑藥(隱) (名詞)　懶惰的(形

To be indicted means t

A tithe is given to a government.　控告 (動詞，被動式)

交稅 (名詞)
A vocation is a job.　When you corroborate a stat
職業 (名詞)　確定 (動詞) A person who is fac

a trace. Egotists think of themselves.　好開玩笑的 (形容詞)
自私 (名詞)

An insolent manner is insulting.　An antido
ubscription is a subscription.　無禮的，侮慢的 (形容詞)　對策，認

自序

　　上冊出版以來，讀者響應非常熱烈，一致認為豐富實用，紛紛要求作者趕快出版中冊。就是在這種讀者的熱情鼓勵之下，筆者勇敢加緊腳步，同時以台灣準備 TOEFL (托福)考試及居美期間所收集之資料，加以整理，完成這本書。

　　很多讀者說道，研讀上冊書之後，使他們信心大增，重燃學習英語文之興趣，對於增進自己英語文之能力懷抱著很大的希望，筆者深感安慰！

　　學習英語文，首先要消除恐懼的心裡，絕對不要有學習無力感的狀態出現。人往往喜歡逃避現實，自認意志薄弱而放棄，想要成功就是要有堅持到底的決心，且要有一直往前的渴望。

　　在學習英語文的過程當中，免不了會碰到困難，遇到失敗，此時一定要勇敢面對，接受挑戰。萬萬不能有一朝被蛇咬，十年怕草繩的害怕心態。

　　其次要增厚自己的臉皮，為什麼小孩子學習語文如此之快，主要在於他們心中不認識「臉皮」這兩個字。我們很多人超會找藉口，經常有人說「我為什麼英語文學不好，因為在台灣沒有學習英語文的環境與條件」，又說「我如果去了美國一定可以將英語文的聽、說、讀和寫學習到呱呱叫」真的是如此嗎？有這種念頭，真是異想天開太天真了。事實上並非那麼簡單，想想看，每天三餐去找華人開的餐館解決，聊天看報找華人與華文報紙，買車、修車及買保險找華人經紀人，甚至理個頭髮也找華人，如此這般，在美國待了十年甚至二十年英語文的進步程度真令人懷疑。讀者如果有機會，不妨去美國任何一個 China Town (中國城) 走一趟，體會一下在那兒居住的華人不管是老人，還是中年人，甚至年輕人，用英語與他們溝通，簡直雞同鴨講。

要比別人優秀就要付出比別人多十倍的努力，勤能補拙，持續不斷地鞭策自己，心無旁鶩地去追求夢想，鍥而不捨專心一致地朝目標邁進。不要讓絆腳石阻礙了我們前進的腳步，要從失敗中學習，而不要被它們擊敗。面臨快被壓力擊潰時，而情緒低落到幾乎要失去信心的情況下，就能抵擋住懦弱的身心繼續往前挺進。

給自己正面的鼓勵，相信自己，對於學習英語文抱有堅定信念，制定一個自己最高目標的學習方案。大膽地走出去，敢聽、敢說、敢讀、敢寫再加上敢問，如能這樣的撐下去，通過時間，失敗以及重重阻礙的嚴酷考驗，最後一定可以嚐到甜蜜果實。

萬分感激讀者們的指教，再度感謝姪女李昭儀及姪子李鍊賦姊弟的大力協助，藉此機會感謝妻子池桂榮及女兒李穎宜的全力支持，讓筆者毫無後顧之憂，使得本書得以提早出版。

TOEFL

托福字彙

2501. The **concurrence** (agreement) of the heads of state was totally unexpected.

> 註解　贊同 (名詞)

2502. The surgeon examined the **gash** (deep cut) in the victim's head.

> 註解　創傷 (名詞)

2503. In spite of medical advances, that disease is usually **fatal** (deadly).

> 註解　致命的 (形容詞)

2504. During the 1930's, a long period of **drought** (dry weather) turned the Midwestern United States into a dustbowl.

> 註解　乾旱 (名詞)

2505. Since federal funds have been **reduced** (cut back), a state program is needed tohelp landowners improve their forest lands.

> 註解　減少 (動詞，完成被動式)

2506. **Affluent** (wealthy) nations have an obligation to help their neighbors.

> 註解　富裕的 (形容詞)

2507. The police **confiscated** (seized) the stolen goods.

> 註解　沒收 (動詞)

2508. In last year's Grand Prix, two cars **overturned** (flipped over), severely injuring both drivers.

> 註解　翻覆 (動詞)

2509. The sculptor, Lorenzo Ghiberti, **blended** (combined) medieval grace with Renaissance realism.

> 註解　溶合 (動詞)

2510. After several near disasters, a **controversy** (dispute) has raged over the safety ofnuclear energy.

> 註解　爭論 (名詞)

2511. The price of gold **fluctuates** (changes) daily.

> 註解　波動 (動詞)

2512. The governor's **impromptu** (unrehearsed) remarks caused his political party much embarrassment.

> 註解　臨時的 (形容詞)

2513. A **conscientious** (careful) teacher spends hours preparing for classes and corecting students' papers.

> 註解　謹慎的 (形容詞)

2514. The last weeks before Christmas are usually **hectic** (very busy), as people rush toget last-minute gifts.
   註解　興奮的 (形容詞)

2515. Identical twins are frequently **inseparable** (not able to be parted), they even seemto think alike.
   註解　不能分離的 (形容詞)

2516. In the 1970's many governments' efforts to **curb** (control) inflation were unsuccessful.
   註解　控制 (不定詞)

2517. The price of gold **changes** (fluctuates) daily.
   註解　改變 (動詞)

2518. Few people like someone who **meddles** (interferes) in the affairs of others.
   註解　干擾 (動詞)

2519. The French detective novelist Georges Simenon is one of the most **prolific**(productive) writers of the twentieth century.
   註解　多生產的 (形容詞)

2520. At the stockholder's meeting, the company spokesperson gave the shareholders the **gist** (main idea) of the annual report.
   註解　要領 (名詞)

2521. His extreme nervousness **impeded** (hindered) his ability to speak in front of large group of people.
   註解　阻礙 (動詞)

2522. The Center for Disease Control reported that the epidemic of the viral disease called acute hemorrhagic conjunctivitis shows no signs of **abating** (subsiding).
   註解　降低 (動名詞)

2523. John pulled over to the side of the road to wait until the storm **abated** (subsided).
   註解　消退 (動詞)

2524. Linda was **baffled** (confused) by the confusing road signs, she did not know whether to turn left or go straight.
   註解　迷惑 (動詞，被動式)

2525. There is no **facile** (easy) solution to this very complicated problem.

> 註解　易得的 (形容詞)

2526. The actors were costumed in the original **garb** (clothing) of sixteenth-century England.

> 註解　衣服 (名詞)

2527. All members of the **cabal** (junta) will be prosecuted for treacon.

> 註解　政黨(名詞)

2528. There are six families living in this **small village** (hamlet).

> 註解　小村莊 (名詞)

2529. Jean and Jane are **exactly the same** (identical) twins.

> 註解　完全相同的 (形容詞)

2530. If she continues to **slander** (malign) the integrity of our company, we will sue herfor slander.

> 註解　誹謗 (不定詞)

2531. The stock market reached its **lowest point** (nadir) on Tuesdy and began to rise again in early trading on Wednesday.

> 註解　最低點 (名詞)

2532. The National Guard was called in to **subdue** (quell) the riot.

> 註解　壓制 (不定詞)

2533. Benjamin Franklin is remembered for his **keenness** (sagacity) and wit.

> 註解　精明 (名詞)

2534. The janitor **fastened with a small nail** (tacked) the rug to the floor so that it would not slide.

> 註解　釘住 (動詞片語)

2535. Since she was alone, she opened the door very **cautiously** (warily), leaving the chain lock fastened.

> 註解　小心地 (副詞)

2536. A religious **zealot** (fanatic), Joseph Smith led his congregation from New York to Salt Lake City where they established the Morman Church.

> 註解　信仰熱心者 (名詞)

2537. It is unlawful to aid and **abet** (aid) a criminal.

> 註解　幫助 (不定詞)

2538. The **bald** (without hair) eagle is so named for the white feathers on top of its head.

　　　註解　光頭的 (形容詞)

2539. Even the most **insensitive** (callous) observer would be moved by the news report about the war.

　　　註解　沒感覺的 (形容詞)

2540. Apparently, the victim has been stabbed with a **dagger** (knife) or some other sharp instrument.

　　　註解　短刀 (名詞)

2541. The boys sat on the edge of the pool and **swung** (dangled) their bare feet in the water.

　　　註解　搖擺 (動詞)

2542. Everyone who wears **eccentric** (odd) clothes is not necessarily a punk rocker.

　　　註解　古怪的 (形容詞)

2543. Since he is shy about speaking in public, his voice always **moves hesitatingly,unsteadily** (falters) a little at the beginning of his speeches.

　　　註解　結結巴巴 (動詞)

2544. Because Barbara had been ill, she was **unaware** (uninformed) of the change in the date for the final examination.

　　　註解　不知道的 (形容詞)

2545. Thomas Jefferson's **mansion** (residence), Monticello, is located near Charlottesville, Virginia.

　　　註解　住宅 (名詞)

2546. Be tactful when you tell him because he has a very **mean** (nasty) temper.

　　　註解　卑鄙的 (形容詞)

2547. With time the author's name faded into **the condition of being completely forgotten** (oblivion) and his books were no longer read.

　　　註解　遺忘 (名詞片語)

2548. Some foods which are considered very **savory** (palatable) in one country are noteaten at all in another country.

　　　註解　可口的 (形容詞，同 savoury)

2549. The New York University research team is collaborating with the Department of Health in its **quest** (search) for a cure for arthritis.

> 註解　搜尋 (名詞)

2550. This composition **rambles** (wanders idly, without purpose) from one subject to another; it does not seem to have any point.

> 註解　漫談 (動詞)

2551. Let us forget our former **spiteful hatred** (rancor) and cooperate to solve the pressing problems at hand.

> 註解　仇恨 (名詞)

2552. If this **scandal** (rumor) appears in the newspapers, it will ruin his political career

> 註解　流言 (名詞)

2553. My sister has no **diplomacy** (tact), she always says the wrong thing.

> 註解　外交手腕，圓滑 (名詞)

2554. she was elected chairperson of the committee by a **unanimous** (full accord) vote.

> 註解　全體一致的 (形容詞)

2555. Since he had no responsibilities he decided to take one year to lead a **vagabond's**(wanderer's) life, traveling from town to town and writing about his experiences.

> 註解　流浪者 (名詞)

2556. The police have issued a written **authorization** (warrant) for his arrest.

> 註解　拘票 (名詞)

2557. She **abhorred** (detested) all forms of discrimination on the basis of race or sex.

> 註解　痛恨 (動詞)

2558. The accounting office sends a bill to all of the company's **debtors** (ones who owe)at the end of the month.

> 註解　負債者 (名詞)

2559. The actor's **persuasive, graceful language** (eloquence) moved his audience totears.

> 註解　口才 (名詞片語)

2560. Paul is so **garrulous** (talkative) that once he starts talking, no one can get a wordin.
註解 愛說話的 (形容詞)

2561. It is obvious that this paper has been written in a very **indifferent** (haphazard)way.
註解 偶然的 (形容詞)

2562. She turned her back and **disregard** (ignored) him as he went by.
註解 不理 (動詞)

2563. Because of her **keen** (eager) interest in ancient history, she plans to major in archaeology in college.
註解 熱心的 (形容詞)

2564. Across the nation and around the world, people **lamented** (expressed sorrow) the death of Dr. Martin Luther King.
註解 哀悼 (名詞)

2565. Most basketball players are **lanky** (tall and thin).
註解 修長的 (形容詞)

2566. The national anthem, "he Star Spangled Banner," **lauds** (praises) the Americanflags.
註解 讚美的 (動詞)

2567. Because the mechanic was **extremely careless** (negligent) about fixing the brakeson her car, she was involved in a serious accident.
註解 粗心的 (形容詞片語)

2568. The children were having such a good time that they were **oblivious** (foretful) totheir mother's calling them.
註解 不注意的 (形容詞)

2569. When the banks failed during the Great Depression, many formerly successful businessmen committed suicide rather than live as **very poor persons** (paupers).
註解 窮人 (名詞片語)

2570. The new math gives **meager** (scant) attention to computation; process is considered more important.
註解 不足的 (形容詞，同 meagre)

2571. The final **tally** (account) showed a score of twenty to eleven.
註解 記錄 (名詞)

2572. The sculpture is still **pliable** (waxy) enough to change it a little if you
like.
註解 柔軟的 (形容詞)

2573. They were living in such **wretched** (abject) poverty that they could not
evenafford the bare necessities.
註解 惡劣的 (形容詞)

2574. After passing his exams, he will be admitted to the **bar** (court of law).
註解 律師業 (名詞)

2575. Their grandmother always **slices** (carves) the Thanksgiving Day Turkey.
註解 切片 (動詞)

2576. Professor Rhode's explanation served to obscure rather than to **elucidate**
(makeunderstandable) the theory.
註解 說明 (不定詞)

2577. The children were **charmed** (fascinated) by the clown's antice.
註解 吸引 (動詞，被動式)

2578. The **gash** (deep cut) above his eye required fifteen stitches.
註解 深傷口 (名詞)

2579. The punishment seemed very **cruel** (harsh) for such a harmless joke.
註解 苛刻的 (形容詞)

2580. Unless it stops raining by tomorrow, a flood appears **impending**
(imminent).
註解 即將來臨的 (形容詞)

2581. Bill likes to fish in his **leisure** (unoccupied) time.
註解 閒暇的 (形容詞)

2582. Dr. Briggs always writes her corrections in the **margines** (verges) of her
students'papers.
註解 邊緣 (名詞)

2583. By the time the mountain climbers had reached the snowy top, their hands
and feet were **paralyzed** (numb) with cold.
註解 麻木的 (形容詞，同 paralysed)

2584. The meaning of this poem is very **obscure** (ambiguous).
註解 不清楚的 (形容詞)

2585. The little boy promised not to **peek** (peep) at his Christmas presents while his parents were gone.

　　| 註解 |　偷看 (不定詞)

2586. The Constitution of the United States was **corroborated** (ratified) by all of the thirteen orginal states during the years 1787-1790.

　　| 註解 |　確定 (動詞，被動式)

2587. If you **scatter** (sprinkle) salt on the sidewalk, it will melt the ice.

　　| 註解 |　撒放 (動詞)

2588. Someone must have **meddled** (tampered) with the TV; the picture was okay a fewminutes ago and now it is fuzzy.

　　| 註解 |　玩弄 (動詞，完成式)

2589. His **uncouth** (boorish) manners made everyone at the table uncomfortable.

　　| 註解 |　粗魯的 (形容詞)

2590. Since chain stores buy merchandise in quantity, they are able to **sell at a lesserprice than** (undercut) their small competitors.

　　| 註解 |　削價 (不定詞片語)

2591. Her **vanity** (vainglory) caused her to lie about her age.

　　| 註解 |　虛榮 (名詞)

2592. The camera followed the **nonconforming** (wayward) flight of the sea gull.

　　| 註解 |　不規則的 (形容詞)

2593. The driver stopped the cab so **abruptly** (unexpectedly) that he was hit by the carbehind him.

　　| 註解 |　突然地 (副詞)

2594. The highway patrol put up a(n) **obstruction** (barricade) in front of the accident.

　　| 註解 |　障礙物 (名詞)

2595. Early every morning the fishermen **cast** (throw out or down) their nets into thesea.

　　| 註解 |　投擲 (動詞)

2596. Mr. Harris did not have the **propriety** (decency) to give us thirty days notice before resigning.

　　| 註解 |　適當行爲 (名詞)

2597. She could only remember part of the **elusive** (elusory) melody.
   註解　難懂的 (形容詞)

2598. Man's first landing on the moon was a **feat** (achievement) of great daring.
   註解　成就 (名詞)

2599. After he had considered the problem more carefully, he regretted having made such a **hasty** (fleet) decision.
   註解　匆忙的 (形容詞)

2600. Mr. Williams is a good referee; he is always as **equitable** (impartial) as possible.
   註解　公平的 (形容詞)

2601. The U.S. **marshal** (law officer) will carry out the orders of this court.
   註解　執法人員 (名詞)

2602. His **servile** (obsequious) submission to his boss's ideas disgusted his fellow workers.
   註解　卑屈的 (形容詞)

2603. The bullet **pierced** (penetrated) the victim's chest and lodged itself just to their right of his heart.
   註解　穿入 (動詞)

2604. A flash-fire **demolished** (razed) the office building before it could be controlled.
   註解　毀壞 (動詞)

2605. She is very **unsophisticated** (ingenuous) for a woman who has traveled so widely.
   註解　天眞的 (形容詞)

2606. Nectarines are **mutation** (variation) of peaches.
   註解　變種 (名詞)

2607. She used every **wile** (maneuver) that she could think of in order to trick him into helping her.
   註解　巧計 (名詞)

2608. Bill did not hear the telephone because he was completely **engrossed** (absorbed)in his reading.
   註解　全神貫注的 (形容詞)

2609. If one has an open mind, it is not difficult to **apperciate** (respect) another's point of view.

註解 尊重 (不定詞)

2610. In spite of his many faults, paul is very **dedicated** (devoted) to his mother.

註解 忠誠的 (形容詞)

2611. There are some people who **advocate** (recommend) relaxation over work.

註解 提倡 (動詞)

2612. The evaluation stated that the secretary's work has been **satisfactory** (adequate).

註解 適當的 (形容詞)

2613. After watching the sunset, I was left with a very **tranquil** (peaceful) feeling.

註解 平靜的 (形容詞)

2614. An employer must verify that the applicants have the proper **qualifications**(credentials).

註解 證件 (名詞)

2615. The columnist's remarks were **inappropriate** (unsuitable) and rude.

註解 不適合的 (形容詞)

2616. Allowing books to be sold at the exhibition would **set a precedent** (establish apattern) for future conventions.

註解 設前例 (動詞片語)

2617. The argument, although understandable, was not very **convincing** (persuasive).

註解 能說服的 (形容詞)

2618. The lawyers obliged the newspaper to **retract** (withdraw) their allegations.

註解 收回 (不定詞)

2619. As a result of the **expansion** (enlargement) of the public transit system, the university will disband its shuttle bus service.

註解 擴張 (名詞)

2620. It is often difficult to **reveal** (divulge) one's true feelings to others.

註解 透露 (不定詞)

2621. Being **meek** (humble), the stranger had difficulty making friends.

註解 溫順的 (形容詞)

2622. After an extended break, the class **resumed** (continued).

註解 繼續 (動詞)

2623. The child **charged** (ran) down the steps.

註解 跑向 (動詞)

2624. The gem is so rare it could be **fake** (simulated).

註解 偽造的 (形容詞)

2625. **Prejudice** (Bias) towards minorities probably stems from fear of the unknown.

註解 偏見 (名詞)

2626. The bank needed some **assurance** (quarantee) that the loan would be repaid.

註解 擔保 (名詞)

2627. Self-confidence is a(n) **integral** (essential) factor for a successful person.

註解 必要的 (形容詞)

2628. When the wind died, the sailboat **drifted** (floated) toward the beach.

註解 沖飄 (動詞)

2629. The sign requested that we **extinguish** (put out) all fires before leaving the camp ground.

註解 撲滅 (動詞)

2630. The theater critics thought the movie was **horrendous** (dreadful), and the audience agreed with them.

註解 恐怖的 (形容詞)

2631. Invitations were **extended** (offered) to everyone who had worked on the project.

註解 贈送 (動詞，被動式)

2632. The politican's manner was **blatantly** (openly) dishonest, so the election result were not a surprise.

註解 非常明顯地 (副詞)

2633. Jane looked at **a(n) assortment of** (variety of) necklaces before choosing one with green beads.

註解 一系列 (名詞片語)

2634. Success is most deserved by **amiable** (good-humored) people.
> 註解 友善的 (形容詞)

2635. The roof of the house was **practically** (almost) falling in and the front steps wererotting away.
> 註解 幾乎 (副詞)

2636. The dog's **furtive** (secretive) actions made me worry about him.
> 註解 偷偷的 (形容詞)

2637. A(n) **ulterior** (Concealed) motive is behind the question.
> 註解 隱藏 (形容詞)

2638. Their **inept** (inappropriate) handing of our account made us reevaluate our relationship with them.
> 註解 不適合的 (形容詞)

2639. Mark is a **kindred** (related) soul, so my friends will like him.
> 註解 類似的 (形容詞)

2640. The chart showed the amount of money spent on food compared with the amount spent on **recreation** (amusement).
> 註解 娛樂 (名詞)

2641. There is no resolution to this **conflict** (disagreement).
> 註解 爭執 (名詞)

2642. The article **alluded to** (referred to) the devastation in the countryside, caused by the wind storm.
> 註解 歸之於 (動詞，通常與 to 連用)

2643. The popular singer was as **ludicrous** (comical) in his dress as he was in his speech.
> 註解 可笑的 (形容詞)

2644. There was a long **interval** (pause) before the music began.
> 註解 中斷時間 (名詞)

2645. The **zealous** (ardent) demonstrators were ignored by the media.
> 註解 熱心的 (形容詞)

2646. The teacher explained the **nuances** (subtleties) in Frost's poetry to the class.
> 註解 微妙，些微差異 (名詞)

2647. A **brisk** (lively) walk in cool weather is invigorating.
> 註解 輕快的 (形容詞)

2648. No one ever knew the reason for the **enmity** (hatred) between the two families.

註解 仇恨 (名詞)

2649. The **opportune** (appropriate) moment had arrived, but few took advantage of it.

註解 合時宜的 (形容詞)

2650. Some tall people often feel **clumsy** (awkward).

註解 笨拙的 (形容詞)

2651. The teacher thought the aspiring writer's essays were **verbose** (redundant).

註解 冗長的、太多字的 (形容詞)

2652. The travel agent tried to **tantalize** (tempt) me with details of a proposed trip to the islands.

註解 折磨、勸誘 (不定詞)

2653. History is best learned from **contemporary** (concurrent) sources.

註解 同時代的 (形容詞)

2654. All typing errors must be **deleted** (erased) from this memo.

註解 消除 (動詞，被動式)

2655. The organizer's **intransigent** (stubborn) manner helped her get her way.

註解 不妥協的 (形容詞)

2656. The natural elements **obliterated** (erased) the writing from the walls of the monument.

註解 消滅 (動詞)

2657. This flag **symbolizes** (represents) what is imporant to our country.

註解 象徵 (動詞)

2658. The name of that **ferocious** (fierce) looking animal is unforgettable.

註解 兇猛的 (形容詞)

2659. The humidity made us more **lethargic** (indifferent) than usual.

註解 昏昏欲睡的 (形容詞)

2660. The **sealed** (closed) chambers of the ancient pharaohs were the goal of the expedition.

註解 封閉的 (形容詞)

2661. The manager was found to be **harassing** (bothering) his employees.

註解 煩惱 (現在分詞)

2662. People usually think cats are naturally **savage** (ferocious), but it depends on the type of cat.

註解 兇猛的 (形容詞)

2663. One is not always able to choose one's **associates** (colleagues).

註解 夥伴 (名詞)

2664. Generosity is believed to be **an innate** (natural) quality of man.

註解 天生的 (形容詞)

2665. The valley, wild and **inaccessible** (impenetrable), had been the haunt of bandits.

註解 難以達到的 (形容詞)

2666. The greatest physical **distinction** (difference) between humans and apes is the hollow space humans have under their chins.

註解 區別 (名詞)

2667. Children often **imitate** (copy) their parents.

註解 模仿 (動詞)

2668. The film rights were **negotiated** (arranged) by the author's lawyers.

註解 商議 (動詞，被動式)

2669. The two personalities have few similarities and are basically **incompatible**(antagonistic).

註解 不能共存的，相反的 (形容詞)

2670. The administration **took for granted** (assumed) that we would agree.

註解 假定 (動詞片語)

2671. The results of experiments on the intelligence of monkeys have not been **conclusive** (final).

註解 確定的 (形容詞)

2672. More responsibility and higher salaries are **incentives** for (inducements for)on-the -job training.

註解 鼓勵 (名詞)

2673. The most recent research **indicates** (suggests) that dinosaurs were warm blooded animals.

註解 指出，認為 (動詞)

2674. The tenor's singing **captivated** (enchanted) the audience.

註解 迷惑 (動詞)

2675. The product to use to **douse** (extinguish) a grease fire is salt or baking soda.

> 註解　去除 (不定詞)

2676. Contrary to popular belief, Cleopatra, the famous Egyptian queen, was Greek,spoke six languages, and was **a(n) brilliant** (intelligent) military strategist.

> 註解　有才能的 (形容詞)

2677. A review of the history of economics shows a recession may **precede** (comebefore) a depression.

> 註解　在前 (動詞)

2678. The use of the microcomputer is as **pedestrian** (common) as the use of thetelephone.

> 註解　平凡的 (形容詞)

2679. The **suspect** (accused) is being held for arraignment witout bail.

> 註解　嫌疑犯 (名詞)

2680. The punishment should reflect the **severity** (seriousness) of the crime.

> 註解　嚴重 (名詞)

2681. The price of gold **fluctuated** (varied) and then plummeted on the world marketlast quarter.

> 註解　浮動 (動詞)

2682. The **quaint** (curious) style of the homes is typical of this region.

> 註解　古怪的 (形容詞)

2683. Many animals **collect a supply of** (accumulate) food for the winter.

> 註解　貯藏 (動詞片語)

2684. Congressional debate over the passage of this **controversial** (disputatious) bill was inevitable.

> 註解　有爭議的 (形容詞)

2685. The picture illustrates the **compassion** (feeling) the artist has for his native land.

> 註解　感情 (名詞)

2686. The **provisions** (clauses) of the contract exclude any division of the property for 50 years.

> 註解　條款 (名詞)

2687. The children in the neighborhood have a club that **excludes** (leaves out) everyone over eight.

註解　排除（動詞）

2688. In the United States a **typical** (characteristic) work day is eight hours long.

註解　典型的（形容詞）

2689. The drought caused escalation of prices and **depletion** (exhaustion) of supplies.

註解　空虛（名詞）

2690. History has shown that rulers do not **relinquish** (abandon) power easily.

註解　放棄（動詞）

2691. What is the **gist** (point) of the article?

註解　要點（名詞）

2692. The worker's **aggressive** (assertive) personality kept him from having many friends.

註解　武斷的（形容詞）

2693. Modern music is usually characterized by a remarkable **dissonance** (discord).

註解　不調和（名詞）

2694. A good magician can make an elephant **vanish** (disappear).

註解　消失（動詞，使役動詞 make 之後接原型動詞）

2695. Because the teenager was **ashamed** (humiliated) that she failed her driving test, she would not come home.

註解　慚愧的（形容詞）

2696. People said that personalities of the young married couple were **discordant**(incompatible).

註解　不一致的（形容詞）

2697. The debate team found their opponents' arguments illogical and consequently **irrefutable** (incontrovertible).

註解　不能反駁的（形容詞）

2698. The fundrarisers claim their motives are **nonpolitical** (nonpartisan).

註解　不同夥的（形容詞）

2699. The manager does not tolerate **imperfections** (defects) in himself or in others.

　註解　不完美，缺點 (名詞)

2700. The soldiers' **disobedience** (insubordination) made them subject to disciplinary action.

　註解　不服從 (名詞)

2701. We all, at times, wish we were **inconspicuous** (invisible).

　註解　不太引人注意的 (形容詞)

2702. The newspaper described the **amoral** (unethical) activities of the terrorist group indetail.

　註解　不道德的 (形容詞)

2703. The **antidote** (remedy) was not where the doctor had left it.

　註解　消毒藥 (名詞)

2704. The **drawback to** (disadvantage of) winning is the notoriety one receives.

　註解　缺點 (名詞片語)

2705. The ercluse's **mistreatment** of (cruelty to) animals did not go unnoticed.

　註解　虐待 (名詞)

2706. The speech, contrary to what we all expected, was **inoffensive** (harmless).

　註解　不令人厭的 (形容詞)

2707. **Inanimate** (inorganic) items are catalogued by their Latin names.

　註解　無生命的 (形容詞)

2708. My aunt's reasoning was clever but **unsubstantiated** (invalid).

　註解　沒有被証實的 (形容詞)

2709. Since an amoeba's old cell will divide into two new cells, it may be called **undying** (immortal).

　註解　不死的 (形容詞)

2710. Eating and drinking too much increases the size of the **belly** (abdomen).

　註解　腹部 (名詞)

2711. **Notification** (Announcement) of taxes due will be sent in the near future.

　註解　通知 (名詞)

2712. Children may **ridicule** (make fun of) other children new to a neighborhood.

　註解　嘲笑 (動詞)

2713. My grandmother always had **kind** (good) words to say about everyone she knew.

註解　慈愛的 (形容詞)

2714. A botanist can identify a flower by its shape and its **scent** (smell).

註解　嗅出 (名詞)

2715. In times of war, the army will draft all **able-bodied** (strong) men.

註解　強壯的 (形容詞)

2716. The comedian has a tendency to be more **absurd** (ridiculous) than funny.

註解　荒謬的 (形容詞)

2717. Regular **upkeep** (maintenance) of an auto will improve its efficiency.

註解　保養 (名詞)

2718. The terrier was **kind of** (somewhat) short with long, black hair.

註解　約略 (名詞)

2719. The **likelihood** (probability) of the strike ending before the tourist season is not high.

註解　可能性 (名詞)

2720. The court **nullified** (annulled) the agreement after months of debate.

註解　廢棄 (動詞)

2721. She **beckoned** (beaconed) them to enter her office.

註解　招手 (動詞)

2722. Shirley was **castigated** (reproved) by her mother for staying out too late.

註解　斥責 (動詞，被動式)

2723. Radiation is **given off** (emitted) as a consequence of a nuclear reaction.

註解　放射 (動詞，被動式)

2724. The old man was too **infirm** (frail) to walk.

註解　虛弱的 (形容詞)

2725. His **gauche** (tactless) manner embarrassed his family.

註解　笨拙的 (形容詞)

2726. Because of the **misty** (hazy) weather, there were only a few sunbathers at the beach.

註解　有霧的 (形容詞)

2727. When the North and the South signed the treaty, which ended the Civil War, they agreed that from that day forth the United States would be one united and **impartible** (indivisible) nation.

　　　註解　不可分的 (形容詞)

2728. You seem to be in a very **pensive** (meditative) mood; I hope that nothing is wrong.

　　　註解　沉思的 (形容詞)

2729. Each team will have a final opportunity to **contradict** (rebut) before the debate isjudged.

　　　註解　否認 (不定詞)

2730. The children **scooped up** (dug) the snow with their hands to build a snow man.

　　　註解　挖掘 (動詞片語)

2731. The centerpiece is a silver candelabra with red roses and six long, **tapered** (sharp) candles.

　　　註解　尖細的 (形容詞)

2732. Let's decide upon a **tentative** (uncertain) date for the next meeting; we can always change it if we need to.

　　　註解　暫時的 (形容詞)

2733. The Sears store has a(n) **assortment** (variety) of styles to choose from.

　　　註解　多種類 (名詞)

2734. Navy blue shoes and gloves would be perfect **increments** (accessories) for this white suit.

　　　註解　配件 (名詞)

2735. He was on his best **demeanour** (deportment) because he wanted to imoress his girl friend's family.

　　　註解　風度，舉止 (名詞，同 demeanor)

2736. In winter the neighborhood children like to go sledding down the **declivity**(decline) at the end of the street.

　　　註解　下斜面 (名詞)

2737. Some universities have been accused of placing too much **significance** (emphasis) on athletics and not enough on academics.

　　　註解　強調，重要 (名詞)

2738. Every hour the captain **conveys over** (ferries) tourists across New York Harbor to see the Statue of Liberty on Liberty Island.

註解 運送 (動詞片語)

2739. We received such a **well-disposed** (genial) welcome that we felt at home immediately.

註解 熱誠的 (形容詞)

2740. Traffic is a always **jammed** (heavy) during rush hours.

註解 擁擠的 (形容詞)

2741. Although he did not say so directly, he **implied** (inferred) that he would be able to help us.

註解 暗示 (動詞)

2742. You should not need more than a **light** (not heavy) coat because the weather isquite warm.

註解 輕便的 (形容詞)

2743. Their landlady likes to **meddle in** (tamper with) her tenants' affairs

註解 干擾 (不定詞)

2744. Jan is such a(n) **mulish** (intractable) person, I know that we will never be able to change her mind.

註解 倔強的 (形容詞)

2745. Please tear along the **perforated** (pierced) line.

註解 穿孔的 (形容詞)

2746. This objective is beyond the **scope** (extent) of our project.

註解 範圍 (名詞)

2747. This tea is **lukewarm** (tepid); please bring me a hot cup.

註解 微溫的 (形容詞)

2748. He spoke with such **vehemence** (intensity) that everyone knew how angry he was.

註解 激烈 (名詞)

2749. The slaves obeyed their master because they feared his **dudgeon** (wrath).

註解 憤怒 (名詞)

2750. The new tourist hotel will have **accommodations** (food and lodging) for more than one thousand people.

註解 住宿 (名詞)

2751. ″You don't need **bawl** (bellow); I'm not going to hurt you″ , said the dentist.

　　註解　大叫 (動詞)

2752. Tornadoes left several Midwestern towns in a state of **tumult** (disarray).

　　註解　騷動 (名詞)

2753. The city buses are in **decrepit** (enfeebled) condition, but the transit company doesnot have funds to purchase new ones.

　　註解　老舊的 (形容詞)

2754. Dennis felt that he had to **emulate** (excel) the success of his famous father.

　　註解　超過 (不定詞)

2755. Romeo's and Juliet's families had been **feuding** (engaging in a long, bitter hostility) for generations.

　　註解　宿仇 (現在分詞)

2756. What I thought was a copy was a **real** (genuine) Rembrandt.

　　註解　眞實的 (形容詞)

2757. Since he did not have time to prepare a talk, his comments were completely **extemporaneous** (improvised).

　　註解　沒準備的 (形容詞)

2758. Several **limbs** (offshoot) fell from the old, dead tree during the storm last night.

　　註解　分枝 (名詞)

2759. Hurricanes periodically **threaten** (menace) the Gulf Coast.

　　註解　威脅 (動詞)

2760. Too many signs and billboards **choke** (clog) the view along the highway.

　　註解　妨礙 (動詞)

2761. Although the acrobat's performance seemed very **perilous** (risky), it was not asdangerous as it looked.

　　註解　危險的 (形容詞)

2762. Mark had his license suspended for **heedless** (rash) driving.

　　註解　不留心的 (形容詞)

2763. After he was promoted to vice president of the company, he became **scornful** (disdainful) of his former friends.

　　註解　輕視的 (形容詞)

2764. Permanent press shirts are convenient because the **wrinkles** (creases) hang out with little or no ironing.

　　 註解　皺紋 (名詞)

2765. The **fissures** (chasms) in this area were caused by glaciers as they receded duringthe Ice Age.

　　 註解　裂縫 (名詞)

2766. Chris **dedicated** (inscribed) her thesis to her father.

　　 註解　獻出 (動詞)

2767. May you have good luck in everything that you **endeavor** (labor) to do.

　　 註解　努力 (動詞)

2768. This photograph does not **eulogize** (flatter) you; you are much more attractive.

　　 註解　稱讚 (動詞)

2769. These seeds will **germinate** (sprout) more quickly if you put them in a warmer place.

　　 註解　發芽 (動詞)

2770. If he had **marked** (observed) his broker's advice, he would not need to borrow money now.

　　 註解　留心 (動詞)

2771. After a week of **incessant** (perpetual) rain, the river overflowed its banks.

　　 註解　不間斷的 (形容詞)

2772. Although he said he had not hurt his leg, he was **laming** (limping) when he left the soccer field.

　　 註解　一跛一跛的 (形容詞)

2773. He asked his mother to **darn** (patch) the hole in the pocket of his jeans.

　　 註解　縫補 (不定詞)

2774. Those dark clouds look **ominous** (portentous); it will probably rain before evening.

　　 註解　徵兆的 (形容詞)

2775. I have had several summer jobs, but I have never been **invariably** (permanently) employed.

　　 註解　永久不變的 (副詞)

2776. It is important to **scrape** (abrade) off all of the old paint before you refinish your furniture.

> 註解 　刮除 (不定詞)

2777. We will repeat the experiment twice in order to **substantiate** (verify) the results.

> 註解 　證實 (不定詞)

2778. The stranger **accosted** (confronted boldly) her as she was unlocking her door.

> 註解 　招呼，面對 (動詞)

2779. Her parents had taught her that she should behave like a **chaste** (elegant) and modest young lady.

> 註解 　純潔的，高雅的 (形容詞)

2780. Because of a **blemish** (flaw) in his hearing the teacher gave him a seat in the front row.

> 註解 　缺陷 (名詞)

2781. Perhaps if you took vitamins you would have more **potency** (vigor).

> 註解 　力量 (名詞)

2782. The thieves **sped** (fled) when they heard the alarm.

> 註解 　逃跑 (動詞)

2783. Besides tuition and books, you will need about one hundred dollars for **contingent** (incidental) expenses.

> 註解 　意外的 (形容詞)

2784. There was only one cloud in an otherwise **limpid** (lucid) sky.

> 註解 　明亮的 (形容詞)

2785. You may **leave out** (omit) questions nine and ten because they do not apply to students.

> 註解 　漏掉 (動詞片語)

2786. It is not **allowable** (permissible) to smoke in the front seats; if you wish to smoke, please move to the back of the bus.

> 註解 　允許的 (形容詞)

2787. When we questioned him about the accident, he did not seem to have any **remembrance** (recollection) of what had happened.

> 註解 　記憶 (名詞)

2788. The pudding should **coagulate** (thicken) as it cools.
   註解　凝固 (動詞)

2789. Danny is a **versatile** (adaptable) athlete; he can compete in either soccer or track.
   註解　多方面的 (形容詞)

2790. **Henceforth** (From now on) at this University we shall observe the first week in February as International week.
   註解　從今以後 (副詞)

2791. While the Lawrence family was on vacation, their mail **heaped up** (piled up) in the box.
   註解　堆積 (動詞)

2792. Since she did not speak a foreign language, she was **nonplussed** (muddled) by the menu at the international restaurant.
   註解　困惑 (動詞，被動式)

2793. According to the Weather Bureau, it will be **chilly** (gelid) tomorrow with a 50 percent chance of showers.
   註解　寒冷的 (形容詞)

2794. In spite of several corrective operations, his foot is still badly **deformed** (malformed).
   註解　變形的 (形容詞)

2795. The diplomate from both countries were **enervated** (debilitated) by the long series of talks.
   註解　衰弱 (動詞，被動式)

2796. A draft caused the candle to **flicker** (shimmer) and go out.
   註解　閃爍 (不定詞)

2797. The finalists in the Miss Universe pageant are all very **fascinating** (glamorous) women.
   註解　迷人的 (形容詞)

2798. We laughed all through the movie; it was **cheerful** (hilarious).
   註解　高興的 (形容詞)

2799. After such **trenchant** (incisive) criticism from the press, it is doubtful that the city council will approve the project.
   註解　尖銳的 (形容詞)

2800. Most **meteors** (celestial bodies) burn up when they enter the Earth's atmosphere.

　　　 |註解| 隕石 (名詞)

2801. Almost everyone was bored by his lengthy **parlance** (oration); it seemes that he would never stop talking.

　　　 |註解| 談話 (名詞)

2802. Bathing in the Fountain of Youth is supposed to assure **imperishable** (eternal) beauty.

　　　 |註解| 忘不掉的，不變的 (形容詞)

2803. Since the couple could not **reconcile** (harmonize) their differences, they decided to get a divorce.

　　　 |註解| 協調 (動詞)

2804. Although the model looks good on the surface, it will not bear **minute inquiry** (scrutiny).

　　　 |註解| 細察 (名詞片語)

2805. Mr. Thompson is so **frugal** (sparing) that he is able to save more than half of his weekly salary.

　　　 |註解| 節儉的 (形容詞)

2806. These ruins are the **vestiges** (tokens) of an ancient civilization.

　　　 |註解| 遺跡 (名詞)

2807. The meeting began with a review of the relevant issues, but it soon dissolved into small group **bickering** (wrangling) over unimportant points of protocol.

　　　 |註解| 爭吵 (現在分詞)

2808. Each of the children had **chores** (tasks) to do before going to school; Kathy had togather the eggs and feed the chickens.

　　　 |註解| 零工 (名詞)

2809. He **deliberately** (intentionally) left the letter on her desk so that she would find it.

　　　 |註解| 有意地 (副詞)

2810. Her beautiful clothes **intensify** (enhance) her appearance.

　　　 |註解| 加強 (動詞)

2811. Newspaper is too **lacking solidarity, strength** (flimsy) to be used for a kite; the wind would tear it to pieces.

註解　脆弱的 (形容詞片語)

2812. The salesman was such **loquacious** (glib) talker the he sold her several items that she did not need.

註解　甜言蜜語的 (形容詞)

2813. Our patient seems more **agile** (spry) today; he must be feeling better.

註解　活潑的 (形容詞)

2814. He arranged the computer cards with **meticulous** (finical) care, making sure that each one was in the correct order.

註解　注意細節的 (形容詞)

2815. Although he offered her a higher salary, he could not **impel** (entice) her to accept aposition with his firm.

註解　驅使 (動詞)

2816. A photographer encourged her to become a model because of her slim figure and **genteel** (refined) features.

註解　優雅的 (形容詞)

2817. A meter is divided into one hundred **ingredients** (fractions) of one centimeter.

註解　組成分 (名詞)

2818. A(n) **assemblage** (horde) of well-wishers gathered at the airport to see him off.

註解　聚集 (名詞)

2819. When a train comes in on the tracks below, the railroad station **oscilates** (vibrates).

註解　震動 (動詞)

2820. This cigarette has an **acrid** (bitter) taste; I guess I have been smoking too much today.

註解　苦苦的 (形容詞)

2821. Jim is eager to see his old school **chums** (intimate friends) at the class reunion.

註解　密友 (名詞)

2822. Although the car was **demolished** (torn down) in the accident, no one was seriously injured.

　　註解　毀壞的 (形容詞)

2823. The smell of breakfast cooking **tempts** (decoy) him to get up.

　　註解　吸引 (動詞)

2824. The truck ran off the road and **flipped** (overturned) over in the ditch.

　　註解　翻覆 (動詞)

2825. Her eyes **glittered** (glinted) with tears as she struggled to control her emotions.

　　註解　閃爍 (動詞)

2826. If you give me an **inkling** (innuendo) I am sure that I can guess the answer.

　　註解　暗示 (名詞)

2827. An **accusation** (indictment) will be handed down by the grand jury when it convenes on Monday.

　　註解　控告，起訴 (名詞)

2828. That **loafer** (idler) will never get the job done.

　　註解　懶惰鬼 (名詞)

2829. It is not easy for him to **mingle** (associate) with people because he is very shy.

　　註解　交往 (不定詞)

2830. Even though no one was seriously injured, the plane crash was a terrible **ordeal** (difficult or painful experience) for the passengers.

　　註解　嚴酷之經驗 (名詞)

2831. When the time limit was up, the examiner **clutched** (grabbed) the tests from those students who were still working.

　　註解　抓緊 (動詞)

2832. The picture fell to the floor with a **dull sound** (thump).

　　註解　砰砰聲 (名詞片語)

2833. Although she had never traveled herself, she received **vicarious** (substitutive) pleasure from reading about interesting places.

　　註解　代替的 (形容詞)

2834. There is parking lot **juxtaposed** (adjacent) to the auditorium.

> 註解　並列的 (形容詞)

2835. No-fault insurance does not require anyone to accept the **blame** (culpability) for an auto accident in order to be reimbursed by the company.

> 註解　責任 (名詞)

2836. Mrs. Ferris **dented** (indented) the fender of her car when she hit the parking meter.

> 註解　弄凹 (動詞)

2837. Mr. Baker is **resentful** (envious) of his neighbor's new swimming pool.

> 註解　嫉妒的 (形容詞)

2838. When they tried to run in the deep snow, they **moved awkwardly** (floundered) and fell.

> 註解　深陷 (動詞片語)

2839. If you do not understand some of the technical terms, refer to the **glossary** (vocabulary).

> 註解　字辭典 (名詞)

2840. The cheerleaders were **husky** (grating) from yelling at the basketball game.

> 註解　喉乾的 (形容詞)

2841. Television commercials **spur** (induce) people to buy new products.

> 註解　鼓吹 (動詞)

2842. She likes her job even though she **loathes** (detests) getting up early in the morning in order to get to work on time.

> 註解　討厭 (動詞)

2843. It will be difficult to **adjust** (reform) the agreement after it has been signed becauseall changes will be subject to Congressional approval.

> 註解　修改 (不定詞)

2844. In order to increase the **output** (yield), a night shift will be hired at the factory.

> 註解　產量 (名詞)

2845. We need one hundred more signatures before we take the **petition** (suit) to the governor.

註解　請願 (名詞)

2846. Before proceeding with the experiment, the lab assistant **reiterated** (iterated) what the professor had said in his last lecture.

註解　重覆的 (形容詞)

2847. General Casey could not convince the **sentry** (guard) to allow him through the gate without proper identification.

註解　哨兵，警衛 (名詞)

2848. Please straighten the lampshade; it is **slant** (sloped) a little bit to the left.

註解　傾斜的 (形容詞)

2849. After a week of constant **vigilance** (watchfulness) and intensive care, the patient began to respond to treatment.

註解　觀察 (名詞)

2850. The army's retreat left the city **vulnerable** (delicate) to enemy attack.

註解　脆弱的 (形容詞)

2851. Her boss **admonished** (forewarned) her against being late for work again.

註解　警告 (動詞)

2852. Despite his sister's **coaxing** (blandishment), he refused to lie to their parents.

註解　誘哄 (名詞)

2853. A **vociferous** (clamorous) contingent of demonstrators marched up the hill to the Capitol.

註解　喧嘩的 (形容詞)

2854. In the classic work, Gone with the Wind, Margaret Mitchell **depicts** (describes) the South during the Civil War and Reconstruction period.

註解　描述 (動詞)

2855. Mrs. Bradley's will divide her estate **equitably** (reasonably) among her three sons.

註解　公平地 (副詞)

2856. Baby chicks have **airy** (fluffy) feathers.

註解　輕快的，絨毛的 (形容詞)

2857. His **intent** (objective) is to receive his Ph. D. in electrical engineering.

註解　計劃，目標 (名詞)

2858. News of an unidentified flying object was a **trick** (hoax).

註解　捏造 (名詞)

2859. This experiment can be repeated with any **immobile** (enert) object, for example, arock or a piece of wood.

註解　固定的，無生命的 (形容詞)

2860. The thieves hid their **plunder** (loot) in a deserted warehouse.

註解　掠奪品 (名詞)

2861. She was offended by his **outrageous** (offensive) remark.

註解　侵害的 (形容詞)

2862. The **overall** (comprehensive) charges for the parts and labor are itemized in your statement.

註解　全部的 (形容詞)

2863. Mr. Jones is so **sluggish** (phlegmatic) that he never gets excited about anything.

註解　遲鈍的 (形容詞)

2864. The doctor told her to stay in bed for a few more days in order to avoid suffering a **relapse** (return of an illness).

註解　復發 (名詞)

2865. Unless an agreement is reached by the end of the week, the two countries will **sunder** (sever) diplomatic relations.

註解　斷絕 (動詞)

2866. The concert had already begun, so he entered the back of the hall **on tiptoe** (stealthily).

註解　悄悄地，用腳趾尖走 (介詞片語，做副詞)

2867. Mr. Moore is quite a family man; he **adores** (idolizes) his wife and children.

註解　非常愛護 (動詞)

2868. In winter, when the trees are bare, and snow covers the ground, the landscape is very **bleak** (desolate).

註解　荒涼的 (形容詞)

2869. I feel that I must **deprecate** (disapprove) the allocation of funds for such an unproductive.

註解　反對 (動詞)

2870. His speeches are so **evasive** (equivocal) that no one is sure of what he really means.

註解　模模糊糊的 (形容詞)

2871. She felt very **asinine** (fatuous) after she realized her mistake.

註解　愚笨的 (形容詞)

2872. George is a very **grasping** (rapacious) man; the more money he acquires, the more he wants.

註解　貪心的 (形容詞)

2873. The picnic area was **infested** (troublesome) with mosquitoes.

註解　困擾的 (形容詞)

2874. The young mother hummed a **cradlesong** (lullaby) to her sleeping baby.

註解　搖籃曲 (名詞)

2875. Tom was fired because his boss caught him **pilfering** (stealing) supplies from the storeroom.

註解　偷竊 (動名詞)

2876. I am happy to recommend her for this position because I have always found her tobe an efficient and **authentic** (trustworthy).

註解　可靠的 (形容詞)

2877. She was **loath** (averse) to accept the invitation because she was not sure that she could find a baby-sitter.

註解　勉強的，不願意的 (形容詞)

2878. Even after he had it drycleaned, his old coat still looked rather **faded** (shabby).

註解　破舊的 (形容詞)

2879. He is not **forbearing** (tolerant) of other people's opinions; he thinks that he is always right.

註解　忍受的 (形容詞)

2880. Under the **deft** (adroit) direction of coach Lewis, the team finished the season with twelve wins and no losses.

註解　熟練的 (形容詞)

2881. This tea is a **blend** (mixturd) of lemon and herbs.

註解　混合 (名詞)

2882. Judge Mccarthy often exercises **clemency** (mercy) with first-offenders.

註解　仁慈 (名詞)

2883. His father **deprived** (took away) him of his allowance as a punishment for misbehaving.

　註解　剝奪 (動詞)

2884. The Salk vaccine has virtually **extirpated** (eradicated) the threat of polio.

　註解　根除 (動詞，完成式)

2885. Please exercise **sufferance** (endurance) in dealing with him because he is still veryill.

　註解　忍耐力 (名詞)

2886. The representatives of the union brought their **grievances** (complaints) before a team of arlitrators.

　註解　苦境 (名詞)

2887. Teams of volunteer are still battling fires from yesterday's **holocaust** (widespreaddevastation); meanwhile the death toll has risen to sixty.

　註解　大規模毀滅 (名詞)

2888. She had planned to bake a pie, but she did not have all of the necessary **elements** (components).

　註解　原料，成分 (名詞)

2889. The dial on this alarm clock is **radiant** (resplendent) so that it can be seen in the dark.

　註解　發光的，輝耀的 (形容詞)

2890. This shampoo is guaranteed to make your hair more **lustrous** (shimmering) than any other brand.

　註解　光亮的 (形容詞)

2891. There was a sign on the gate which read: "Do not **plague** (molest) the dog."

　註解　干擾，惹起 (動詞)

2892. That such a **horrible** (monstrous) crime could occur in their neighborhood shocked them.

　註解　恐怖的 (形容詞)

2893. In spite of his having graduated from a respected university, he often behaves like a **moron** (foolish, silly person).

　註解　低能的人 (名詞)

2894. The dinner must have been good because there is not even a **scrap** (morsel) of it leftover.

註解　殘屑(名詞)

2895. It is hard to understand him because he has a tendency to **mumble** (mutter).

註解　喃喃自語 (不定詞)

2896. The boys always **chew** (munch) popcorn while they watch the movie.

註解　啃咬 (動詞)

2897. Although Bob and his father do not agree on the issues, they have a **reciprocal** (mutual) respect for each other's opinions.

註解　相互的 (形容詞)

2898. The Lincoln Memorial is supported by thirty-six **pilasters** (piers), one of each of the states of the Union at the time of Lincoln's presidency.

註解　建築方柱 (名詞)

2899. After she had finished cutting out the pattern, she still had enough **residua** (remnants) of cloth to make a scarf.

註解　剩餘物料 (名詞)

2900. To **shiver** (shatter) a mirror accidentally is considered bad luck.

註解　打破 (不定詞)

2901. The guards were accused of **torturing** (tormenting) the prisoners in order to make them confess.

註解　折磨 (動名詞)

2902. Mr. Wilson must be very wealthy because his address is in the most **will-to-do**(affluent) neighborhood in the city.

註解　富裕的 (形容詞)

2903. Connie's father calls her his **blithe** (sprightly) spirit because she is very lighthearted and carefree.

註解　快樂的 (形容詞)

2904. The secretary's desk was **littered** (cluttered) up with papers and reference materials.

註解　雜亂的 (形容詞)

2905. The other boys **jeered** (derided) him because of his funny haircut.

註解　嘲笑 (動詞)

2906. The editor did not want to publish such a(n) **erudite** (learned) article because he was afraid that no one would understand it.

註解 博學的 (形容詞)

2907. Before the bridge was built, people used to cross the river at this **bank** (ford).

註解 河岸，淺灘 (名詞)

2908. When the storm caused a power failure, he had to **grope** (search blindly, uncertainly) around in the kitchen for candles and matches.

註解 瞎摸 (不定詞)

2909. The nation paid **obeisance** (homage) to their dead leader by lowering the flag to half-mast.

註解 尊崇 (名詞)

2910. More than four billion people **inhabit** (dwell) the earth.

註解 居住 (動詞)

2911. As she was getting out of the car she accidentally **pinched** (pressed) her fingerin the door.

註解 挾住 (動詞)

2912. Ladies and gentlemen, I am very privileged to present to you the **renowned**(famous) star of stage and screen, John Wayne.

註解 著名的 (形容詞)

2913. Take your **shawl** (covering) with you because it will probably be chilly when you come back.

註解 大圍巾 (名詞)

2914. That is a very **tourchy** (irritable) subject and I prefer not to discuss it.

註解 棘手的 (形容詞)

2915. Smoking **aggravates** (intensifies) a cold.

註解 加重 (動詞)

2916. The hijackers tried to **coerce** (compel) the crew into cooperating with them.

註解 強迫 (不定詞)

2917. Having **designated** (named) his closest friends as members of the committee, the chairman was assured of support.

註解 指定 (動詞，完成式)

2918. The president will be **escorted** (accompanied) by several secret service officers when he participates in the Fourth of July parade.

　註解　護航 (動詞，被動式)

2919. I do not **anticipate** (foresee) any problems in transferring funds from your savings account to your checking account.

　註解　預期 (動詞)

2920. Anne thought that her brother was angry because he had been **grouchy** (sulky) all day.

　註解　不悅的 (形容詞)

2921. His opening comment caused such a **hubbub** (clamor) that he had to wait until the noise subsided to continue his lecture.

　註解　喧鬧 (名詞)

2922. Based upon the **tentative theory** (hypothesis) that the world was round, explorers sailed west in order to reach the East.

　註解　假設理論 (名詞片語)

2923. She felt **compassion** (pity) for the was orphans regardless of what their parents, polotical associations had been.

　註解　同情 (名詞)

2924. The army **ward off** (repelled) the enemy.

　註解　抵擋，逐退 (動詞片語)

2925. When the wind **shifted** (changed direction) from south to north it began to get cold.

　註解　移動 (動詞)

2926. The sea was so **tranquil** (peaceful) that the little boat barely moved.

　註解　平靜的 (形容詞)

2927. A dancer must do strenuous exercises in order to execute the **brisk** (agile) movements of his art.

　註解　輕快的 (形容詞)

2928. I think that I committed a **slip** (blunder) in asking her because she seemed very upset by my question.

　註解　失誤 (名詞)

2929. His ideas were so **cogent** (sound) that no one offered an argument against them.

　註解　使人信服的 (形容詞)

2930. When it is **detected** (descried) in its early stages, cancer can be cured.

   | 註解 |　發現 (動詞被動式)

2931. It is **indispensable** (intrinsic) that you have these transcripts translated and not arized.

   | 註解 |　不可缺少的 (形容詞)

2932. Despite the unfairness with which he was treated, he did not hold a **resentment** (grudge) against his former employer.

   | 註解 |　憤恨 (名詞)

2933. In his inauguration speech, the new dean promised to **commence** (initiate) many changes in the administration of the college.

   | 註解 |　開始 (不定詞)

2934. Some of the **innovations** (changes) on display at the World Science Fair will not be practical until the twenty-first century.

   | 註解 |　改革 (名詞)

2935. The manager tried to **placate** (conciliate) the angry customer by offering to exchange his purchase.

   | 註解 |　安慰 (不定詞)

2936. She **reproached** (reprimanded) him for drinking too much.

   | 註解 |　責備 (動詞)

2937. Although he has had no formal education, he is one of the **most sagacious** (shrewdest) businessmen in the company.

   | 註解 |　最精明的 (形容詞)

2938. Since it involves bringing plants into the country, this sale cannot be **transacted** (enacted) without special permission from the Department of Agriculture.

   | 註解 |　處理，發生 (動詞，被動式)

2939. Rumors of a strike **disturbed** (agitated) the workers.

   | 註解 |　擾亂 (動詞)

2940. She always **blushes** (flushes) when she is embarrassed.

   | 註解 |　面紅耳赤 (動詞)

2941. A marked **depreciation** (deterioration) in his health forced him to retire.

   | 註解 |　衰退 (名詞)

2942. We hold Senator Adams in great **esteem** (honor); he is one of the most respected members of Congress.

註解   尊敬 (名詞)

2943. Everyone **whines** (grumbles) about paying more taxes.

註解   抱怨 (動詞)

2944. His hat was blown off by a sudden **gust** (blast) of wind.

註解   一陣強風 (名詞)

2945. Stevie is a very **inquisitive** (inquiring) child; he never tires of asking questions.

註解   好奇的 (形容詞)

2946. The new airport will be constructed on a **high, broad plain** (plateau) overlooking the capital.

註解   高地 (名詞)

2947. The view is so lovely, that it **transcends** (exceeds) any description of it.

註解   超越 (動詞)

2948. There was only one candle **aglow** (glowing) on the baby's first birthday cake.

註解   發光的 (形容詞)

2949. The crew was able to haul away the smaller rocks, but there are still some **large rocks** (boulders) at the construction site which were too heavy to move without bigger equipment.

註解   大石頭 (名詞，同 boulders)

2950. Although his **colloquies** (dialogues) are very interestion, I prefer a more informal class.

註解   談話 (名詞)

2951. Mr. Jackson eats out every night because he **execrates** (detest) cooking.

註解   討厭 (動詞)

2952. His brother was chosen to give the funeral **eulogy** (laudation) for the late President Kennedy.

註解   頌揚 (名詞)

2953. He did not think that he had broken his arm, but the x-rays revealed a slight **fracturd** (break).

註解   骨折 (名詞)

2954. Roger and his brother are **inseparable** (not able to be disjoined); you never seeone without the other.

   註解　不能分離的 (形容詞)

2955. Even though it is a **plausible** (specious) explanation, I am not completely convinced.

   註解　似乎可靠的 (形容詞)

2956. In order to pay a lesser fee at a state university, you must **reside** (sojourn) in the state for one year.

   註解　定居 (動詞)

2957. Put the windows down and close the **shutters** (valances) before the storm comes.

   註解　窗板 (動詞)

2958. The dress **metamorphoses** (transforms) her from a little girl into a young woman.

   註解　改觀 (動詞)

2959. Mrs. Thompson is a hypochondriac; she has a new **mild illness** (ailment) every week.

   註解　疾病 (名詞)

2960. Because our speaker cannot stay for the entire meeting, we will **deviate** (veer) slightly from the agenda in order to begin with his address.

   註解　轉向，離題 (動詞)

2961. According to Darwin's theory, man has **evolved** (developed gradually) from lower animals.

   註解　演化 (動詞，完成式)

2962. This identification is **guile** (duplicity); the signatures do not match.

   註解　詐術 (名詞)

2963. Despite opposition from his family, he remained **resolute** (steadfast) in his decision.

   註解　堅決的 (形容詞)

2964. The model tests in this book **counterfeit** (simulate) the TOEFL examination.

   註解　仿造 (動詞)

2965. She left the door **ajar** (partly and slightly open) so that she could hear the conversation in the other room.

　　　註解　微開的 (形容詞)

2966. Although he displays **diffidence** (timidity) with strangers, he is veryself-confident with friends.

　　　註解　害羞 (名詞)

2967. Accounting is a very **meticulous** (exacting) profession; there is no room forerror.

　　　註解　一絲不苟的，精準的 (形容詞)

2968. Do not **fret** (fume) about getting a job; with your qualifications I am sure that you have noting to worry about.

　　　註解　煩躁 (動詞)

2969. It has been very difficult to **integrate** (coordinate) all of the local agencies into the national organization.

　　　註解　整合 (不定詞)

2970. These tomatoes are **plump** (portly) and juicy.

　　　註解　圓胖的 (形容詞)

2971. Please **rejoin** (respond) to this memorandum by Friday.

　　　註解　回答 (動詞)

2972. Seen from an airplane, the river is as **sinuous** (curving) as a snake.

　　　註解　彎彎曲曲的 (形容詞)

2973. The wagon trains had to **move along** (traverse) Indian territory in order to reach California.

　　　註解　經過 (不定詞片語)

2974. Be careful driving home because the road is quite **perfidious** (treacherous) when it is icy.

　　　註解　不可靠的 (形容詞)

2975. Jealousy is often **akin** (cognate) to love.

　　　註解　同性質的 (形容詞)

2976. When he **brandishes** (flourish) a knife, the clerk agreed to give him the money in the cash drawer.

　　　註解　揮舞 (動詞)

2977. She felt **commiseration** (clemency) for the people who were living in the disaster area.

註解 同情 (名詞)

2978. The lecture **rambled** (digressed) from the subject often that it was difficuly totake notes.

註解 漫談，離題 (動詞)

2979. Professor Patterson was **infuriated** (exasperated) by his student, constant lateness.

註解 激怒 (動詞，被動式)

2980. The **very cold** (frigid) temperatures in the Arctic caused many hardships for the men in the expedition.

註解 苦冷的 (形容詞)

2981. While they were taking a test, Peter cast a **surreptitious** (furtive) glance at his friend's paper.

註解 秘密的 (形容詞)

2982. Unfortunately, all efforts to rescure the survivors were **futile** (unavailing).

註解 無用的 (形容詞)

2983. Many lakes and rivers have been **contaminated** (befouled) by industrial waste.

註解 污染 (動詞，完成被動式)

2984. He was so angry that he could not **byidle** (restrain) himself from Pushing the mout of his way.

註解 克制 (動詞)

2985. Although some people work until they are sixty-five, the **trend** (tendency) is to retire after thirty years of service.

註解 趨勢 (名詞)

2986. The **affray** (altercation) got louder and louder until the police arrived.

註解 騷動，口角 (名詞)

2987. Her **complexion** (appearance) is so flawless that she seldom wears makeup.

註解 氣色 (名詞)

2988. The shutter of a camera will **dilate** (extend) in darkness in a way similar to the pupil of one's eye.

註解 擴大 (動詞)

2989. The runners were **enervated** (exhausted) after the marathon.

> 註解　精疲力盡的 (形容詞)

2990. Their leader remained **intrepid** (bold) even in the face of great danger.

> 註解　勇猛的 (形容詞)

2991. Each class player will have five minutes to **meditate** (ruminate) his next move.

> 註解　考慮 (不定詞)

2992. In the United States most married women do not **retain** (preserve) their maiden names.

> 註解　保留 (動詞)

2993. I am **skeptical** (indeterminate) of his methods; they do not seem very scientific to me.

> 註解　懷疑的 (形容詞)

2994. The Ohio River is a **tributary** (stream) of the Mississippi River.

> 註解　支流 (名詞)

2995. Although he was almost ninety years old, he was still active and **alert** (perceptive).

> 註解　敏捷的 (形容詞)

2996. She receives many **panegyrics** (compliments) on her taste in clothes.

> 註解　誇獎 (名詞)

2997. Mr. Carson's secretary is a very **diligent** (industrious) worker; she always stays at the office long after everyone else has gone home.

> 註解　勤勞的 (形容詞)

2998. Dr. Taylor's fees are **exorbitant** (extravagant); he charges twice as much as anyone else.

> 註解　過份的 (形容詞)

2999. A(n) **intricate** (labyrinthine) system of interstate, state, and county highways connects all of the major towns and cities in the Unites States.

> 註解　錯綜複雜的 (形容詞)

3000. We ordain this Constitution for ourselves and our future **generation** (posterity).

> 註解　後代 (名詞)

3001. A reduction of resources will considerably **retard** (impede) the progress of our project.

   註解　妨礙 (動詞)

3002. Since he did not have time to read the article before class, he just **gave a cursory glance** (skimmed) through it.

   註解　匆匆瞄閱 (動詞片語)

3003. In general, your test was very good; you only made a few trivial (frivolous)mistakes.

   註解　不重要的 (形容詞)

3004. The nurse will give you something to **alleviate** (lessen) the pain.

   註解　減輕 (不定詞)

3005. Attendance in the public schools is **mandatory** (compulsory) until age sixteen.

   註解　義務的 (形容詞)

3006. Bill is a **diminutive** (teeny) form of the name William.

   註解　極小的 (形容詞)

3007. Please forgive me; I did not mean to **intrude** (infringe) (trespass).

   註解　侵犯 (不定詞)

3008. Her angry **retort** (retaliate) to his question suspended their conversation.

   註解　報復 (動詞)

3009. He **hit her with an open hand** (slapped her) because she was hysterical.

   註解　摑耳光 (動詞片語)

3010. The **troupe** (band) of actors are playing.

   註解　團隊 (名詞)

3011. She looked very **seductive** (inviting) in her black evening dress.

   註解　誘惑的 (形容詞)

3012. The tourists walked over to the **brink** (verge) of the cliff to take a picture.

   註解　邊緣 (名詞)

3013. He tried to **conceal** (screen) his identity by disguising his voice.

   註解　隱藏 (不定詞)

3014. Despite its **dingy** (dismal) exterior, the little house was very bright and cheerful inside.

   註解　昏暗的 (形容詞)

3015. Pictures of the moon show vast **expanses** (large areas) of crater and rock.

　　註解　一大片 (名詞)

3016. Mrs. Warner has been a(n) **invalid** (sick person) since her last heart attack.

　　註解　病人 (名詞)

3017. On April Fool's Day people like to play **pranks** (tricks) on their friends.

　　註解　戲弄 (名詞)

3018. State universities get most of their **revenue** (income) from taxes.

　　註解　收入 (名詞)

3019. When he went hunting with his older brothers, he did not want them to **slay** (massacre) the deer.

　　註解　屠殺 (不定詞)

3020. A small boat **tugged** (hauled) a ship into the harbor.

　　註解　拖拉 (動詞)

3021. Our neighbors are so **aloof** (reserved) and unfriendly that they never speak to anyone.

　　註解　冷漠的 (形容詞)

3022. My fingernails are so **frail** (frangible) that they break off before they gey long enough to polish.

　　註解　脆弱的 (形容詞)

3023. When Mrs. Davis was learning to cook, she **concocted** (devised) some rather strange dishes.

　　註解　調製，發明 (動詞)

3024. After the elections, the nominating committee will be **disbanded** (dissolved).

　　註解　解散 (動詞，被動式)

3025. He does his work with such **invariable** (immutable) accuracy that it is never necessary to make any corrections.

　　註解　不變的 (形容詞)

3026. When he has a headache, even the slightest noise **piques** (infuriates) him.

　　註解　引起，激怒 (動詞)

3027. The Supreme Court can **reverse** (invert) the decision of any lower court.

　　註解　改變 (動詞)

3028. I like the style and the color, but the material seems a little **sleazy** (gauzy) tome.
   註解　輕薄的 (形容詞)

3029. She tripped and **plunged headlong** (tumbled) down the stairs.
   註解　跌落 (動詞片語)

3030. If a **concord** (covenant) is not reached by the end of the month, the ambassador and his staff will withdraw from the embassy.
   註解　盟約 (名詞)

3031. I would like to **cast aside** (discard) the old texts and purchase the revised editions for next semester.
   註解　拋棄 (不定詞片語)

3032. Her directions are always so **explicit** (unequivocal) that everyone understands what to do immediately.
   註解　明確的 (形容詞)

3033. Because of advances in medical technology heart surgery is not as **perilous** (risky) as it formerly was.
   註解　危險的 (形容詞)

3034. As the temperature dropped, the rain turned to **a mixture of snow, hail and rain** (sleet).
   註解　雨雪 (名詞片語)

3035. He could not be heard over the **tumult** (ado) of angry voices.
   註解　喧鬧 (名詞)

3036. The murder was so **brutal** (savage) that the jury was not allowed to see the police photographs.
   註解　殘忍的 (形容詞)

3037. The President and the Congress are in **concurrence** (accordance) concerning this appointment.
   註解　贊同 (名詞)

3038. It was so dark that he could not **perceive** (discern) the identity of his attacker.
   註解　辨識 (動詞)

3039. He became rich by **exploiting** (utilizing) his workers.
   註解　剝削 (動詞)

3040. The following **precept** (directive) is worth remembering: "If at first you don't succeed, try, try again."

註解 教訓，指令 (名詞)

3041. Since these two teams have played each other for the championship for five consecutive years, they have built up an intense **rivalry** (emulation).

註解 競爭 (名詞)

3042. She **slit** (fissured) the envelope with a letter opener.

註解 割裂 (動詞)

3043. A convertible couch has a **twofold** (double) purpose; it can be used for a sofa during the day and a bed at night.

註解 雙重的 (形容詞，同 bifold)

3044. He is a **neophyte** (tyro) in art, but he shows great promise.

註解 生手 (名詞)

3045. After months of negotiations, they arrived at an **amicable** (peaceable) settlement.

註解 和平的 (形容詞)

3046. Eddie likes to **bully** (domineer) the younger boys, but he never tries to fight with anyone his own age.

註解 作威作福 (不定詞)

3047. When the little boy fell down, he skimned his knees and got a **bump** (jolt) on his head.

註解 腫塊 (名詞)

3048. Since I can no longer **condone** (overlook) the activities of this organization, I am removing my name from the membership.

註解 原諒 (動詞)

3049. Professor Mathews **set forth** (expounded) upon her theory by giving detailed examples of applications.

註解 說明 (動詞片語)

3050. He had to put up a fence to keep his cattle from **roaming** (straying) onto his neighbor's farm.

註解 流浪 (動名詞)

3051. This drain is **moving slowly** (sluggish) (slothful) because there is something caught in the pipe.

註解 緩慢的 (形容詞片語)

3052. He suffered from temporary **amnesia** (lapse of memory) as the result of a head injury.

註解 健忘症 (名詞)

3053. When they were children, she always **confided** (entrusted) her problems to her big sister.

註解 信賴 (動詞)

3054. The literary critics **dissect** (anatomize) every sentence in the essay.

註解 分析 (動詞)

3055. Since I did not expect to address you this evening, my remarks will have to be **extempore** (extemporaneous).

註解 臨時的 (形容詞)

3056. Although the weatherman had **prophesied** (predicted) snow, it was a beautiful weekend.

註解 預告 (動詞，完成式)

3057. Allen Burns will portray the **role** (character) of Macbeth in the Shakespearean Festival.

註解 角色 (名詞)

3058. The forest rangers found a fire **burning with little smoke and no flame** (smoldering) in an abandoned campsite.

註解 悶燒 (動名詞片語)

3059. Richard's scholarship includes a very **ample** (liberal) living allowance.

註解 充足的 (形容詞)

3060. The World Cup Soccer Games will be **disseminated** (dispersed) internationally by television satellites.

註解 傳播 (動詞，被動式)

3061. The fire caused **spacious** (extensive) damage to the factory.

註解 廣大的 (形容式)

3062. Organ music is often a **prelude** (preliminary action) to church services.

註解 前奏曲 (名詞)

3063. When the Smiths moved to the country, they were surprised by their neighbors'**rustic** (unsophisticated) manners.

註解 農村的，單純的 (形容詞)

3064. Benjamin Franklin is remembered for his **sagacity** (keenness) and wit.

註解 精明 (名詞)

3065. As she was waiting on the corner for the light to change, a young boy tried to **snatch** (seize) her purse.

　註解　搶奪 (不定詞)

3066. Please **confine** (restrict) your comments to the topic assigned.

　註解　限制 (動詞)

3067. While it was raining out, the children **diverted** (entertained) themselves by playing games in their room.

　註解　轉向 (動詞)

3068. Some of the traditional customs still **preponderate** (privail) among members ofthe older generation.

　註解　超過 (動詞)

3069. The reporter could not **impart** (divulge) the source of his information.

　註解　告知 (動詞)

3070. This article **extols** (exalts) the application of linguistics to language teaching.

　註解　頌揚 (動詞，同 extolls)

3071. Smog is more **prevalent** (widespread) in urban centers.

　註解　普遍的 (形容詞)

3072. The Christmas candles **congeald** (curdled) in the molds.

　註解　凝結 (動詞)

3073. Several passengers were still **dozing** (napping) when the bus prlled into the station.

　註解　打瞌睡 (動詞，進行式)

3074. **Prior to** (Preceding) the Revolutionary War, the United States was an English colony.

　註解　先前的 (形容詞片語)

3075. A hot cloth pressed against your jaw will usually **tranquilize** (soothe) a tooth ache.

　註解　鎮定 (動詞)

3076. It is an **anomalous** (abnormal) situation; he is the director of the personnel office, but he does not have the authority to hire and dismiss staff.

　註解　反常的 (形容詞)

3077. Margaret is a very **congenial** (complaisant) person; everyone likes her.
註解　彬彬有禮的 (形容詞)

3078. We were **drenched** (damped) by the sudden downpour.
註解　溼透 (動詞，被動式)

3079. A second car is an excessive **expenditure** (extravagance) we cannot afford.
註解　經費 (名詞)

3080. When the home team scored the winning goal, the crowd gave a(n) **exultant** (jubilant) shout.
註解　狂歡的 (形容詞)

3081. Everyone felt very **dejected** (sorrowful) about the misunderstanding.
註解　失望的 (形容詞)

3082. Regular prenatal checkups can help to reduce **congenital** (hereditary) birth defects.
註解　先天的 (形容詞)

3083. Golden Gate Bridge **spans** (extends over) the entrance to San Francisco Bay.
註解　跨過 (動詞)

3084. I always take the bus to work because the **congestion** (crowding) in the city makes it difficult to find a parking place.
註解　擁擠 (名詞)

3085. Since this medicine may cause you to fell **somnolent** (drowsy), do not drive a car or operate machinery.
註解　昏睡的 (形容詞)

3086. Hemingway was a very **teeming** (prolific) writer; during his brief career he published seven major novels, six volumes of short stories and poems, and two travel sketches.
註解　豐富的 (形容詞)

3087. Pine trees, of which there are almost one hundred **species** (classes), are found through out the North Temperate zone.
註解　種類 (名詞)

3088. Fifty thousand dollars would be a fair **appraisal** (valuation) of their new house.
註解　估價 (名詞)

3089. That is only a **supposition** (conjecturd) on your part, not a certainly.

   註解　推測 (名詞)

3090. I am very **obscure** (dubious) about signing this contract because I am not sure about some of the fine print.

   註解　模糊的 (形容詞)

3091. As soon as the mayor **promulgates** (announces) the new law, Market Place will be a one-way street going south.

   註解　公佈 (動詞)

3092. I think I have a **small particle** (speck) of dust in my eye.

   註解　小東西 (名詞片語)

3093. An arrangement of flowers is always a **befitting** (becoming) gift for someone in the hospital.

   註解　適當的 (形容詞)

3094. Mike is a very **scrupulous** (conscientious) student, he studies in the library every night.

   註解　謹慎的 (形容詞)

3095. The basement in the old house was so damp and dark that it looked like a **dungeon** (cell).

   註解　地牢 (名詞)

3096. He used a brick as a rigid **support** (prop) to keep the door open.

   註解　支柱 (名詞)

3097. Shoveling deep snow is far too **arduous** (toilsome) a task for a man of his age.

   註解　費力的 (形容詞)

3098. Hundreds of cans of tuna were recalled by the factory because some of them were found to be **sullied** (defiled).

   註解　污染 (不定詞，被動式)

3099. The candidate's speech was interrupted by **sporadic** (occasional) applause.

   註解　斷斷續續的 (形容詞)

3100. His refusal to walk through the metal detector before boarding the plane **aroused** (inspirit) the guard's suspicion.

   註解　引起 (動詞)

3101. Metal **contracts** (reduces) as it cools.
　　註解　收縮 (動詞)

3102. Their business began to **proper** (thrive) when they moved to their new location.
　　註解　興旺 (不定詞)

3103. Iris's pet cat likes to **sprawl out** (stretch out) in front of the fireplace to sleep.
　　註解　伸懶腰 (不定詞)

3104. The suspects will be **arraigned** (censured) by the district court.
　　註解　提訊 (動詞，被動式)

3105. When he saw the lone **protruding** (projecting) through her skin, he knew that she had a very serious fracture.
　　註解　突出物 (動名詞)

3106. The checkout girl always puts the bread on top of the other groceries so that it does not get **squashed** (crushed).
　　註解　壓扁的 (形容詞)

3107. The union officials resented the **arrogance** (haughtiness) with which the company president dismissed their demands.
　　註解　傲慢 (名詞)

3108. His lecture **called forth** (instigated) an interesting discussion.
　　註解　煽動 (動詞片語)

3109. She **stacked** (piled) the dishes in the sink because she did not have time to wash them.
　　註解　堆積 (動詞)

3110. Three candidates **yearned** (aspired) to win the election.
　　註解　渴望 (動詞)

3111. Overpopulation is at the **midst** (core) of many other problems, including food shortages and inadequate housing.
　　註解　中心點 (名詞)

3112. The witness **avowed** (asserted) that the salesman was dishonest.
　　註解　公開宣稱 (動詞)

3113. **Proximity** (Nearness) to the new shopping center should increase the value of our property.
　　註解　接近 (名詞)

3114. In order to make a **sober** (prudent) decision, you must consider all of the possibilities carefully.

註解　謹慎的 (形容詞)

3115. It is not necessary to boil the drinking water because it has already been **cleansed** (purified) chemically.

註解　清淨 (動詞，完成被動式)

3116. This part may move, but that one must remain **static** (stationary) in order for the machine to run smoothly.

註解　固定的 (形容詞)

3117. After his friends called him a **dastard** (poltroom), he agreed to fight.

註解　膽小鬼 (名詞)

3118. When she was expecting her first baby, she **longed for** (craved) pickles.

註解　渴望 (動詞片語)

3119. Nothing could **assuage** (mitigate) his anger.

註解　平息 (動詞)

3120. Donna is so **gullible** (credulous) that she will believe anything you tell her.

註解　易受騙的 (形容詞)

3121. The cowboy **sat straddling** (sat astride) the fence at the rodeo waiting for his turn to ride.

註解　跨坐 (動詞片語)

3122. The results of his test **amazed** (astounded) him; he had not expected to pass, and he received one of the highest possible scores.

註解　吃驚 (動詞)

3123. Equal rights regardless of sex, race, or **creed** (faith) are guaranteed by the Constitution.

註解　宗教信仰 (名詞)

3124. The **strain** (tension) of meeting a daily deadline made the columnist very nervous.

註解　緊張 (名詞)

3125. Their neighbor asked them to keep their dog tied so that it would not go **out ofthe right way** (astray).

註解　迷途地 (副詞片語)

3126. **Crude** (Coarse) oil is refined by heating it in a closed still.
  註解 原始的 (形容詞)

3127. We must **struggle vigorously** (strive) to finish this report before we leave because it is due tomorrow morning.
  註解 努力 (動詞)

3128. The men who are chosen to become astronauts must be perfectly healthy, highly skilled in engineering, and **audacious** (daring).
  註解 勇敢的 (形容詞)

3129. A police car **drives slowly** (cruises) past the school every hour.
  註解 巡邏 (動詞片語)

3130. This one is not as large as the others; something have **stunted** (dwarfed) its growth.
  註解 阻礙 (動詞，完成式)

3131. The problem will be discussed at length in **succeeding** (subsequent) chapters.
  註解 隨後的 (形容詞)

3132. Miss White **swelled** (augmented) her income by typing theses and dissertations.
  註解 增大 (動詞)

3133. Just before the outbreak of the Civil War, the South declared itself to be a(n) **free** (autonomous) nation.
  註解 自治的 (形容詞)

3134. She agreed to marry the aging millionarie more because of **cupidity** (avarice) than because of love.
  註解 貪財 (名詞)

3135. He must have a(n) **repugnance** (aversion) to work because he is always out of a job.
  註解 厭惡 (名詞)

3136. In spite of efforts by several universities, the **occult** (cryptic) symbols on the mural remained a mystery.
  註解 神秘的 (形容詞)

3137. Whether or not he is **culpable** (censurable) will be determined by the jury.
  註解 受譴責的 (形容詞)

3138. He was offended by the telephone operator's **snappish** (curt) reply.

註解　尖刻的，草率的 (形容詞)

3139. Bus service will have to be **docked** (curtailed) because of the transit strike.

註解　縮減 (不定詞，被動式)

3140. Southern Florida is very **sultry** (sweltering) during the summer months.

註解　酷熱的 (形容詞)

3141. A new judge will be appointed to **supersede** (supplant) the late Judge Taylor.

註解　替代 (不定詞)

3142. After **satiating** (surfeiting) himself at the banquet, he felt too sleepy to enjoy the entertainment.

註解　享樂，飽足 (動名詞)

3143. His **arrogant** (surly) manner keeps him from having many friends.

註解　自大的，粗暴的 (形容詞)

3144. Since she is not at home, I **surmise** (suspect) that she is on her way here.

註解　猜測 (動詞)

3145. When the baseball landed in their hive, a **swarm** (horde) of bees flew onto the field.

註解　大群 (名詞)

3146. The driver had to **swerve** (veer) his car in order to avoid hitting a little boy on a bicycle.

註解　轉向 (不定詞)

3147. In order not to be late to work, she **caused to coincide** (synchronized) her watch with the clock at the office.

註解　對時一致 (動詞片語)

3148. Although I have not seen the entire script, I have read a(n) **epitome** (condensation) of the plot.

註解　概要，濃縮 (名詞)

3149. He is a very **taciturn** (reticent) person; he never speaks unnecessarily.

註解　沉默的 (形容詞)

3150. The old soldier was **inured** (habituated) to hard work and danger.

註解　習慣的 (形容詞)

3151. He is not used to such **servile** (menial) tasks as washing pots and pans.
　　　註解　奴隸的 (形容詞)

3152. Hiring a new teacher will **ameliorate** (reform) the condition, but we still need more books and desks.
　　　註解　改善 (動詞)

3153. We **foiled** (thwarted) his attempt to sell the house.
　　　註解　阻止 (動詞)

3154. The speech he gave last night has considerably **solidified** (consolidated) his influence among all the party members.
　　　註解　結合 (動詞，完成式)

3155. He was making a(n) **all-out** (total) effort to win the race.
　　　註解　全力的 (形容詞)

3156. He is the popular candidate; **consequently** (therefore), he will be elected.
　　　註解　因此 (副詞)

3157. Jose and Reynaldo are **compatriots** (fellow countrymen) because they both come from Mexico.
　　　註解　同胞 (名詞)

3158. Giving money to the poor is an act of **charitableness** (benevolence).
　　　註解　仁慈 (名詞)

3159. He died without making a **testament** (will).
　　　註解　遺囑 (名詞)

3160. President Chiang Kai-Shek urged Chinese to **rejuvenate** (freshen) their national culture.
　　　註解　恢復 (不定詞)

3161. The policeman **admonished** (warned) him not to drive too fast.
　　　註解　警告 (動詞)

3162. His success cannot be evaluated only **in terms of** (from the standpoint of) money.
　　　註解　條件 (介詞片語)

3163. He spoke in parliament with **fidelity** (constancy) of purpose.
　　　註解　精確，堅定 (名詞)

3164. The panel discussion will be **moderated** (pacified) by Dr. Johson, our teacher of English literature.
　　　註解　主持會議 (動詞，未來被動式)

3165. What you have in mind is only **a pie in the sky** (a dream); you can't put it into real practice.

> 註解   一場夢 (名詞片語)

3166. His refusal to **humiliate** (abase) himself in the eyes of his followers irritated the king, who wanted to lower the proud leader.

> 註解   屈辱 (不定詞)

3167. Even though the Red Cross had **assigned** (allocated) a large sum for the relief of the sufferers of the disaster, many people perished.

> 註解   分配 (動詞，完成式)

3168. He can recognize by his **crooked** (hooked) nose, curved like the beak of the eagle.

> 註解   彎曲的 (形容詞)

3169. I will not be **wheedled** (cajoled) into granting you your wish.

> 註解   勸誘 (動詞，被動式)

3170. The paramecium is a **ciliated** (having minute hairs), one celled animal.

> 註解   有纖毛的 (形容詞)

3171. He was present at all their **private meeting** (conclaves) as a sort of unofficial observer.

> 註解   秘密會議 (名詞片語)

3172. The people rebelled against the **despotism** (tyranny) of the king.

> 註解   暴政 (名詞)

3173. The **dissimilitude** (diversity) of colleges in this country indicates that many levels of ability are being cared for.

> 註解   不同點，多樣化 (名詞)

3174. The monotonous routine of hospital life induced a feeling of **ennui** (boredom) which made him moody and irritable.

> 註解   倦怠 (名詞)

3175. While conditions are in such a state of **flux** (flowing), I do not wish to commit myself too deeply in this affair.

> 註解   變化，流動 (名詞)

3176. I want this photograph printed on **sleek** (glossy) paper.

> 註解   光滑的 (形容詞)

3177. Educators try to put pupils of similar abilities into classes because they believe that this **not heterogeneous** (homogeneous) grouping is advisable.
　　　| 註解 |　不是混雜的 (形容詞片語)

3178. The fire spread in such an unusual manner that the fire department chiefs were certain that it had been set by an **incendiary** (arsonist).
　　　| 註解 |　放火者 (名詞，同 arsonite)

3179. They found his **lewd** (lustful) stories objectionable.
　　　| 註解 |　淫蕩的 (形容詞)

3180. To find the **perimeter** (outer boundary) of any quadrilateral, we add the foursides.
　　　| 註解 |　周邊 (名詞)

3181. You should be ashamed of your **fainthearted** (pusillanimous) conduct during this dispute.
　　　| 註解 |　膽小的 (形容詞)

3182. He recited the passage by **rote** (repetition) and gave no indication he understood what he was saying.
　　　| 註解 |　固定程序 (名詞)

3183. Lemurs are nocturnal mammals and have many **simian** (monkeylike) characteristics, although they are less intelligent than monkeys.
　　　| 註解 |　似猿猴的 (形容詞)

3184. Forgive us our **transgressions** (sins).
　　　| 註解 |　犯規 (名詞)

3185. I do not understand how you can **live in a monotonous way** (vegetate) in this quiet village after the adventurous life you have led.
　　　| 註解 |　單調過活 (動詞片語)

3186. In designing a good lens for a camera, the problem of correcting chromatic and rectilinear **divergence** (aberration) was a serious one.
　　　| 註解 |　相差，差異(名詞)

3187. The waiter preparing the salad poured oil and vinegar from two **cruets** (glassbottles) into the bowl.
　　　| 註解 |　調味瓶 (名詞)

3188. With the **excision** (resection) of the dead and dying limbs of this tree, you have not only improved its appearance, but you have enhanced its chances of bearing fruit.

　註解　切除 (名詞)

3189. In his inaugural address, the President stated that he had a(n) **mandate** (order)from the people to seek an end to social evils such as poverty, poor housing, etc.

　註解　命令 (名詞)

3190. Their relationship could not be explained as being based on mere **propinquity** (kinship); they were more than relatives; they were true friends.

　註解　親近關係 (名詞)

3191. I can overlook his **simpering** (smirking) manner, but I cannot ignore his stupidity.

　註解　傻笑的 (形容詞)

3192. The Taming of the Shrew is one of many stories of the methods used in changing a **virago** (termagant) into a demure lady.

　註解　悍婦 (名詞)

3193. He was not at all **abashed** (embarrassed) by her open admiration.

　註解　困窘的 (形容詞)

3194. The land was no longer **arable** (fit for plowing); erosion had removed the valuable topsoil.

　註解　可耕種的 (形容詞)

3195. They found the **baroque** (highly ornate) architecture amusing.

　註解　巴洛克式的，高度華麗的 (形容詞)

3196. A man of such **caliber** (capacity) should not be assigned such menials tasks.

　註解　才幹 (名詞)

3197. This tiny **circlet** (band) is very costly because it is set with precious stones.

　註解　小圓環，小帶 (名詞)

3198. How did you ever **concoct** (contrive) such a strange dish?

　註解　調製 (動詞)

3199. He was **stripped** (divested) of his power to act.
　　　註解　剝除的 (形容詞)

3200. He did not realize the **hugeness** (enormity) of his crime until he saw what suffering he had caused.
　　　註解　巨大 (名詞)

3201. His speeches were famous for his **exuberant** (lavish) language and vivid imagery.
　　　註解　豐富的 (形容詞)

3202. We can overlook the **foibles** (weakness) of our friends.
　　　註解　缺點 (名詞)

3203. The many manufacturers **glutted** (overstocked) the market and could not find purchasers for the many articles they had produced.
　　　註解　過多供應 (動詞)

3204. Students who dislike school must be given a(n) **incentive** (spur) to learn.
　　　註解　鼓勵 (名詞)

3205. They are going to **inter** (bury) the body tomorrow.
　　　註解　埋葬 (不定詞)

3206. I cannot find this word in any **lexicon** (dictionary) in the library.
　　　註解　字典 (名詞)

3207. During this very trying period, he could not have had a better **mentor** (teacher), for the teacher was sympathetic and understanding.
　　　註解　教師 (名詞)

3208. He refused to celebrate his **pertaining to birth** (natal) day because it reminded him of the few years he could look forward to.
　　　註解　出生的 (動名詞片語，當形容詞)

3209. The **roving** (peripatetic) school of philosophy derives its name from the fact that Aristotle walked with his pupils while discussing philosophy with them.
　　　註解　逍遙的，遊行的 (形容詞)

3210. Do not be **rash** (precipitate) in this matter; investigate further.
　　　註解　輕率的 (形容詞)

3211. The gangrenous condition of the wound was indicated by the **putrid** (decayed) smell when the bandages were removed.
　　　註解　腐爛的 (形容詞)

3212. If we **relegate** (banish) there experienced people to positions of unimportance because of their political persuasions, we shall lose the services of valuably trained personnel.

註解 拋棄 (動詞)

3213. Washington Irving emphasized the **rotundity** (roundness) of the governor by describing his height and circumference.

註解 肥胖 (名詞)

3214. I resent your **haughty** (supercilious) and arrogant attitude.

註解 傲慢的 (形容詞)

3215. This hotel caters to a **transient** (fleeting) trade.

註解 片刻的 (形容詞)

3216. He spoke with **vehement** (impetuous) eloquence in defense of his client.

註解 猛烈的 (形容詞)

3217. Since I do not wish to be **beholden** (indebted) to anyone, I cannot accept this favor.

註解 感恩 (不定詞,被動式)

3218. These shoes are so ill-fitting that they will **excoriate** (flay) the feet and createblisters.

註解 磨皮 (動詞)

3219. The special **terms used in a science or art** (terminology) developed by some authorities in the field has done more to confuse the layman than to enlighten him.

註解 專門術語 (名詞)

3220. When Edward V III **abdicated** (renounced) the British throne, he surprised the entire world.

註解 放棄 (動詞)

3221. Try not to **allude** (refer indirectly) to this matter in his presence because it annoys him to hear of it.

註解 提及 (不定詞)

3222. Coal is much more **heat-producing** (calorific) than green wood.

註解 生熱的 (形容詞)

3223. Because of the traffic congestion on the main highways, he took a **roundabout** (circuitous) route.

註解 繞遠的 (形容詞)

3224. Every month the farmer **culls** (picks out) the nonlaying hens from his flock and sells them to the local butcher.

註解　揀出 (動詞)

3225. I base my opinions not on any special gift of **augury** (divination) but on the laws of probability.

註解　先兆 (名詞)

3226. The audience was **please intensely** (enraptured) by the freshness of the voices and the excellent orchestration.

註解　歡欣若狂的 (形容詞片語)

3227. I will not permit you to **foist** (palm off) such ridiculous ideas upon the membership of this group.

註解　混騙 (不定詞)

3228. Molasses is a **viscous** (glutinous) substance.

註解　黏黏的 (形容詞)

3229. Travelers interested in economy should stay at **hostelries** (inns) and pensions rather than fashionable hotels.

註解　旅館 (名詞)

3230. Before the Creation, the world was a(n) **rudimentary** (inchoate) mass.

註解　未開發的 (形容詞)

3231. The company will not consider our proposal until next week; in the **interim** (meantime), let us proceed as we have in the past.

註解　同時間 (名詞)

3232. I am more interested in the opportunities available in the **mercantile** (commercial) field than I am in those in the legal profession.

註解　商業的 (形容詞)

3233. The Red Cross emphasizes the need for courses in **natation** (swimming).

註解　游泳 (名詞)

3234. Passing a red light is a violation of a city **ordinance** (decree).

註解　法令 (名詞)

3235. He sensed that there was something just beyond the **periphery** (perimeter) of his vision.

註解　外圍 (名詞)

3236. We must be patient as we cannot **precipitate** (hasten) these results.

註解　催促 (動詞)

3237. I was impressed by the **pertinence** (relevancy) of your remarks.

　　　註解　恰當，中肯 (名詞)

3238. Ten years after World War II, some of the **rubbles** (fragments) left by enemy bombings could be seen.

　　　註解　瓦礫，碎片 (名詞)

3239. Since your report gave only a **trivial** (superficial) analysis of the problem, I cannot give you more than a passing grade.

　　　註解　微小的 (形容詞)

3240. Bound in **vellum** (parchment) and embossed in gold, this book is a beautiful example of the binder's craft.

　　　註解　羊皮紙 (名詞)

3241. No act of **abnegation** (self-sacrifice) was more pronounced than his refusal of any rewards for his discovery.

　　　註解　棄權，自我犧牲 (名詞)

3242. Where our estates **abut** (adjoin), we must build a fence.

　　　註解　鄰接處 (名詞)

3243. Although I do not wish to **depreciate** (disparage) your contribution, I feel we must place it in its proper perspective.

　　　註解　輕視 (不定詞)

3244. After his many hours of intensive study in the library, he retired to his **cubicle** (small chamber).

　　　註解　小臥室 (名詞)

3245. The world **expresses abhorrence for** (execrates) the memory of Hitler and hopes that genocide will never again be the policy of any nation.

　　　註解　仇恨 (動詞片語)

3246. I can eveluate the data gathered in this study; the **imponderable** (weightless) items are not so easily analyzed.

　　　註解　無法衡量的 (形容詞)

3247. Enlightened slave owners were willing to **emancipate** (manumit) their slaves and thus put an end to the evil of slavery in the country.

　　　註解　解放 (不定詞)

3248. The medieval knight in full **panoply** (set of armor) found his movements limited by the weight of his armor.

　　　註解　盔甲 (名詞)

3249. The flesh of the diamondback **terrapin** (American marsh tortoise) is considered by many epicures to be a delicacy.
註解 烏龜 (名詞)

3250. He was accused of being an aider and **abettor** (encourager) of the criminal.
註解 教唆者 (名詞)

3251. Any **despotic** (arbitrary) action on your part will be resented by the members of the board whom you do not consult.
註解 專制的 (形容詞)

3252. Galsworthy started as a **barrister** (counselor-at-law), but when he found the practice of law boring, turned to writing.
註解 律師 (名詞)

3253. Shakespeare wrote that love and friendship were subject to envious and **slandering** (calumniating) time.
註解 誹謗的 (形容詞)

3254. Although I do not wish to **circumscribe** (confine) your activities, I must insist that you complete this assignment before you start anything else.
註解 限制 (不定詞)

3255. The animals, **desultory** (aimless) behavior indicated that they had no awareness of their predicament.
註解 無目地的 (形容詞)

3256. The parents thought that their children were **ensconced** (settled securely) in the private school and decided to leave for Europe.
註解 安置 (動詞，被動式)

3257. If we **fabricate** (construct) the buildings inf this project, we can reduce the cost considerably.
註解 建造 (動詞)

3258. This report will **stir up** (instigate) dissension in the club.
註解 鼓動 (動詞)

3259. The **voracious** (gluttonous) boy ate all the cookies.
註解 貪吃的 (形容詞)

3260. His **benignant** (humane) and considerate treatment of the unfortunate endeared him to all.
註解 親切的 (形容詞)

3261. I will sleep early for I want to break an **incipient** (initial) cold.

   註解　初期的 (形容詞)

3262. **Interment** (Burial) will take place in the church cemetery at 2 P.M. Wednesday.

   註解　埋葬 (名詞)

3263. He sued the newspaper because of its **defamatory** (libelous) story.

   註解　中傷的 (形容詞，同 libellous)

3264. I am certain that your action was prompted by **covetous** (mercenary) motives.

   註解　貪心的 (形容詞)

3265. The foul smells began to **nauseate** (sicken) him.

   註解　作嘔 (不定詞)

3266. The Howe Caverns were discovered when someone observed that a cold wind was issuing from a(n) **orifice** (vent) in the hillside.

   註解　小孔 (名詞)

3267. This hill is difficult to climb because it is so **precipitous** (perpendicular).

   註解　陡峭的 (形容詞)

3268. Do not be misled by the exorbitant claims of this **charlatan** (quack).

   註解　騙子 (名詞)

3269. His **rubicund** (ruddy) complexion was the result of an active outdoor life.

   註解　紅潤的 (形容詞)

3270. We must defeat the **inauspicious** (sinister) forces that seek our downfall.

   註解　不利的 (形容詞)

3271. We have a definite lack of sincere workers and a **superfluity** (overabundance) of leaders.

   註解　多餘 (名詞)

3272. We could not recognize the people in the next room because of the **partly transparent** (translucent) curtains which separated us.

   註解　半透明的 (形容詞)

3273. The **corruptible** (venal) policeman accepted the bribe offered him by the speeding motorist whom he had stopped.

   註解　可賄賂的，貪污的 (形容詞)

3274. His arrogance is exceeded only by his **abysmal** (bottomless) ignorance.

   註解　無底的 (形容詞)

3275. We have endowed our Creator with a **benignity** (graciousness) which permits forgiveness of our sins and transgressions.

註解 仁慈 (名詞)

3276. The soldiers were unaware that they were marching into a **cul-de-sac** (trap) when they entered the canyon.

註解 陷阱，無後退之路 (名詞)

3277. I can follow your **exegesis** (interpretation) of this passage to a limited degree; some of your reasoning eludes me.

註解 解釋 (名詞)

3278. He tried to hide him from his **importunate** (urgent) creditors until his allowance arrived.

註解 緊急的 (形容詞)

3279. She sought a divorce on the grounds that her busband had a(n) **illicit** lover (paramour) in another town.

註解 情婦 (名詞)

3280. The crude typewriter on display in this museum is the **prototype** (pattern) of the elaborate machines in use today.

註解 典型 (名詞)

3281. Unless you can prove your allegations, your remarks constitute **defamation** (slander).

註解 誹謗 (名詞)

3282. I recall seeing a table with a **mosaic** (tessellated) top of bits of stone and glass in a very interestion pattern.

註解 鑲入的 (形容詞)

3283. The deal was held in **temporary inactivity** (abeyance) until his arrival.

註解 中止 (名詞片語)

3284. The **trafficker** (barterer) exchanged trinkets for the natives, furs.

註解 商人 (名詞)

3285. He could endure his financial failure, but he could not bear the malicious **misrepresentation** (calumny) that his foes heaped upon him.

註解 虛偽陳述 (名詞)

3286. Investigating before acting, he tried always to be **circumspect** (prudent).

註解 愼重的 (形容詞)

3287. Corrupt politicians who condone the activities of the gamblers are equally **culpable** (reprehensible).
　　　註解　該受譴責的 (形容詞)

3288. From the moment he saw her picture, he was **enthralled** (enslaved) by her beauty.
　　　註解　迷住 (動詞，被動式)

3289. Don't be **foolhardy** (heedless). Get the advice of experienced people before undertaking this venture.
　　　註解　魯莽的 (形容詞)

3290. The **twisted** (gnarled) oak tree had been a landmark for years and was mentioned in several deeds.
　　　註解　纏繞的(形容詞)

3291. After his years of adventure, he could not settle down to a **monotonous** (humdrum) existence.
　　　註解　單調的 (形容詞)

3292. The demagogue **goaded** (provoked) the mob to take action into its own hands.
　　　註解　刺激的 (形容詞)

3293. Although his speech lasted for only twenty minutes, it seemed **interminable** (endless) to his bored audience.
　　　註解　無終止的 (形容詞)

3294. Although she was aware of his reputation as a **libertine** (debauchee), she felt she could reform him and help him break his dissolute way of life.
　　　註解　放蕩者 (名詞)

3295. He was of a **fickle** (mercurial) temperament and therefore unpredictable.
　　　註解　多變的 (形容詞)

3296. Furniture of of the Baroque period can be recognized its **showy** (ornate) carvings.
　　　註解　華麗的 (形容詞)

3297. Glass is **porous** (permeable) to light.
　　　註解　可穿透的 (形容詞)

3298. This contract does not **forestall** (preclude) my being employed by others at the same time that I am working for you.
　　　註解　阻止 (動詞)

3299. I **relish** (savor) a good joke as much as anyone else.

　　　 | 註解 |　喜好 (動詞)

3300. His **healthy-looking** (reddish) features indicated that he spent much time in the open.

　　　 | 註解 |　微紅的 (形容詞)

3301. The snake moved in a **serpentine** (sinuous) manner.

　　　 | 註解 |　彎曲的 (形容詞)

3302. He was unable to **transmute** (change) his dreams into actualities.

　　　 | 註解 |　變化 (不定詞)

3303. Casual acquaintances were deceived by his **thin layer** (veneer) of sophistication and failed to recognize his fundamental shallowness.

　　　 | 註解 |　外表 (名詞)

3304. If I **accede** (agree) to this demand for blackmail, I am afraid that I will be the victim of future demands.

　　　 | 註解 |　同意 (動詞)

3305. Let us pray that the **benison** (blessing) of peace once more shall prevail among the nations of the world.

　　　 | 註解 |　祝福 (名詞)

3306. If we build a **sewer** (culvert) under the road at this point, we will reduce the possibility of the road's being flooded during the rainy season.

　　　 | 註解 |　下水道 (名詞)

3307. Although he wished to break the nicotine habit, he found himself **impotent** (ineffectual) in resisting the craving for a cigarette.

　　　 | 註解 |　無效的 (形容詞)

3308. You do not make sense; you **talk incoherently** (maunder) and garble your words.

　　　 | 註解 |　嘮嘮叨叨 (動詞片語)

3309. I am not interested in its **provenance** (origin); I am more concerned with its usefulness than with its source.

　　　 | 註解 |　起源 (名詞)

3310. If you persist in wearing such sloppy clothes, people will call you a **slattern**(slut).

　　　 | 註解 |　懶散的女人 (名詞)

3311. The attorney called in his secertary and his partner to witness the signature of the **maker of a will** (testator).

　　註解　立遺囑之人 (名詞片語)

3312. He **recant** (abjured) his allegiance to the king.

　　註解　撤銷 (動詞)

3313. He remained **aloof** (apart) while all the rest conversed.

　　註解　遠離地 (副詞)

3314. Until it was time to open the presents, the children had to **bate** (let down) their curiosity.

　　註解　減弱 (不定詞)

3315. In order to **outwit** (circumvent) the enemy, we will make two preliminary attacks in other sections before starting our major campaign.

　　註解　欺詐 (不定詞)

3316. The public approved the **condign** (fitting) punishment.

　　註解　適宜的 (形容詞)

3317. The defeated people could not satisfy the **avarice** (cupidity) of the conquerors,who demanded excessive tribute.

　　註解　貪財 (名詞)

3318. The **detonation** (explosion) could be heard miles away.

　　註解　爆炸聲 (名詞)

3319. He **doffed** (took off) his hat to the lady.

　　註解　脫去 (動詞)

3320. The stonecutter decided to improve the rough diamond by providing it with several **facets** (sides).

　　註解　刻面 (名詞)

3321. In medieval mythology, **gnomes** (dwarfs) were the special guardians and inhabitants of subterranean mines.

　　註解　小矮人 (名詞)

3322. I like to read a good book in **inclement** (stormy) weather.

　　註解　暴風雨(或雪)的 (形容詞)

3323. Our picnic was marred by **on and off** (intermittent) rains.

　　註解　斷斷續續的 (形容詞片語)

3324. They objected to his **lustful** (libidinous) behavior.

　　註解　好色的 (形容詞)

3325. Her jewels were inexpensive but not **tawdry** (meretricious).
　　　註解　外表美麗的 (形容詞)

3326. Your theories are too **nebulous** (hazy); please clarify them.
　　　註解　模糊的 (形容詞)

3327. The odor of frying onions **permeated** (pervaded) the air.
　　　註解　擴散 (動詞)

3328. He was afraid that he would **quail** (cower) in the face of danger.
　　　註解　畏縮 (動詞)

3329. Let us be grateful that the damage is **remediable** (reparable).
　　　註解　可以補救的 (形容詞)

3330. His dancing was limited to a few **rudimentary** (elementary) steps.
　　　註解　基本的 (形容詞)

3331. They were forced to **skimp** (scrimp) on necessities in order to make their imited supplies last the winter.
　　　註解　節省 (不定詞)

3332. He could not resist the dog's **suppliant** (beseeching) whimpering, and he gaveit some food.
　　　註解　哀求的 (形容詞)

3333. The members of the board of trustees of the museum expected the new **curator** (superintendent) to plan events and exhibitions which would make the museum more popular.
　　　註解　主持人 (名詞)

3334. Your **mawkish** (insipid) sighs fill me disgust.
　　　註解　淡而無味的 (形容詞)

3335. We have to overcome their **provincial** (rustic) attitude and get them to become more cognizant of world problems.
　　　註解　粗俗的 (形容詞)

3336. The magician amazed the audience with his **dexterity** (sleight) of hand.
　　　註解　機巧 (名詞)

3337. I would have to be a **thaumaturgist** (magician) and not a mere doctor to find a remedy for this disease.
　　　註解　魔術師 (名詞)

3338. His daily **ablutions** (washings) were accompanied by loved noises which he humorously labeled 〝Opera in the Bath.〞

    註解　沐浴 (名詞)

3339. Throughout the entire **altercation** (wordy quarrel), not one sensible word was suttered.

    註解　口角 (名詞)

3340. These notions are **archaic** (antiquated).

    註解　古代的 (形容詞)

3341. We cannot accept a system where a favored few can **batten** (grow fat) in extreme comfort while others toil.

    註解　長肥 (動詞)

3342. It is almost impossible to protect oneself from such a base **canard** (hoax).

    註解　謠言 (名詞)

3343. The **fortress** (citadel) overlooked the city like a protecting angel.

    註解　城堡 (名詞)

3344. Spanish food is full of **condiments** (seasonings).

    註解　調味品 (名詞)

3345. The courtier **dressed** (curried) favors of the king.

    註解　調製 (動詞)

3346. He is offended by your frequent **slanderings** (detractions) of his ability as a leader.

    註解　誹謗 (名詞)

3347. Although we find occasional snatches of genuine poetry in his work, most of his writing is mere **doggerel** (poor verse).

    註解　打油詩 (名詞)

3348. Because of his wealth and social position, he had **entree** (entrance) into the most exclusive circles.

    註解　進入 (名詞)

3349. Your **jocular** (facetious) remarks are not appropriate at this serious moment.

    註解　好笑的 (形容詞)

3350. The company staged a a midnight **foray** (raid) against the enemy outpost.

    註解　搶掠 (名詞)

3351. He was **urged on** (prodded) by his friends until he yielded to their wishes.

  註解 督促 (動詞，被動式)

3352. He spoke with a **humility** (meekness) and lack of pride which impressed his listeners.

  註解 謙卑 (名詞)

3353. The **obituary notice** (necrology) of those buried in this cemetery is available in the office.

  註解 訃聞 (名詞)

3354. It is interesting to note how public opinion **vibrates** (oscillates) between the extremes of optimism and pessimism.

  註解 回響 (動詞)

3355. He argues that these books had a **pernicious** (deleterious) effect on young and susceptible minds.

  註解 有害的 (形容詞)

3356. Gray and Burns were **forerunner** (precursor) of the Romantic Movement in English literature.

  註解 先驅 (名詞)

3357. His **qualms** (misgivings) of conscience had become so great that he decided to abandon his plans.

  註解 焦慮不安 (名詞)

3358. Because he was a slow reader, he decided to take a course in **curative** (remedial) reading.

  註解 矯正的 (形容詞)

3359. The artist has captured the sadness of childhood in his portrait of the boy with the **dejected** (rueful).

  註解 悲傷的 (形容詞)

3360. He is as **skittish** (frisky) as a kitten playing with a piece of string.

  註解 活潑的 (形容詞)

3361. We **supplicate** (solicit) your majesty to grant him amnesty.

  註解 懇求 (動詞)

3362. In spite of all our efforts to keep the meeting a secret, news of our conclusions **exhaled** (transpired).

  註解 散發 (動詞)

3363. In China, the people **venerate** (revere) their ancestors.

註解 敬奉 (動詞)

3364. We must suppress our **bestial** (beastlike) desires and work for peaceful and civilized ends.

註解 獸性的 (形容詞)

3365. Although he reguarded by many as a **curmudgeon** (churlish person), a few of us were aware of the many kindesses and acts of charity which he secretly performed.

註解 守財奴 (名詞)

3366. The sergeant's remarks were filled with **profane oaths** (expletives) which refected on the intelligence and character of the new recruits.

註解 咒罵語 (名詞)

3367. If I wished to **impute** (ascribe) blame to the officers in change of this program, I would come out and state it definitely and without hesitation.

註解 歸罪於 (不定詞)

3368. I find your analogy inaccurate because I do not see the **parity** (equality) between the two illustrations.

註解 相同 (名詞)

3369. During the recent ice storm, many people **slithered** (slided) down this hill as they walked to the station.

註解 滑倒 (動詞)

3370. Moses scolded the idol worshippers in the tribe because he **abominated** (execrated) the custom.

註解 痛恨 (動詞)

3371. The philanthropist was noted for his **generosity** (altruism).

註解 慷慨 (名詞)

3372. The child was delighted with the **trinket** (bauble) she had won in the grab bag.

註解 小玩具 (名詞)

3373. The **candor** (frankness) and simplisity of his speech imressed all.

註解 坦誠 (名詞)

3374. He could **cite** (quote) passages in the Bible from memory.

註解 引用 (動詞)

3375.　A **cursory** (casual) examination of the ruins indicates the possibility of arson; amore extensive study should be undertaken.
　　註解　粗略的 (形容詞)

3376.　Your acceptance of his support will ultimately prove to be a **detriment** (damage) rather than an aid to your cause.
　　註解　損害 (名詞)

3377.　Do not be so **arbitrary** (dogmatic) about that statement; it can be easily refuted.
　　註解　武斷的 (形容詞)

3378.　Opponents of our present tax program argue that it discourages **entrepreneurs**(contractors) from trying new fields of business activity.
　　註解　企業家 (名詞)

3379.　Because he was a **facile** (glib) speaker, he never refused a request to address an organization.
　　註解　隨和的 (形容詞)

3380.　Caesar ridiculed his wife's **forebodings** (presentiments) about the Ides of March.
　　註解　預感 (名詞)

3381.　The gluttonous guest **gorged** (cramed) himself with food as though he had not eaten for days.
　　註解　狼吞虎嚥 (動詞)

3382.　A ruler who maintains his power by **intimidation** (fear) is bound to develop clandestine resistance.
　　註解　脅迫 (名詞)

3383.　The **lewd** (licentious) monarch helped bring about his country's downfall.
　　註解　放縱的 (形容詞)

3384.　Because he was able to perform feats of **necromancy** (conjuration), the natives thought he was in league with the devil.
　　註解　巫術，魔術 (名詞)

3385.　Only an insane person could **execute** (perpetrate) such a horrible crime.
　　註解　犯行 (動詞)

3386.　The hawk is a **predatory** (plundering) bird.
　　註解　食肉的，搶奪的 (形容詞)

TOEFL

3387. When the two colleges to which he had applied accepted him, he was in a
dilemma (quandary) as to which one he should attend.

註解　左右爲難 (名詞)

3388. Her **reminiscences** (recollections) of her experiences are so fascinating
that she ought to write a book.

註解　回憶 (名詞)

3389. We cannot afford to wait while you **ruminate** (ponder) upon these planes.

註解　考慮 (動詞)

3390. He **skulked** (slinked) through the less fashionable sections of the city in
order to avoid meeting any of his former friends.

註解　溜走 (動詞)

3391. I find no similarity between your **supposititious** (hypothetical)
illustration andthe problem we are facing.

註解　推論的 (形容詞，同 hypothetic)

3392. How long do you think a man can endure such **toil** (travail) and
degradation without rebelling?

註解　辛勞 (名詞)

3393. We may regard a hungry man's stealing as a **venial** (trivial) crime.

註解　可原諒的，不重要的 (形容詞)

3394. With a bifurcated (forked) branch and a piece of elastic rubber, he made a
crude but effective slingshot.

註解　分叉的 (形容詞)

3395. In normal writing we run our letters together in **cursive** (flowing) form; in
printing, we separate the letters.

註解　草書的，流暢的 (形容詞)

3396. Your remarks are **explicit** (open); no one can misinterpret them.

註解　明白的 (形容詞)

3397. This anthology provides a **medley** (miscellany) of the author's output in
the fields of satire, criticism and political analysis.

註解　混合 (名詞)

3398. In this **perilous** (parlous) times, we must overcome the work of saboteure
and propagandists.

註解　危險的 (形容詞)

3399. His studies of the primitive art forms of the **aboriginal** (native) Indians were widely reported in the scientific journals.

註解 土著的 (形容詞)

3400. The unions will attempt to **amalgamate** (combine) their groups into national body.

註解 合併 (不定詞)

3401. His **zeal** (ardor) was contagious; soon everyone was eagerly working.

註解 熱心 (名詞)

3402. The **beatific** (blissful) smile on the child's face made us very happy.

註解 快樂的 (形容詞)

3403. Poverty is a **canker** (sore) in the body politic; it must be sured.

註解 傷害 (名詞)

3404. Your **erratic** (devious) behavior in this matter puzzles me since you are usually direct and straightforward.

註解 古怪的 (形容詞)

3405. He found the **dolorous** (sorrowful) lamentations of the bereaved family emotionally disturbing and the left as quickly as he could.

註解 悲傷的 (形容詞)

3406. In medieval days, Paris was **environed** (enclosed) by a wall.

註解 包圍 (動詞，被動式)

3407. He tried to **facilitate** (make less difficult) matters at home by getting a part-time job.

註解 使容易 (不定詞)

3408. The audience shuddered as they listened to the details of the **gory** (bloody) massacre.

註解 血腥的 (形容詞)

3409. Mendel's formula explains the appearance of **hybrid** (mongrel) and pure species in breeding.

註解 雜種 (名詞)

3410. In their **incommodious** (not spacious) quarters, they had to improvise for closet space.

註解 不方便的，不寬敞的 (形容詞)

3411. The strike settlement has clooapsed because both sides are **adamant** (intransigent).

　　　註解　不妥協的 (形容詞)

3412. He was universally feared because of his many **nefarious** (wicked) deeds.

　　　註解　兇惡的 (形容詞)

3413. Although the **professed** (ostensible) purpose of this expedition is to discover new lands, we are really interested in finding new markets for our products.

　　　註解　表面的 (形容詞)

3414. Although the artist used various media from time to time, he had a **predilection**(partiality) for watercolor.

　　　註解　偏好 (名詞)

3415. Because of the captain's carelessness, the ship crashed inot the **quay** (dock).

　　　註解　碼頭 (名詞)

3416. He was accused of being **remiss** (negligent) in his duty.

　　　註解　不小心的 (形容詞)

3417. When we **ransacked** (rummaged) through the trunks in the attic, we found many souvenirs of our childhood days.

　　　註解　搜索 (動詞)

3418. When we reached the oasis, we were able to **quench** (slake) our thirst.

　　　註解　結束，緩和 (不定詞)

3419. He begged the doctors to grant him **cessation** (surcease) from his suffering.

　　　註解　斷絕，停止 (名詞)

3420. The decision of the jury has arrived at is a **travesty** (comical parody).

　　　註解　歪曲 (名詞)

3421. His attempts at pacifying the mob were met by angry hoots and **vituperation** (billingsgate).

　　　註解　兇罵，下流話 (名詞)

3422. The incessant drone seemed to **hypnotize** (mesmerize) him and place him in a hypnotic trance.

　　　註解　催眠 (不定詞)

3423. The difficulties anticipated by the obstetriciance at **parturition** (childbirth) did not materialize; it was a normal delivery.

　　|註解| 分娩 (名詞)

3424. I don't know whether it is better to be ignorant of a subject or to have a mere **smattering** (slight knowledge) of information about it.

　　|註解| 一知半解 (名詞)

3425. We had to abandon our **abortive** (fruitless) attempts.

　　|註解| 無結果的 (形容詞)

3426. The miser's aim is to **amass** (collect) and hoard as much gold possible.

　　|註解| 積聚 (不定詞)

3427. In the **argot** (slang) of the underworld, he "was taken for a ride."

　　|註解| 暗語 (名詞)

3428. The **shrewd** (canny) Scotsman was more than a match for the swindlers.

　　|註解| 精明的 (形容詞)

3429. In such (a)n **agglomeration** (conglomeration) of miscellaneous slatistice, it was impossible to find single area of analysis.

　　|註解| 結塊 (名詞)

3430. He was **devoid** (lacking) of any personal desire for gain in his endervor to secure improvement in the community.

　　|註解| 缺乏的 (形容詞)

3431. I thought I was talking to mature audience; instead, I find myself addressing a pack of **dolts** (blockheads) and indiots.

　　|註解| 傻瓜 (名詞)

3432. The may fly is an **ephemeral** (evanescent) creature.

　　|註解| 短命的 (形容詞)

3433. The quarrels and bickering of the two small **cliques** (factions) within the club distured the majority of the members.

　　|註解| 派系 (名詞)

3434. We must not treat the battle lightly for we are facing a **formidable** (menacing) foe.

　　|註解| 險惡的 (形容詞)

3435. Nylon can be woven into **gossamer** (sheer) or thick fabrics.

　　|註解| 輕薄的 (形容詞)

3436. You are **hypercritical** (overcritical) in your demands for perfection; we all make mistakes.

　註解　苛求的 (形容詞)

3437. The married couple agreed incessantly and finally decided to separate because they were **inharmonious** (incompatible).

　註解　不協調的 (形容詞)

3438. Although the **inherent** (intrinsic) value of this award is small, I shall always cherish it.

　註解　固有的 (形容詞)

3439. He was satisfied with his attempts to **limn** (portray) her beauty on canvas.

　註解　描畫 (不定詞)

3440. The **metamorphosis** (mutations) of caterpillar to butterfly is typical of many such changes in animal life.

　註解　變形 (名詞)

3441. I must accept his argument since you have been unable to present any **negation** (denial) of his evidence.

　註解　否定 (名詞)

3442. The real hero is never **pretentious** (ostentatious).

　註解　驕傲的 (形容詞)

3443. This **banter** (persiflage) is not appropriate when we have such serious problems to discuss.

　註解　嘲弄 (名詞)

3444. The king traveled to Boston because he wanted the **preeminent** (peerless) surgeon in the field to perform the operation.

　註解　卓越的 (形容詞)

3445. His classmates were repelled by his **whining** (querulous) and complaining statements.

　註解　抱怨的 (形容詞)

3446. I must **remonstrate** (protest) about the lack of police protection in this area.

　註解　抗議 (動詞)

3447. You will not be able to fool your friends with such an obvious **ruse** (stratagem).

　註解　詐術 (名詞)

3448. This is a **sleazy** (flimsy) material; it will not wear well.
　　　註解　粗薄的 (形容詞)

3449. One of the difficulties of our present air age is the need of travelers to **adjust toclimate** (acclimate) themselves to their new and often strange environments.
　　　註解　適應 (不定詞片語)

3450. Because the country was in a state of anarchy and lacked a leader, it was described as a(n) **acephalous** (headless) monstrosity.
　　　註解　無領袖的 (形容詞)

3451. It is impossible to obtain their **compliance** (acquiescence) to the proposal because it abhorrent to their philosophy.
　　　註解　聽從 (名詞)

3452. I will entertain this concept as a(n) **adjunct** (appendix) to the proposal because it is abhorrent to their philosophy.
　　　註解　附錄 (名詞)

3453. Although age had **blanched** (whitened) his hair, he was still vigorous and energetic.
　　　註解　變白 (動詞，完成式)

3454. This **debacle** (downfall) in the government can only result in anarchy.
　　　註解　災難 (名詞)

3455. In his **feverish** (febrile) condition, he was subject to nightmares hallucinations.
　　　註解　發燒的 (形容詞)

3456. Even though he disscouress on the matter like a **pundit** (authority), he is actually rather ignorant about this topic.
　　　註解　權威 (名詞)

3457. Despite all his protests, his classmates continued to call him by that unflattering **sobriquet** (nickname).
　　　註解　綽號 (名詞)

3458. His **craven** (timorous) manner betrayed the fear he felt at the moment.
　　　註解　膽小的 (形容詞)

3459. The skin of his leg was **eroded** (abraded) by the sharp rocks.
　　　註解　磨擦 (動詞，被動式)

3460. Medieval sailing vessels brought **fragrant** (aromatic) herbs from China to Europe.

註解　芳香的 (形容詞)

3461. Many listeners were fooled by the pious **phraseology** (cant) and hypocrisy of his speech.

註解　措辭，用語 (名詞)

3462. After avoiding their chaperon, the lovers had a **clandestine** (underhand) meeting.

註解　秘密的 (形容詞)

3463. It **deputized** (devolved) upon us, the survivors, to arrange peace terms with the enemy.

註解　委託 (動詞)

3464. **Epicures** (Connoisseurs) frequent this restaurant because it features exotic wines and dishes.

註解　美食者，行家 (名詞)

3465. Your statement is **dissentient** (factious) and will upset the harmony that now exists.

註解　持異議的 (形容詞)

3466. The **absurdity** (incongruity) of his wearing sneakers with formal attire amused the observers.

註解　荒謬，不合適 (名詞)

3467. As soon as the newspapers carried the story of his connection with the criminals, his friends began to **ostracize** (exile) him.

註解　排斥 (不定詞)

3468. We admired his **astute** (perspicacious) wisdom and sagacity.

註解　機敏的 (形容詞)

3469. The chairman made a few **prefatory** (introductory) remarks before he called on the first speaker.

註解　開場的 (形容詞)

3470. Do not **equivocate** (quibble); I want a straightforward and definite answer.

註解　推托，模稜兩可 (動詞)

3471. I find my new work so **compensating** (remunerative) that I may not return to my previous employment.

註解 有報酬的 (形容詞)

3472. I like city so much that I can never understand how people can **rusticate** (dwellin the country) in the suburbs.

註解 定居鄉村 (動詞)

3473. Such **sloth** (laziness) in a young person is deplorable.

註解 懶惰 (名詞)

3474. News of their **surreptitious** (covert) meeting gradually leaked out.

註解 秘密的 (形容詞)

3475. The tribe **trekked** (migrated) further north that summer in search of available.

註解 移居 (動詞)

3476. We shall now examine the **abdominal** (ventral) plates of this serpent.

註解 腹部的 (形容詞)

3477. I suspect that this area is infested with malaria as I can readily smell the **miasma** (swamp gas).

註解 瘴氣 (名詞)

3478. In his **purblind** (obtuse) condition, he could not identify the people he saw.

註解 遲鈍的 (形容詞)

3479. I hope you will find **solace** (consolation) in the thought that all of us share your loss.

註解 安慰 (名詞)

3480. I am here not to **titillate** (tickle) my audience but to enlighten it.

註解 刺激 (不定詞)

3481. "**Arrant** (Unmitigated) knave," an epithet found in books dealing with the age of chivalry, is a term of condemnation.

註解 徹底的 (形容詞)

3482. He **deluded** (beguiled) himself during the long hours by playing solitaire.

註解 迷惑 (動詞)

3483. We work to the **clear and shrill** (clarion) call of the bugle.

註解 清晰而尖銳的 (形容詞片語)

3484. According to geologists, the **conifers** (pine trees) to bear flowers.

  註解 結球樹 (名詞)

3485. Laertes told Ophelia that Hamlet could only **procrastinate** (dally) with her affections.

  註解 拖延 (動詞)

3486. The **saintly** (devout) man prayed daily.

  註解 虔誠的 (形容詞)

3487. Sometimes **lethargic** (torpid) talents in our friends' surprise those of us who never realized how gifted our a acquaintances really are.

  註解 昏睡的 (形容詞)

3488. Hollywood actresses often create **sham** (factitious) tears by using glycerine.

  註解 人工的 (形容詞)

3489. He was awarded the medal for his **fortitude** (bravery) in the battle.

  註解 勇敢 (名詞)

3490. Your objections are **inconsequential** (trivial) and may be disregarded.

  註解 不重要的 (形容詞)

3491. He was able to **liquidate** (clear up) all his debts in a short period of time.

  註解 清償 (不定詞)

3492. He tried to be impartial in his efforts to **mete** (measure) our justice.

  註解 衡量 (不定詞)

3493. This mountain slope contains slides that will challenge experts as well as an **neophytes** (tiroes).

  註解 新手 (名詞，同 tyroes)

3494. According to the United States Constitution, a person must commit an **overt** (apparent) act before he may be tried for treason.

  註解 明顯的 (形容詞)

3495. I think your **forward** (pert) and impudent remarks call for an apology.

  註解 魯莽的 (形容詞)

3496. We ignored these **forewarnings** (premonitions) of disaster because they appeared to be based on childish fears.

  註解 預告 (名詞)

3497. After this geyser erupts, it will remain **quiescent** (dormant) for twenty-four hours.

> 註解　安靜的 (形容詞)

3498. In his grief, he tried to **rend** (tear apart) his garments.

> 註解　割裂 (不定詞)

3499. The escaped convict was a dangerous and **pitiless** (ruthless) murderer.

> 註解　無情的 (形容詞)

3500. Each spring, the snake **sloughs off** (casts off) its skin.

> 註解　蛻去 (動詞片語)

3501. The five **venturous** (enterprising) young men decided to look for a approach to the mountain top.

> 註解　大膽的 (形容詞)

3502. After repeated rejections of its **admonitions** (cautions), the country was forced to issue an ultimatum.

> 註解　警告 (名詞)

3503. Your **clownish** (boorish) remarks to the driver of the other car were not warranted by the situation and served merely to enrage him.

> 註解　粗野的 (形容詞)

3504. We do more to **decimate** (kill) our population in automobile accidents than we do in war.

> 註解　殺害 (不定詞)

3505. He did not **flinch** (shrink) in the face of danger but fought back bravely.

> 註解　退縮 (動詞)

3506. These remarks do not have any relationship to the problem at hand; they are **incongruous** (absurd) and should be stricken from the record.

> 註解　不合適的 (形容詞)

3507. In the **little world** (microcosm) of our small village, we find illustrations of all the evils that beset the universe.

> 註解　小天地 (名詞片語)

3508. As we study the **morbid** (pathological) aspects of this disease, we must not overlook the psychological elements.

> 註解　病理的 (形容詞)

3509. Although there are some doubts, the **reputed** (putative) author of this work is Massinger.

　註解　推定的 (形容詞)

3510. Why do you ignore the spiritual aspects and emphasize only the corporeal and the **somatic** (physical)?

　註解　身體的 (形容詞)

3511. Awakened by the sound of the **tocsin** (alarm bell), we rushed to our positions to await the attack.

　註解　警鈴 (名詞)

3512. The teller **decamped** (absconded) with the bonds and was not found.

　註解　逃亡 (動詞)

3513. He was described as a(n) **ambulatory** (capable walking) patient because he was not confined to his bed.

　註解　能走的 (形容詞)

3514. In this time of crisis, it **behooves** (be incumbent upon) all of us to remain calmand await the instructions of our superiors.

　註解　應該 (動詞，同 behoves)

3515. Because the racehorse had outdistanced its competition so easily, the reporter wrote that the race was won in a **canter** (slow gallop).

　註解　慢跑 (名詞)

3516. Their dreams of **nuptial** (conjugal) bliss were shattered as soon as their temperaments clashed.

　註解　婚姻的 (形容詞)

3517. The walls of the dungeon were **dank** (damp) and slimy.

　註解　陰濕的 (形容詞)

3518. The magician was so **dexterous** (nimble) that we could not follow him as he performed his tricks.

　註解　靈活的 (形容詞)

3519. A shark may be identified by its **dorsal** (back) fin, which projects above the surface of the ocean.

　註解　背脊的 (形容詞)

3520. Although we had hired him as a messenger, we soon began to use him as ageneral **factotum** (handyman) around the office.

　註解　雜役 (名詞)

3521. There is no connection between these two events; their timing is extremely **fortuitous** (accidental).

　　　註解　意外的 (形容詞)

3522. We must yield to the **incontrovertible** (indisputable) evidence which you have presented and free your client.

　　　註解　明確的 (形容詞)

3523. The tremendous waves **inundated** (overflowed) the town.

　　　註解　淹沒 (動詞)

3524. Her figure was **supple** (lithe) and willowy.

　　　註解　柔軟的 (形容詞)

3525. Every evening this terminal is filled with the thousands of commuters who are going from this **metropolis** (large city) to their homes in the suburbs.

　　　註解　大都會 (名詞)

3526. John left his position with the company because he felt that advancement was based on **favoritism** (nepotism) rather than ability.

　　　註解　偏袒 (名詞，同 favouritism)

3527. The **antimilitarisms** (pacifists) urged that we reduce our military budget and recall our troops stationed overseas.

　　　註解　反軍事主義者，和平主義者 (名詞)

3528. He is bound to succeed because his **pertinacious** (persistent) nature will not permit him to quit.

　　　註解　堅持的 (形容詞)

3529. I feel confident that the forces of justice will **preponderate** (outweigh) eventually in this dispute.

　　　註解　佔優勢 (動詞)

3530. He was impressed by the air of **quietude** (tranquillity) and peace that pervaded the valley.

　　　註解　安靜 (名詞，同 tranquility)

3531. He **rendered** (delivered) aid to the needy and indigent.

　　　註解　供給 (動詞)

3532. The priest decided to abandon his **sacerdotal** (priestly) duties and enter the field of politics.

　　　註解　僧侶的 (形容詞)

3533. Such **untidy** (slovenly) work habits will never produce good products.

> 註解 雜亂的 (形容詞)

3534. In the tropics, the natives find **nourishment** (sustenance) easy to obtain.

> 註解 營養料 (名詞)

3535. She was **tremulous** (trembling) more from excitement than from fear.

> 註解 發抖的 (形容詞)

3536. I can recommend him for this position because I have always found him **veracious** (truthful) and reliable.

> 註解 誠實的 (形容詞)

3537. Since you **advert to** (refer to) this matter so frequently, you must regard it as important.

> 註解 注意 (動詞片語)

3538. After the film editors had **bowdlerized** (expurgated) the language in the script, the motion picture's rating was changed from "R" to "PG".

> 註解 刪去 (動詞，完成式)

3539. His **licentious** (incontinent) behavior off stage shocked many people and they refused to attend the plays and movies in which he appeared.

> 註解 放縱的 (形容詞)

3540. His **milieu** (environment) is watercolor although he has produced excellent oil paintings and lithographs.

> 註解 環境 (名詞，法國字)

3541. Most mammals are **four-footed animals** (quadrupeds).

> 註解 四腳動物 (名詞片語)

3542. You are using all the devices of a **sophist** (quibbler) in trying to prove your case; your argument is specious.

> 註解 巧辯家 (名詞)

3543. The father confessor **absolved** (pardoned) him of his sins.

> 註解 原諒 (動詞)

3544. Many social workers have attempted to **ameliorate** (improve) the conditions of people living in the slums.

> 註解 改善 (不定詞)

3545. The Trojan war proved to the Greeks that cunning and **trickery** (artifice) were often more effective than military might.

> 註解 詭計 (名詞)

3546. He **was belaboring** (assailed verbally) his opponent.

　　　　註解　　重擊 (動詞，進行式)

3547. Even though he wore shoulder pads, the football player broke his **clavicle** (collarbone) during a practice scrimmage.

　　　　註解　　鎖骨 (名詞)

3548. With the **connivance** (assistance) of his friends, he plotted to embarrass the teacher.

　　　　註解　　默許 (名詞)

3549. This sneak attack is the work of a **dastard** (coward).

　　　　註解　　膽小鬼 (名詞)

3550. This scheme is so **diabolical** (devilish) that I must reject it.

　　　　註解　　殘酷的 (形容詞，同 diabolic)

3551. In his **senility** (dotage), the old man bored us with long tales of events in his childhood.

　　　　註解　　年老 (名詞)

3552. The audience was so disappointed in the play that many did not remain to hear the **epilogue** (speech).

　　　　註解　　收場白 (名詞，同 epilog)

3553. The knight said, "I would **fain** (gladly) be your protector."

　　　　註解　　樂意的 (形容詞)

3554. According to the legend, Romulus and Remus were **reared** (fostered) by ashe-wolf.

　　　　註解　　養育 (動詞，被動式)

3555. We have reason to be thankful, for our crops were good and our **granaries** (repositories) are full.

　　　　註解　　穀倉 (名詞)

3556. We must devote time to the needs of our **incorporeal** (immaterial) mind as well as our corporeal body.

　　　　註解　　精神的，非物質的 (形容詞)

3557. He became **insured** (accustomed) to the Alaskan cold.

　　　　註解　　習慣的 (形容詞)

3558. Try to settle this amicably; I do not want to start **litigation** (lawsuit).

　　　　註解　　訴訟 (名詞)

3559. When challenged by the other porses in the race, the thoroughbred proved its **mettle** (spirit) by its determination to hold the lead.

註解　勇氣 (名詞)

3560. Do not let him **nettle** (vex) you with his sarcastic remarks.

註解　激怒 (動詞，使役動詞 let 之後接原型動詞)

3561. They sang **paeans** (songs) of praise.

註解　讚美歌 (名詞，同 peans)

3562. The lawyer wanted to know all the **pertinent** (suitable) details.

註解　適當的 (形容詞)

3563. The excuse he gave for his lateness was so **ridiculous** (preposterous) that everyone laughed.

註解　奇妙的 (形容詞)

3564. These books display the **quintessence** (embodiment) of wit.

註解　精髓，體系(名詞)

3565. The two fleets met at the **meeting place** (rendezvous) at the appointed time.

註解　集會地 (名詞片語)

3566. His stealing of the altar cloth was a very **profane** (sacrilegious) act.

註解　污神的 (形容詞)

3567. "You are a **sluggard** (lazy person), a drone, a parasite," the angry father shouted at his lazy son.

註解　懶人 (名詞)

3568. When I visited him in the hospital, I found him **swathed** (wrapped around) inbandages.

註解　包緊的 (形容詞)

3569. I am afraid his **cutting** (trenchant) wit for it is so often sarcastic.

註解　銳利的 (形容詞)

3570. After we had waded through all the **verbiage** (verbosity), we discovered that the writer had said very little.

註解　冗長，贅詞 (名詞)

3571. He found the only wells in the area were **brackish** (saline); drinking the water made him nauseated.

註解　有鹽味的 (形容詞)

3572. I was unpretared for the state of **decrepitude** (feebleness) in which I had found my old friend; he seemed to have aged twenty years in six months.
註解 衰老 (名詞)

3573. The **incredulous** (skeptical) judge refused to accept the statement of the defendant.
註解 不肯相信的，多疑的 (形容詞)

3574. Although at this time he was advocating a policy of neutrality, one could usually find him adopting a more **bellicose** (militant) attitude.
註解 好戰的 (形容詞)

3575. His years of study of the language at the university did not enable him to understand the **patois** (dialects) of the natives.
註解 方言 (名詞)

3576. Our soldiers who served in Vietnam will never forget he drudgery of marching through the **bogs** (quagmires) of the delta country.
註解 沼澤地 (名詞)

3577. **Sophistication** (Artificiality) is an acquired characteristic, found more frequently among city dwellers than among residents of rural areas.
註解 摻雜，人工 (名詞)

3578. The drunkards mocked him because of his **abstemious** (temperate) habits.
註解 適度的 (形容詞)

3579. He was **amenable** (tractable) to any suggestions which came from those he looked up to; he resented advice from his inferiors.
註解 肯接受的，溫順的 (形容詞)

3580. Artists and **craftsmen** (artisans) alike are necessary to the development of aculture.
註解 手工匠 (名詞)

3581. He apologizes for his **belated** (delayed) note of condolence to the widow of his friend and explained that he had just learned of her husband's untimely death.
註解 延誤的 (形容詞)

3582. The lightning **splits asunder** (cleaves) the tree in two.
註解 劈開 (動詞片語)

3583. He had developed into a(n) **aesthete** (connoisseur) of fine china.
註解 審美家 (名詞，同 esthete)

3584. Your threats cannot **daunt** (intimidate) me.

> 註解 恐嚇 (動詞)

3585. The king's **diadem** (crown) was on display at the museum.

> 註解 王冠 (名詞)

3586. Many folk tales have sprung up about this **doughty** (courageous) pioneer who opened up the New World for his followers.

> 註解 堅強的 (形容詞)

3587. In his will, he dictated the **epitaph** (inscription) he wanted placed on his tom-stone.

> 註解 墓誌銘 (名詞)

3588. Your reasoning must be **fallacious** (misleading) because it leads to a ridiculous answer.

> 註解 不可靠的 (形容詞)

3589. The **fractious** (unruly) horse unseated its rider.

> 註解 性情暴烈的 (形容詞)

3590. The politician could never speak simply; he was always **pompous** (grandiloquent).

> 註解 誇大的 (形容詞)

3591. Because he was an **incorrigible** (uncontrollable) criminal, he was sentenced tolife imprisonment.

> 註解 任性的 (形容詞)

3592. He had expected criticism but not the **invective** (contumely) which greeted hisproposal.

> 註解 大罵，無禮 (名詞)

3593. His face was so **livid** (black and blue) with rage that we were afraid that he might have an attack of apoplexy.

> 註解 死灰色的 (形容詞)

3594. I fail to see the **nexus** (connection) which binds these two widely separated events.

> 註解 連結 (名詞)

3595. He proudly showed us through his **palatial** (magnificent) home.

> 註解 壯麗的 (形容詞)

3596. I am afraid this news will **perturb** (agitate) him.

> 註解 擾亂 (動詞)

3597. The vultures flying overhead **presaged** (forecasted) the discovery of the corpsein the desert.

　　註解　預測 (動詞)

3598. You are unpopular because you are too free with your **taunts** (quips) and sarcastic comments.

　　註解　笑罵，雙關語 (名詞)

3599. Because he refused to support his fellow members in their drive, he was shunned as a(n) **apostate** (renegade).

　　註解　背叛者 (名詞)

3600. The brash insurance salesman invaded the **inviolable** (sacrosanct) privacy of the office of the president of the company.

　　註解　神聖不可侵犯的 (形容詞)

3601. The solemnity of the occasion filled us with **sobriety** (soberness).

　　註解　節制 (名詞)

3602. We must face the enemy without **perturbation** (trepidation) if we are to win this battle.

　　註解　混亂，驚恐 (名詞)

3603. This article is too **verbose** (wordy); we must edit it.

　　註解　冗長的 (形容詞)

3604. Most Americans were unaware of the **advent** (arrival) of the Nuclear Age until the news of Hiroshima reached them.

　　註解　來臨 (名詞)

3605. The **debased** (degraded) wretch spoke only of his past glories and honors.

　　註解　貶低的 (形容詞)

3606. The military police stopped the **melees** (fracas) in the bar and arrested the belligerents.

　　註解　混戰 (名詞)

3607. I do not expect the **millennium** (thousand-year period) to come during my lifetime.

　　註解　千年 (名詞)

3608. His **embezzlements** (peculations) were not discovered until the auditors found discrepancies in the financial statements.

　　註解　盜用公款 (名詞)

3609. We will have to place this house under **strict isolation** (quarantine) until we determine the exact nature of the disease.
> 註解 | 隔離 (名詞片語)

3610. Your **sophomoric** (immature) remarks indicate that you have not given much thought to the problem.
> 註解 | 一知半解的，未成熟的 (形容詞)

3611. What **criterion** (touchstone) can be used to measure the character of a person?
> 註解 | 標準，試金石 (名詞)

3612. The doctor recommended total **sobriety** (abstinence) from salted foods.
> 註解 | 節制 (名詞)

3613. He observed the social **amenities** (courtesies).
> 註解 | 溫柔 (名詞)

3614. Please **make clear** (ascertain) his present address.
> 註解 | 確定 (動詞片語)

3615. As soon as the city was **beleaguered** (besieged), life became more subdued as the citizens began their long wait for outside assistance.
> 註解 | 包圍 (動詞，被動式)

3616. In the **capacious** (spacious) areas of the railroad terminal, thousands of travelers lingered while waiting for their train.
> 註解 | 廣大的 (形容詞)

3617. There was a **fissure** (cleft) in the huge boulder.
> 註解 | 裂縫 (名詞)

3618. Foreigners frequently are unaware of the **connotations** (implied meanings) ofthe words they use.
> 註解 | 內涵，暗示 (名詞)

3619. Despite the dangerous nature of the undertaking, the **indomitable** (dauntless) soldier volunteered for the assignment.
> 註解 | 不屈不撓的 (形容詞)

3620. The man was **dour** (sullen) and taciturn.
> 註解 | 頑固的 (形容詞)

3621. I know I am **liable to err** (fallible), but I feel confident that I am right this time.
> 註解 | 易犯錯的 (形容詞片語)

3622. Hamlet says, "**Frailty** (Delicacy), thy name is woman."

　　註解　脆弱 (名詞)

3623. His **grandiose** (imposing) manner impressed those who met him for the first time.

　　註解　華麗的 (形容詞)

3624. I could not understand their **idioms** (usages) because literal translation made no sense.

　　註解　習慣語 (名詞)

3625. Your **incredulity** (disbelief) in the face of all the evidence is hard to understand.

　　註解　懷疑 (名詞)

3626. He was **wheedled** (inveigled) into joining the club.

　　註解　誘騙 (動詞，被動式)

3627. They were both **averse** (loath) for him to go.

　　註解　反對的 (形容詞)

3628. She had the gracious **mien** (demeanor) of a queen.

　　註解　風采 (名詞，同 demeanour)

3629. The **nibs** (points) of fountain pens often became clotted and corroded.

　　註解　筆尖 (名詞)

3630. In spite of all the **palaver** (chatter) before the meeting, the delegates were ableto conduct serious negotiations when they sat down at the conference table.

　　註解　談判，喋喋不休 (名詞)

3631. I fail to understand why such an innocent remark should create such **perturbation** (agitation).

　　註解　混亂，焦慮 (名詞)

3632. Hamlet felt a **foreboding** (presentiment) about his meeting with Laertes.

　　註解　預感 (名詞)

3633. By **caprice** (quirk) of fate, he found himself working for the man whom he had discharged years before.

　　註解　反覆無常 (名詞)

3634. Joan of Arc refused to **disown** (repudiate) her statements even though she knew she would be burned at the stake as a witch.

　　註解　否認 (不定詞)

3635. If we are to improve conditions in this prison, we must first get rid of the **inclined to cruelty** (sadistic) warden.
> 註解　虐待的 (形容詞片語)

3636. The king enjoyed the **servilely flattering** (sycophantic) attentions of his followers.
> 註解　奉承的 (形容詞片語)

3637. After all the trials and **distresses** (tribulations) we have gone through, we need this rest.
> 註解　憂愁 (名詞)

3638. The **green** (verdant) meadows in the spring are always an inspiring sight.
> 註解　綠油油的 (形容詞)

3639. Under the **aegis** (shield) of the Bill of Rights, we enjoy our most treasured freedoms.
> 註解　保護 (名詞)

3640. He was disappointed in the litter because the puppies were **brindled** (variegated); he had hoped for animals of a uniform color.
> 註解　斑紋的 (形容詞)

3641. After the storm the beach was littered with the fronds (frondages) of palm trees.
> 註解　樹葉 (名詞)

3642. Because of his **inebriety** (habitual intoxication), he was discharged from his position as family chauffeur.
> 註解　酒醉 (名詞)

3643. As the ship left the harbor, he became **squeamish** (queasy) and thought that he was going to suffer from seasickness.
> 註解　想嘔吐的 (形容詞)

3644. I do not need a **sleep producer** (soporific) when I listen to one of his speeches.
> 註解　安眠藥 (名詞片語)

3645. He read **profound** (abstruse) works in philosophy.
> 註解　深奧的 (形容詞)

3646. His **amiable** (lovable) disposition pleased all who had dealings with him.
> 註解　友愛的 (形容詞)

3647. The cavalier could not understand the **ascetic** (austere) life led by the monks.

　　　註解　修道者的，苦修的 (形容詞)

3648. His **bellicose** (warlike) disposition alienated his friends.

　　　註解　好戰的 (形容詞)

3649. The audience admired the **caparison** (trappings) of the horses as they made their entrance into the circus ring.

　　　註解　馬的服飾 (名詞)

3650. In his telegram, he wished the newlyweds a lifetime of **connubial** (matrimonial) bliss.

　　　註解　夫婦的 (形容詞)

3651. In as much as we must meet a deadline, do not loiter (dawdle) over this work.

　　　註解　浪費光陰 (動詞)

3652. They admired her **diaphanous** (sheer) and colorful dress.

　　　註解　透明的 (形容詞)

3653. The **sediments** (dregs) of society may be observed in this slum area of the city.

　　　註解　殘渣 (名詞)

3654. This final book is the **epitome** (abstract) of all his previous books.

　　　註解　縮影，摘要 (名詞)

3655. Farmers have learned that it is advisable to permit land to lie **fallow** (uncultivated) every few years.

　　　註解　休耕的 (形容詞)

3656. The city issued a **franchise** (privilege) to the company to operate surface transitlines on the streets for ninety-nine years.

　　　註解　經銷權 (名詞)

3657. One of his personal **eccentricities** (idiosyncrasies) was his habit of rinsing allcutlery given him in a restaurant.

　　　註解　怪癖性 (名詞)

3658. The new contract calls for a 10 person **increment** (increase) in salary for each employee for the next two years.

　　　註解　增長 (名詞)

3659. There is an **inverse** (opposite) ratio between the strength of light and its distance.
　註解　相反的 (形容詞)

3660. If this **lode** (vein) which we have discovered extends for any distance, we have found a fortune.
　註解　礦脈　(名詞)

3661. These **migrant** (migratory) birds return every spring.
　註解　移居的 (形容詞)

3662. I cannot distinguish between such **niceties** (precisions) of reasoning.
　註解　細小差異，精確 (名詞)

3663. I am certain that you have missed important details in your rapid **perusal** (reading) of this document.
　註解　閱讀 (名詞)

3664. She had the **arrogance** (effrontery) to disregard our advice.
　註解　自大 (名詞)

3665. Let us be on the **qui vive** (expectant).
　註解　期待之人 (名詞，法國字)

3666. The Halloween cake was decorated with **saffron** (yellow-orange) icing.
　註解　橘黃色的 (形容詞)

3667. I must give this paper a failing mark because it contains many **ungrammaticalusages** (solecisms).
　註解　違反文法用語 (名詞片語)

3668. His paintings of nymphs in **sylvan** (rustic) background were criticized as overly sentimental.
　註解　森林的 (形容詞)

3669. The decision of the **tribunal** (court of justice) was final.
　註解　裁判 (名詞)

3670. It has taken **aeons** (ages) for our civilization to develop.
　註解　世世代代 (名詞)

3671. If we become frightened by such **bugaboos** (bugbears), we are no wiser than the birds who fear scarecrows.
　註解　鬼怪 (名詞)

3672. Keats is referring to epic poetry when he mentions Homer's "proud **demesne** (domain)."

註解 領域 (名詞)

3673. He felt that his face was **ineluctable** (irresistible) and refused to make any attempt to improve his lot.

註解 不能抵抗的 (形容詞)

3674. All abusive and **minatory** (threatening) letters received by the mayor and other public officials were examined by the police.

註解 恐嚇的 (形容詞)

3675. I am worried about the possibility of a(n) **spate** (outpouring) if the rains do not diminish soon.

註解 暴雨 (名詞)

3676. We find **asceticism** (austerities) carried on in many parts of the world.

註解 苦行 (名詞)

3677. The appearance of the sun after the many rainy days was like a **benediction** (blessing).

註解 祝福 (名詞)

3678. The enemy was warned to **capitulate** (surrender) face annihilation.

註解 投降 (不定詞)

3679. The lawsuit developed into a test of the **kinship** (consanguinity) of the claimant to the estate.

註解 血親關係 (名詞)

3680. The **scarcity** (dearth) of skilled labor compelled the employers to open trade schools.

註解 缺乏 (名詞)

3681. He was a popular guest because his **droll** (waggish) anecdotes were always amusing.

註解 有趣的 (形容詞)

3682. The glacial **epoch** (era) lasted for thousands of years.

註解 年代 (名詞)

3683. The leader of the group was held responsible even though he could not control the **excessive zeal** (fanaticism) of his followers.

註解 狂熱 (名詞片語)

3684. At the time of the collision, many people became **frantic** (wild) with fear.
　　　註解　發狂的 (形容詞)

3685. I was particularly impressed by the **delineating** (graphic) presentation of the storm.
　　　註解　記述的 (形容詞)

3686. The evidence gathered against the racketeers **incriminates** (accuses) some high public officials as well.
　　　註解　牽累，控告 (動詞)

3687. He is a(n) **inveterate** (deep-rooted) smoker.
　　　註解　成癖的 (形容詞)

3688. The old man was proud of his **longevity** (long life).
　　　註解　長命 (名詞)

3689. The return of the **migrating** (wandering) birds to the northern sections of this country is a harbinger of spring.
　　　註解　徘徊的 (形容詞)

3690. The **parsimonious** (niggardly) pittance the widow receives from the government cannot keep her from poverty.
　　　註解　極小的 (形容詞)

3691. I do not feel that your limited resources will permit you to carry out such a **pretentious** (ostentatious) program.
　　　註解　虛飾的 (形容詞)

3692. He is constantly presenting these **quixotic** (fanciful) schemes.
　　　註解　傳奇的 (形容詞)

3693. Do not sign this **renunciation** (repudiation) of your right to sue until you have consulted a lawyer.
　　　註解　放棄 (名詞)

3694. This is a **saga** (tale) of the sea and the men who risk their lives on it.
　　　註解　冒險故事 (名詞)

3695. The employer was very **solicitous** (concerned) about the health of his employees as replacements were difficult to get.
　　　註解　焦慮的 (形容詞)

3696. We have many examples of scientists in different parts of the world who have made **synchronous** (simultaneous) discoveries.
　　　註解　同時的 (形容詞)

3697. The colonists refused to pay **tribute** (impost) to a foreign despot.

註解 關稅 (名詞)

3698. The four **verities** (realities) were revealed to Buddha during his long meditation.

註解 眞理 (名詞)

3699. Although he held a position of responsibility, he was a(n) **affable** (cordial) individual and could be reached by anyone with a complaint.

註解 友善的 (形容詞)

3700. He lamented the passing of aristocratic society and maintained that a **demotic** (popular) society would lower the nation's standards.

註解 通俗的 (形容詞)

3701. In the **radiant** (fulgent) glow of the early sunrise everything seemed bright and gleaming.

註解 明亮的 (形容詞)

3702. Our **inertia** (sluggishness) in this matter may prove disastrous; we must move to aid our allies immediately.

註解 遲鈍 (名詞)

3703. He was always accompanied several of his **minions** (subordinates) because he enjoyed their subservience and flattery.

註解 屬下 (名詞)

3704. His use of **prejudiced** (depreciating) language indicated his contempt for his audience.

註解 輕視的 (形容詞)

3705. **Treacle** (Syrup) is more highly refind than molasses.

註解 糖漿 (名詞，英國用語)

3706. The car could not go up the **acclivity** (ascent) in high gear.

註解 向上的斜坡 (名詞)

3707. He was frightened by the **amorphous** (shapeless) mass which had floated in from the sea.

註解 無形的 (形容詞)

3708. I can **ascribe** (attribute) no motive for his acts.

註解 認爲 (動詞)

3709. Scrooge later became Tiny Tim's **benefactor** (patron).

註解 恩人，保護人 (名詞)

3710. Do not act on **whim** (caprice). Study your problem.

註解 幻想 (名詞)

3711. He charged that a **clique** (coterie) had assumed control of school affairs.

註解 派系，小集團 (名詞)

3712. We shall **consecrate** (sanctify) our lives to this people purpose.

註解 尊崇 (動詞)

3713. Do not **debase** (demean) yourself by becoming maudlin.

註解 貶低 (動詞)

3714. He repeated the statement as though it were the **dictum** (maxim) of the most expert worker in the group.

註解 格言 (名詞)

3715. Many methods have been devised to separate the valuable metal from the **dross** (waste matter).

註解 金屬渣滓 (名詞)

3716. After the hot summers and cold winters of New England, he found the climate of the west Indies **tranquil** (equable) pleasant.

註解 平靜的 (形容詞)

3717. You are resenting **fancied** (imagined) insults. No one has ever said such things about you.

註解 想像的 (形容詞)

3718. The government seeks to prevent **fraudulent** (deceitful) and misleading advertising.

註解 不誠實的 (形容詞)

3719. The company offered to give one package **gratis** (free) to every purchaser of one of their products.

註解 免費的 (形容詞)

3720. Lava, pumice, and other **volcanic** (igneous) rocks are found in great abundance around Mount Vesuvius near Naples.

註解 火山的，火成的 (形容詞)

3721. In as much as our supply of electricity is cut off, we shall have to rely on the hens to **incubate** (hatch) these eggs.

註解 孵蛋 (不定詞)

3722. We disregarded her **invidious** (hateful) remarks because we realized how jealous she was.

   註解 怨恨的 (形容詞)

3723. As the horses **gallop slowly** (loped) along, we had an opportunity to admire theever-changing scenery.

   註解 慢跑 (動詞片語)

3724. Doctors must **palliate** (alleviate) that which they cannot cure.

   註解 減輕病痛 (動詞)

3725. Because of your **intractable** (perverse) attitude, I must rate you as deficient incooperation.

   註解 倔強的 (形容詞)

3726. Some people believe that to **prevaricate** (lie) in a good cause is justifiable andregard the statement as a "White lie."

   註解 說謊 (不定詞)

3727. Will Rogers, **quizzical** (comical) remarks endeared him to his audiences.

   註解 奇怪的 (形容詞)

3728. Fortunately, the damages we suffered in the accident were **capable of being repaired** (reparable).

   註解 可以修復的 (形容詞片語)

3729. He is much too **shrewd** (sagacious) to be fooled by a trick like that.

   註解 精明的 (形容詞)

3730. The **soliloquy** (talking to oneself) is a device used by the dramatist to reveal acharacter's innermost thoughts and emotions.

   註解 自言自語 (名詞)

3731. Neptune is usually depicted as rising from the sea, carrying his **trident** (three-pronged spear) on his shoulder.

   註解 三尖叉 (名詞)

3732. we may expect **vernal** (spring like) showers all during the month of April.

   註解 春天的 (形容詞)

3733. Wearing the **buskin** (cothurnus) gave the Athenian tragic actor a larger-than-life appearance and enhanced the intensity of the play.

   註解 半統靴 (名詞)

3734. All attempts to **denigrate** (blacken) the character of our late President have failed; the people still love him and cherish his memory.

　　　　註解　　侮辱 (不定詞)

3735. We must be particularly cautious when we **deduce** (infer) that a person is guilty on the basis of circumstantial evidence.

　　　　註解　　推論 (動詞)

3736. The **pendulous** (suspended) chandeliers swayed in the breeze and gave the impression that they were about to fall from the ceiling.

　　　　註解　　下垂的 (形容詞)

3737. "From the **ramparts** (barricades) we watched" as the fighting continued.

　　　　註解　　障礙物 (名詞)

3738. He is not finicky about his food; he is a **good eater** (trencherman).

　　　　註解　　食客 (名詞片語)

3739. In Hollywood, an "Oscar" is the highest **accolade** (award of merit).

　　　　註解　　賞賜 (名詞)

3740. Frogs are classified as **amphibian** (amphibious).

　　　　註解　　水陸兩棲動物 (名詞)

3741. His face was **ashen** (ashy) with fear.

　　　　註解　　灰色的 (形容詞)

3742. His **charitable** (benevolent) nature prevented him from refusing any beggar who accosted him.

　　　　註解　　慈悲的 (形容詞)

3743. The storm was **incalculable** (capricious) and changed course constantly.

　　　　註解　　難預測的 (形容詞)

3744. The nuns lived in the **monastery** (cloister).

　　　　註解　　修道院 (名詞)

3745. A vicious newspaper can **debauch** (seduce) public ideals.

　　　　註解　　誘導 (動詞)

3746. Your composition suffers from a **diffusion** (wordiness) of ideas; try to be more compact.

　　　　註解　　散漫，冗長 (名詞)

3747. Cinderella's fairy godmother rescued her from a life of **drudgery** (menial work).

　　　　註解　　沉悶的或低賤的工作 (名詞)

3748. In his later years, he could look upon the foolishness of the world with **equanimity** (equilibrium) and humor.

   註解 平靜 (名詞)

3749. The dog **fancier** (breeder) exhibited his prize collie at the annual Kennel Clubshow.

   註解 玩賞家，養動物者 (名詞)

3750. Since this enterprise is **fraught** (filled) with danger, I will ask for volunteers who are willing to assume the risks.

   註解 充滿的 (形容詞)

3751. I resent your **gratuitous** (unwarranted) remarks because no one asked for them.

   註解 無理由的 (形容詞)

3752. This plan is inspired by **ignoble** (unworthy) motives and I must, therefore, oppose it.

   註解 下流的 (形容詞)

3753. The **incubus** (nightmare) of financial worry helped bring on his nervous breakdown.

   註解 惡夢 (名詞)

3754. They respected the **inviolability** (incorruptibility) of her faith and did not try to change her manner of living.

   註解 看不見，不腐朽 (名詞)

3755. She is very **voluble** (loquacious) and can speak on the telephone for hours.

   註解 健談的 (形容詞)

3756. Yum-Yum walked across the stage with **mincing** (affectedly dainty).

   註解 不自然 (動名詞)

3757. I never could stand the **unwholesome** (noisome) atmosphere surrounding the slaughter houses.

   註解 不健康的 (形容詞)

3758. Because his occupation required that he work at night and sleep during the day, he had an exceptionally **wan** (pallid) complexion.

   註解 蒼白的 (形容詞)

3759. In as much as he had no motive for his crimes, we could not understand his **perversion** (corruption).

> 註解 敗壞 (名詞)

3760. Many people commented on the contrast between the **prim** (starched) attire of the young lady and the inappropriate clothing worn by her escort.

> 註解 端正的，呆板的 (形容詞)

3761. He was a **rabid** (furious) follower of the Dodgers and watched them play whenever he could go to the ball park.

> 註解 狂熱的 (形容詞)

3762. At the peace conference, the defeated country promised to pay **amends** (reparations) to the victors.

> 註解 賠償 (名詞)

3763. One of the **salient** (prominent) features of that newspaper is its excellent editorial page.

> 註解 顯著的 (形容詞)

3764. Romain Rolland's novel Jean Christophe was first published as a **trilogy** (group of three works).

> 註解 三部曲 (名詞)

3765. Let us drop a perpendicual line from the **vertex** (summit) of the triangle to thebase.

> 註解 頂點 (名詞)

3766. As we examine ancient manuscrips, we become impressed with the **penmanship** (calligraphy) of the scribes.

> 註解 書法 (名詞)

3767. A dictionary will always give us the **denotation** (meaning) of a word; frequently, it will also give us its connotation.

> 註解 意義 (名詞)

3768. The car lost **momentum** (impetus) as it tried to ascend the steep hill.

> 註解 動力 (名詞)

3769. The **pennate** (winged) leaves of the sumac remind us of feathers.

> 註解 羽狀的 (形容詞)

3770. We regard this unwarranted attack on a neutral nation as an act of **depredation** (spoliation) and we demand that it cease at once and that proper restitution bemade.

> 註解　劫掠 (名詞)

3771. Your **asinine** (stupid) remarks prove that you have not given this problem any serious consideration.

> 註解　愚笨的 (形容詞)

3772. In the **benighted** (unenlightened) Middle Ages, intellectual curiosity was discouraged by the authorities.

> 註解　未開發的 (形容詞)

3773. I find the **captions** (titles) which accompany these cartoons very clever and humorous.

> 註解　標題 (名詞)

3774. He was assigned as **coadjutor** (assistant) of the bishop.

> 註解　助手 (名詞)

3775. We frequently judge people by the company with whom they **consort** (associate with).

> 註解　連結 (動詞)

3776. Over indulgence **enfeebles** (debilitates) character as well as physical stamina.

> 註解　使衰老 (動詞)

3777. People were shocked and dismayed when they learned of his **hypocrisy** (duplicity) in this affair for he had always seemed honest and straightforward.

> 註解　偽善，口是心非 (名詞)

3778. This is a **whimsical** (visionary) scheme because it does not consider the facts.

> 註解　幻想的 (形容詞)

3779. The three musketeers were in the thick of the **fray** (brawl).

> 註解　爭吵 (名詞)

3780. He was not **gregarious** (sociable) and preferred to be alone most of the time.

> 註解　群居的，愛交際的 (形容詞)

3781. The country smarted under the **ignominious** (disgraceful) defeat and dreamed of the day when it would be victorious.

　註解　屈辱的 (形容詞)

3782. In an effort to **inculcate** (teach) religious devotion, the officials ordered that the school day begin with the singing of a hymn.

　註解　教誨 (不定詞)

3783. Ackilles was **incapable of injury** (invulnerable) except in his heel.

　註解　不會傷害的 (形容詞片語)

3784. The lost prospector was fooled by a **mirage** (optical illusion) in the desert.

　註解　妄想 (名詞)

3785. Several **nomadic** (wandering) tribes of Indians would hunt in this area each year.

　註解　遊牧的 (形容詞)

3786. I cannot understand how you could overlook such a **tangible** (palpable) blunder.

　註解　眞實的 (形容詞)

3787. The Neanderthal Man is one of our **primordial** (rudimentary) ancestors.

　註解　原始的 (形容詞)

3788. He felt sorry for the **ragamuffin** (tatterdemalion) who was begging for food and gave him money to buy a meal.

　註解　衣衫襤褸之人 (名詞)

3789. He was famous for his witty **repartee** (banter) and his sarcasm.

　註解　機智應答 (名詞)

3790. By dint of very frugal living, he was finally able to become **able to pay alldebts** (solvent) and avoid bankruptcy proceedings.

　註解　清償的 (形容詞片語)

3791. We have a **tacit** (understood) agreement.

　註解　心照不宣的 (形容詞)

3792. The **hackneyed** (trite) and predictable situations in many television programs alienate many viewers.

　註解　陳腐的 (形容詞)

3793. We test potential plane pilots for susceptibility to spells of **vertigo** (dizziness).

　　註解　頭昏 (名詞)

3794. The poet boasted of his divine **afflatus** (inspiration) as the source of his greatness.

　　註解　靈感 (名詞)

3795. In that youthful movement, the leaders were only a little less **callow** (unfledged) than their immature followers.

　　註解　不成熟的 (形容詞)

3796. The play was childishly written; the **denouement** (outcome) was obvious to sophisticated theatergoers as early as the middle of the first act.

　　註解　結局 (名詞)

3797. Your **insouciant** (indifferent) attitude at such a critical moment indicates that you do not understand the gravity of the situation.

　　註解　漫不經心的 (形容詞，法國語)

3798. These marshy **wastelands** (moors) can only be used for hunting; they are too barren for agriculture.

　　註解　不毛之地 (名詞，同 waste lands)

3799. His **peregrinations** (journeys) in foreign lands did not bring understanding; he mingled only with fellow tourists and did not attempt to communicate with the native population.

　　註解　旅行 (名詞)

3800. His program was reactionary (retrograde) since it sought to abolish many of the social reforms instituted by the previous administration.

　　註解　保守的 (形容詞)

3801. We knew that the first men in this area were **troglodytes** (cave dwellers) by the artifacts we have discovered.

　　註解　古代穴居人 (名詞)

3802. The fisherman was **accoutred** (equipped) with the best that the sporting goods store could supply.

　　註解　裝備 (動詞，被動式，同 accoutered)

3803. When the doctors decided to **prune** (amputate) his leg to prevent the spread of gangrence, he cried that he preferred death to incapacity.

　　註解　剪掉 (不定詞)

3804. Looking **askance** (sideways) at her questioner, she displayed her scorn.

　　註解　懷疑地，側目 (副詞)

3805. The old man was well liked because of his **benign** (favorable) attitude toward friend and stranger alike.

　　註解　親切的 (形容詞)

3806. His criticisms were always **faultfinding** (captious) and frivolous, never offering constructive suggestions.

　　註解　找碴的 (形容詞)

3807. The brooks **coalesce** (fuse) into one large river.

　　註解　會合 (動詞)

3808. There was a feeling of **constraint** (compulsion) in the room because no one dared to criticize the speaker.

　　註解　拘束，強迫 (名詞)

3809. The **debonair** (friendly) youth was liked by all who met him, because of his cheerful and obliging manner.

　　註解　快樂的 (形容詞，同 debonaire)

3810. Your fears are **grotesque** (fantastic) because no such animal as you have described exists.

　　註解　古怪的 (形容詞)

3811. This town is a rather dangerous place to visit as it is frequented by pirates, **freebooters** (buccaneers), and other plunderers.

　　註解　流寇，海盜 (名詞)

3812. She shuddered at the **grisly** (ghastly) sight.

　　註解　可怕的 (形容詞)

3813. Man, having explored the far corners of the earth, is now reaching out into **illimitable** (infinite) space.

　　註解　無邊際的 (形容詞)

3814. The newly elected public official received valuable advice from the present **incumbent** (officeholder).

　　註解　在職者，公務員 (名詞)

3815. He hadn't a(n) **iota** (mite) of common sense.

　　註解　一點點 (名詞)

3816. The moon's **lucent** (shining) rays silvered the river.

　　註解　明亮的 (形容詞)

3817. The young explorer met death by **misadventure** (mischance).

　　註解　災難，不幸 (名詞)

3818. Few people could understand how he could listen to the news of the tragedy with such **nonchalance** (indifference); the majority regarded him as callous and unsympathetic.

　　註解　漠不關心 (名詞)

3819. As he became excited, his heart began to **palpitate** (flutter) more and moreerratically.

　　註解　抖動 (不定詞)

3820. He has a **pervious** (penetrable) mind and readily accepts new ideas.

　　註解　有理智的 (形容詞)

3821. This area has been preserved in all its **pristine** (unspoiled) wildness.

　　註解　原始的 (形容詞)

3822. We must examine all the **ramifications** (subdivisions) of this problem.

　　註解　枝枝節節 (名詞)

3823. Mosquitoes find the odor so **repellent** (unattractive) that they leave any spot where this liquid has been sprayed.

　　註解　不吸引人的 (形容詞)

3824. We were disturbed by his **sallow** (yellowish) complexion.

　　註解　病黃色的 (形容詞)

3825. The most famous **somnambulist** (sleepwalker) in literature is Lady Macbeth; her monologue in the sleepwalking scene is one of the highlights of Shakespeare's play.

　　註解　夢遊者 (名詞)

3826. His calloused hands had lost their **tactile** (tangible) sensitivity.

　　註解　有觸覺的 (形容詞)

3827. He gave her his **troth** (loyalty) and vowed he would cherish her always.

　　註解　承諾 (名詞)

3828. There was a variety of **viands** (foods) at the feast.

　　註解　食物 (名詞)

3829. The turtle takes advantage of its hard **integument** (cortex) and hides within itsshell when threatened.

　　註解　外殼 (名詞)

3830. The **spume** (foam) at the base of the waterfall extended for a quarter of a miledownriver.

註解 泡沫 (名詞)

3831. The **accretion** (growth) of wealth marked the family's rise in power.

註解 增大 (名詞)

3832. When he placed his hat **askew** (awry) upon his head, his observers laughed.

註解 歪斜地 (副詞)

3833. He feared she would **berate** (vituperate) him for his forgetfulness.

註解 痛罵 (動詞)

3834. He works on five days a week and has **every Saturday and Sunday off** (freetime every Saturday and Sunday).

註解 每週六和週日休息 (名詞片語)

3835. He said that he had not the wish for his daughter to marry **into the purple** (aprince or a nobleman).

註解 王子或貴族 (名詞片語)

3836. He cares not for justice, but **pays all his debts with the roll of the drum** (doesnot pay at all).

註解 不付 (動詞片語)

3837. He played his part to **a nail** (a nicety).

註解 精準 (名詞片語)

3838. The fact that he is a rich man will cut **no ice** (no effect) with that particular judge.

註解 不太重要 (名詞片語)

3839. If I **construe** (interpret) your remarks correctly, you disagree with the theory already advanced.

註解 推斷 (動詞)

3840. Your **dilatory** (delaying) tactics may compel me to cancel the contract.

註解 拖延的 (形容詞)

3841. His **earthy** (coarse) remarks often embarrased the women in his audience.

註解 粗俗的 (形容詞)

3842. The **equipage** (carriage) drew up before the inn.

註解 馬車 (名詞)

3843. The waitresses disliked serving him dinner because of his very **fastidious** (squeamish) taste.

註解　吹毛求疵的 (形容詞)

3844. His **frenzied** (frenetic) activities convinced us that he had no organized plan of operation.

註解　暴怒的 (形容詞)

3845. The nightly **incursions** (invasions) and hit-and-run raids of our neighbors across the border tried the patience of the country to the point where we decided to retaliate in force.

註解　侵入 (名詞)

3846. His **irascible** (choleric) temper frightened me.

註解　暴燥的 (形容詞)

3847. We were annoyed by his **noncommittal** (neutral) reply for we had been led to expect definite assurances of his approval.

註解　含糊的 (形容詞)

3848. This is a **paltry** (petty) sum to pay for such a masterpiece.

註解　微小的 (形容詞)

3849. The good news we have been receiving lately indicates that there is little reason for your **gloominess** (pessimism).

註解　沮喪，悲觀 (名詞)

3850. we do not care for **privy** (hidden) chamber government.

註解　私用的 (形容詞)

3851. I am afraid that this event will have serious **reverberation** (repercussions).

註解　反應 (名詞)

3852. Many people with hay fever move to more **salubrious** (healthful) sections of the country during the months of August and September.

註解　健康的 (形容詞)

3853. The heavy meal and the overheated room made us all **half-asleep** (somnolent) and indifferent to the speaker.

註解　昏昏欲睡的 (形容詞)

3854. Health authorities are always trying to prevent the sale and use of **contaminated** (tainted) food.

註解　污染的 (形容詞)

3855. They are a **truculent** (savage) race, ready to fight at any moment.

註解　兇猛的 (形容詞)

3856. I am accustomed to life's **vicissitudes** (mutations), having experienced poverty and wealth, sickness and health, and failure and success.

註解　變化 (名詞)

3857. We felt that he was responsible for the **agitation** (excitement) of the mob because of the inflammatory report he had issued.

註解　煽動 (名詞)

3858. With each dinner, the patron receives a **decanter** (carafe) of red or white wine.

註解　玻璃瓶 (名詞)

3859. During the lengthy **invective** (diatribe) delivered by his opponent he remained calm and self-controlled.

註解　痛罵 (名詞)

3860. Behind his front of **gasconade** (bluster) and pompous talk, he tried to hide his inherent uncertainty and nervousness.

註解　吹牛 (名詞)

3861. Civilized nations must **interdict** (prohibit) the use of nuclear weapons if we expect our society to live.

註解　禁止 (動詞)

3862. The cloister was surrounded by a **colonnade** (peristyle) reminiscent of the Parthenon.

註解　一列柱子 (名詞)

3863. His **staccato** (discontinuous) speech reminded one of the sound of a machine gun.

註解　斷斷續續的 (形容詞)

3864. If you **truckle** (curry favor) to the lord, you will be regarded as a sycophant; if you do not, you will be considered arrogant.

註解　屈服 (動詞)

3865. Around his neck he wore the **talisman** (amulet) which the witch doctor had given him.

註解　護身符 (名詞)

3866. These remarks, spoken with **asperity** (sharpness), stung the boys to whom they had been directed.

   註解　刻薄 (名詞)

3867. The foolish gambler soon found himself **bereft** (deprived) of funds.

   註解　被剝奪的 (形容詞)

3868. The **burlesques** (caricatures) he drew always emphasized or personal weakness of the people he burlesqued.

   註解　諷刺圖畫 (名詞)

3869. I have never seen anyone who makes as many stupid errors as you do; you must be a **consummate** (complete) idiot.

   註解　完全的 (形容詞)

3870. The moral **decadence** (decay) of the people was reflected in the lewd literature of the period.

   註解　衰落 (名詞)

3871. In this **dilemma** (problem), he knew no one to whom he could turn for advice.

   註解　左右為難的狀況 (名詞)

3872. His **high-spirited** (ebullient) nature could not be repressed; he was always laughing and gay.

   註解　熱情的 (形容詞)

3873. Our courts guarantee **equity** (justice) to all.

   註解　公平 (名詞)

3874. As soon as they smelled smoke, the madly **excited** (frenzied) animals milled about in their cages.

   註解　激怒的 (形容詞)

3875. I am amazed at the **imbecility** (silliness) of the readers of these trashy magazines.

   註解　愚笨 (名詞)

3876. He was **indefatigable** (tireless) in his constant efforts to raise funds for the Red Cross.

   註解　不屈不撓的 (形容詞)

3877. He turned his hobby into a **lucrative** (profitable) profession.

   註解　可賺錢的 (形容詞)

3878. To avoid **misapprehension** (error), I am going to ask all of you to repeat the instructions I have given.

　　 註解　誤解 (名詞)

3879. Of course you are a **nonentity** (nonexistence); you will continue to be one until you prove your value to the community.

　　 註解　無足輕重之人 (名詞)

3880. There is no easy **panacea** (cure-all) that will solve our complicated international situation.

　　 註解　萬靈丹 (名詞)

3881. People were afraid to explore the **pestilential** (baneful) swamp.

　　 註解　致病的 (形容詞)

3882. Everyone took his **probity** (incorruptibility) for granted; his defalcations, therefore, shocked us all.

　　 註解　正直，廉潔 (名詞)

3883. The **rampant** (unrestrained) weeds in the garden killed all the flowers which had been planted in the spring.

　　 註解　蔓延的 (形容詞)

3884. The punishment had a **salutary** (wholesome) effect on the boy, as he became a model student.

　　 註解　有益的 (形容詞)

3885. His **resonant** (sonorous) voice resounded through the hall.

　　 註解　共鳴的 (形容詞)

3886. She wore the **talisman** (charm) to ward off evil.

　　 註解　護身符 (名詞)

3887. Many **platitudes** (truism) are well expressed in proverbs.

　　 註解　陳腐話，老生常談 (名詞)

3888. The **didactic** (instructional) qualities of his poetry overshadow its literary qualities; the lesson he teaches is more memorable than the lines.

　　 註解　教訓的 (形容詞)

3889. This **interlocutory** (conversational) decree is only a temporary setback; the case has not been settled.

　　 註解　對話的，中間的 (形容詞)

3890. When he refused to support his party's nominees, he was called a **defector from a party** (mugwump) and deprived of his seniority privileges in Congress.

　　註解　獨立分子 (名詞片語)

3891. Negotiations between the union and the employers have reached a **stalemate** (deadlock); neither side is willing to budge from previously stated positions.

　　註解　停頓 (名詞)

3892. The top of a cone which has been **truncated** (cut short) in a plane paralled to itsbase is a circle.

　　註解　修短 (動詞，完成被動式)

3893. The salad had an exceedingly **acetic** (vinegary) flavor.

　　註解　醋酸的 (形容詞)

3894. He called our attention to the things that had been done in a(n) **analogous** (comparable) situation and recommended that we do the same.

　　註解　類似的 (形容詞)

3895. Do not cast **slanderous remarks** (aspersions) on his character.

　　註解　惡毒的批評 (名詞片語)

3896. Angered, he went **berserk** (frenzied) and began to wreck the room.

　　註解　發狂的 (形容詞)

3897. **Carmine** (purplish-red) in her lipstick made her lips appear black in the photographs.

　　註解　深紅色 (名詞)

3898. I will not tolerate those who **contemn** (disregard) the sincere efforts of this group.

　　註解　輕視 (名詞)

3899. Be sure to **pour off gently** (decant) this wine before serving it.

　　註解　輕輕倒出 (不定詞片語)

3900. He was not serious in his painting; he was rather a **dabbler** (dilettante).

　　註解　涉足之人，業餘愛好者 (名詞)

3901. Some of his friends tried to account for his rudeness to strangers as the **eccentricity** (idiosyncrasy) of genius.

　　註解　古怪性格 (名詞)

3902. Macbeth was misled by the **equivocal** (ambiguous) statements of the witches.

> 註解 模稜兩可的 (形容詞)

3903. He is far too intelligent to utter such **fatuous** (inane) remarks.

> 註解 愚昧的 (形容詞)

3904. The marathon is a(n) **grueling** (exhausting) race.

> 註解 費力的 (形容詞)

3905. The dry soil **drank in** (imbibed) the rain quickly.

> 註解 吸取 (動詞片語)

3906. The city will **indemnify** (recompense) all home owners whose property is spoiled by this project.

> 註解 賠償 (動詞)

3907. It is **sardonic** (sarcastic) that his success came when he least wanted it.

> 註解 諷刺的 (形容詞)

3908. Preferring **lucre** (money) to fame, he wrote stories of popular appeal.

> 註解 金錢 (名詞)

3909. Some states passed laws against **intermarriage between races** (miscegenation).

> 註解 異族通婚 (名詞片語)

3910. When the ships collided in the harbor, **pandemonium** (wild tumult) broke out among the passengers.

> 註解 騷亂 (名詞)

3911. His sudden and unexpected appearance seemed to **benumb** (petrify) her.

> 註解 嚇呆 (不定詞)

3912. The elephant uses his **proboscis** (nose) to handle things and carry them from place to place.

> 註解 鼻子 (名詞)

3913. The end of rationing enabled us to **replenish** (fill up again) our supply of canned food.

> 註解 補充 (不定詞)

3914. A **soupcon** (suggestion) of garlic will improve this dish.

> 註解 少量 (名詞)

3915. Tom loved to **tantalize** (tease) his younger brother.

> 註解 折磨 (不定詞)

3916. All this finery is mere **trumpery** (rubbish).

> 註解 | 毫無價值 (名詞)

3917. When we **vie** (contend) with each other for his approval, we are merely weakening ourselves and strengthening him.

> 註解 | 競爭 (動詞)

3918. I will attempt to **disabuse** (undeceive) you of your impression of my client'sguilt; I know he is innocent.

> 註解 | 矯正，說明 (不定詞)

3919. Such remarks are **boorish** (gauche) and out of place; you should apologize for making them.

> 註解 | 粗野的 (形容詞)

3920. The rising death toll on both sides indicates the **internecine** (mutually destructive) nature of this conflict.

> 註解 | 兩敗俱傷的 (形容詞)

3921. "A **murrain** (plague) on you" was a common malediction in that period.

> 註解 | 瘟疫 (名詞)

3922. The **perquisites** (bonus) attached to this job make it even more attractive than the salary indicates.

> 註解 | 津貼 (名詞)

3923. His consistent support of the party has proved that he is a **stalwart** (brawny) and loyal member.

> 註解 | 堅定的 (形容詞)

3924. James was unpopular because of his sarcastic and **acidulous** (caustic) remarks.

> 註解 | 乖僻的，刻薄的 (形容詞)

3925. Your **parallelism** (analogy) is not a good one because the two situations are notsimilar.

> 註解 | 對應，類推 (名詞)

3926. The scandalous remarks in the newspaper besmirch (soil) the reputations of every member of the society.

> 註解 | 糟蹋，污辱 (動詞)

3927. The carnage (butchery) that can be caused by atomic warfare adds to the responsibilities of our statesmen.

> 註解 | 大屠殺 (名詞)

3928. We heard loud and **contentious** (quarrelsome) noises in the next room.

> 註解 爭吵的 (形容詞)

3929. The blockaders hoped to achieve victory as soon as the **diminution** (lessening) of the enemy's supplies became serious.

> 註解 減少 (名詞)

3930. The minister donned his **ecclesiastic** (ecclesiastical) garb and walked to the pulpit.

> 註解 教會的 (形容詞)

3931. The audience saw through his attempts to **equivocate** (prevaricate) on the subject under discussion and ridiculed his remarks.

> 註解 推托，搪塞 (不定詞)

3932. The scientist could visualize the **fauna** (animals) of the period by examining the skeletal remains and the fossils.

> 註解 動物 (名詞)

3933. Motorists were warned that spring **freshets** (floods) had washed away several small bridges and that long detours would be necessary.

> 註解 洪水 (名詞)

3934. People screamed when his **gruesome** (grisly) appearance was flashed on the screen.

> 註解 可怕的 (形容詞)

3935. He was called in to settle the **imbroglio** (perplexity) but failed to bring harmony into the situation.

> 註解 糾紛，困惑 (名詞)

3936. Because the separated couple were **irreconcilable** (incompatible), the marriage counselor recommended a divorce.

> 註解 不能妥協的 (形容詞)

3937. The **lugubrious** (mournful) howling of the dogs added to our sadness.

> 註解 悲哀的 (形容詞)

3938. These spring flowers will make an attractive **nosegay** (posy).

> 註解 花束 (名詞)

3939. The feverish patient was **petulant** (peevish) and restless.

> 註解 性急的 (形容詞)

3940. He has a(n) **proclivity** (inclination) to grumble.

> 註解 脾氣，傾向 (名詞)

3941. As we heard him **rant** (rave) on the platform, we could not understand his strange popularity with many people.

註解 怒吼 (動詞，感官動詞 hear 之後接原型動詞)

3942. This book is **replete** (filled) with humorous situations.

註解 充滿的 (形容詞)

3943. The captain's **sangfroid** (composure) helped to allay the fears of the passengers.

註解 鎮定 (名詞，法國字)

3944. The **periodic** (spasmodic) coughing in the auditorium annoyed the performers.

註解 不時發生的，間斷的 (形容詞)

3945. The child learned that he could have almost anything if he went into **caprices** (tantrums).

註解 發怒，善變 (名詞)

3946. The lovers kept their **tryst** (meeting) even though they realized their danger.

註解 約會 (名詞)

3947. Eternal **vigilance** (watchfulness) is the price of liberty.

註解 警戒，注意 (名詞)

3948. Because he was certain that he would have no visitors, he lounged around the house in a state of **dishabille** (undress), wearing only his pajamas and a pair of old bedroom slippers.

註解 便裝 (名詞)

3949. He was proud of his **genealogy** (lineage) and constantly referred to the achievements of his ancestors.

註解 家譜，血統 (名詞)

3950. The mountain climber sought to obtain a foothold in the **crevices** (interstices) of the cliff.

註解 裂縫 (名詞)

3951. In thinking only of your present needs and ignoring the future, you are beingrather **nearsighted** (myopic).

註解 短視的，近視旳 (形容詞)

3952. The man I am seeking to fill this position must be **personable** (handsome) since he will be representing us before the public.

註解 英俊的 (形容詞)

3953. The flood left a deposit of mud on everything; it was necessary to **renovate** (refurbish) our belongings.

註解 刷新 (不定詞)

3954. Man's **aspirations** (ambitions) should be as lofty as the stars.

註解 渴望 (名詞)

3955. He wishes to **bestow** (confer) great honors upon the hero.

註解 贈與 (不定詞)

3956. The public was more interested in **carnal** (fleshly) pleasures than in spiritual matters.

註解 肉體的 (形容詞)

3957. During the election campaign, the two candidates were kept in full **cognizance** (knowledge) of the international situation.

註解 認知 (名詞)

3958. The children loved to ski down the **declivity** (slpoe).

註解 下坡 (名詞)

3959. By **dint** (effort) of much hard work, the volunteers were able to place the raging forest fire under control.

註解 努力 (名詞)

3960. The announcement that the war had ended brought on a (n) **ecstasy** (rapture).

註解 狂歡 (名詞)

3961. The limestone was **eaten away** (eroded) by the dripping water.

註解 侵蝕 (動詞，被動式)

3962. Your tactless remarks during dinner were a(n) **faux pas** (impropriety).

註解 失禮，不適當 (名詞，法國字)

3963. Although he was blunt and **gruff** (brusque) with most people, he was always gentle with children.

註解 粗暴的 (形容詞)

3964. His visits to the famous Gothic cathedrals **saturated** (imbued) him with feelings of awe and reverence.

註解 滲透 (動詞)

3965. This statement is **irrelevant** (unrelated) and should be disregarded by the jury.

　　　註解　不相關的 (形容詞)

3966. By **mishap** (mischance), he lost his week's salary.

　　　註解　災禍 (名詞)

3967. The first settlers found so much work to do that they had little time for **nostalgia** (homesickness).

　　　註解　思鄉病 (名詞)

3968. The modest hero blushed as he listened to the **panegyrics** (eulogies) uttered by the speakers about his valorous act.

　　　註解　頌詞 (名詞)

3969. Even though it is small, this **phial** (bottle) of perfume is expensive.

　　　註解　小瓶 (名詞)

3970. It is wise not to **procrastinate** (postpone); otherwise, we find ourselves bogged down in a mass of work which should have been finished long ago.

　　　註解　拖延 (不定詞)

3971. Hawks and **rapacious** (plundering) birds play an important role in the "balanceof nature;" therefore, they are protected from hunting throughout North America.

　　　註解　捕食的，獵食的 (形容詞)

3972. Are you going to hang this **replica** (facsimile) of the Declaration of Independence in the classroom or in the auditorium?

　　　註解　複製品 (名詞)

3973. The battle of Iwo Jima was unexpectedly **sanguinary** (bloody).

　　　註解　血腥的 (形容詞)

3974. In the sentence "It was visible to the eye," the phrase "to the eye" is **needlesslyrepetitious** (tautological).

　　　註解　同義語重複的，不必要的 (形容詞片語)

3975. The **tumbrels** (tipcarts) became the vehicles which transported the condemned people from the prisons to the guillotine.

　　　註解　拖肥車 (名詞，同 tumbrils)

3976. Why is he always trying to **vilify** (calumniate) my reputation?

　　　註解　詆毀，中傷 (不定詞)

3977. Even since the days of Greek mythology we refer to strong and aggressive women as **amazons** (female warrior).

    註解　男子氣慨的女人，女戰士 (名詞)

3978. In a(n) **dispassionate** (uninvolved) analysis of the problem, he carefully examined the causes of the conflict and proceedes to suggest suitable remedies.

    註解　沒有偏見的 (形容詞)

3979. You have made the mistake of thinking that his behavior is **generic** (common); actually, very few of his group behave the way he does.

    註解　一般的 (形容詞)

3980. The horse was **refractory** (intractable) and refused to enter the starting gate.

    註解　倔強的 (形容詞)

3981. If we could identify these revolutionary movements in their **nascent** (incipient) state, we would be able to eliminate serious trouble in later years.

    註解　初期的 (形容詞)

3982. One of the outstanding features of this book is the **perspicuity** (clarity) of its author; his meaning is always clear.

    註解　敏銳，明晰 (名詞，同 perspicacity)

3983. The audience cheered enthusiastically as she completed her **rendition** (translation) of the aria.

    註解　翻譯，解釋 (名詞)

3984. My chief objection to the book is that the characters are **stereotyped** (commonplace).

    註解　老套的，平凡的 (形容詞)

3985. I am acting in my **tutelary** (protective) capacity when I refuse to grant you permission to leave the campus.

    註解　保護的 (形容詞)

3986. He heaped **anathema** (solemn curse) upon his foe.

    註解　詛咒 (名詞)

3987. He asked the court to change his **family name** (cognomen) to a more American-sounding name.

    註解　姓 (名詞片語)

3988. Her **decorous** (proper) behavior was praised by her teachers.
   註解　有禮的 (形容詞)

3989. Although his purpose was to **edify** (instruct) and not to entertain his audience, many of his listeners were amused and not enlightened.
   註解　教化 (不定詞)

3990. The loud **guffaws** (laughters) that came from the closed room indicated that the members of the committee had not yet settled down to serious business.
   註解　哄笑 (名詞)

3991. The West Point cadets were **immaculate** (pure) as they lined up for inspection.
   註解　無瑕的 (形容詞)

3992. Tobacco is one of the **indigenous** (native) plants which the early explorers found in this country.
   註解　固有的，土產的 (形容詞)

3993. The error he made was **irremediable** (incurable).
   註解　不能補救的 (形容詞)

3994. The **sensational** (lurid) stories he told shocked his listeners.
   註解　恐怖的，驚人的 (形容詞)

3995. His kindness to the **miscreant** (villain) amazed all of us who had expected to hear severe punishment pronounced.
   註解　惡棍 (名詞)

3996. Captain Kidd was a(n) **outstandingly bad** (notorious) pirate.
   註解　惡名昭彰的 (形容詞片語)

3997. Do not **philander** (flirt) with my affections because love is too serious.
   註解　調戲，玩弄 (動詞)

3998. The **prodigal** (wasteful) son squandered his inheritance.
   註解　浪費的 (形容詞)

3999. Both sides were eager to effect a **rapprochement** (reconciliation) but did not know how to undertake a program designed to bring about harmony.
   註解　恢復友誼 (名詞，同 reconcilement)

4000. Libraries are **repositories** (storehouses) of the world's best thoughts.
   註解　倉庫 (名詞)

4001. Let us not be too **sanguine** (hopeful) about the outcome.

  > 註解 樂天的，期望的 (形容詞)

4002. He won a few **meretricious** (tawdry) trinkets in Coney Island.

  > 註解 虛有其表的 (形容詞)

4003. I especially dislike his **tumid** (pompous) style; I prefer writing which is less swollen and bombastic.

  > 註解 浮誇的 (形容詞)

4004. I hope to **exonerate** (vindicate) my client and return him to society as a free man.

  > 註解 免罪，辯明 (不定詞)

4005. The **amoral** (nonmoral) individual lacks a code of ethics; he should not be classified as immoral.

  > 註解 超道德的 (形容詞)

4006. His ancestors on the **distaff** (female) side were equally as famous as his father's progenitors; his mother's father and grandfather were both famous judges.

  > 註解 女性 (名詞)

4007. As a proud democrat, he refused to **bend the knee as in worship** (genuflect) to any man.

  > 註解 屈膝 (不定詞片語)

4008. His **perspicuous** (explicit) comments eliminated all possibility of misinterpretation.

  > 註解 顯明的 (形容詞)

4009. In an **ancillary** (auxiliary) capacity he was helpful; however, he could not be entrusted with leadship.

  > 註解 附屬的 (形容詞)

4010. When they **assayed** (evaluated) the ore, they found that they had discovered avery rich vein.

  > 註解 分析 (動詞)

4011. The announcement that they had become **affianced** (betrothed) surprised their friends who had not suspected any romance.

  > 註解 訂婚的 (形容詞)

4012. The party degenerated into an ugly **carousal** (drunken revel).

  > 註解 狂歡的酒會 (名詞)

4013. Solids have a greater tendency to **cohere** (stick together) than liquids.

　　註解　凝結 (不定詞)

4014. He vowed to lead a life of **sexual chastity** (continence).

　　註解　節慾 (名詞片語，同 continency)

4015. The wild ducks were not fooled by the **decoy** (bait).

　　註解　誘餌 (名詞)

4016. People ignored his **dire** (disastrous) predictions of an approaching depression.

　　註解　不幸的 (形容詞)

4017. He could not **educe** (elicit) a principle that would encompass all the data.

　　註解　推斷 (動詞)

4018. The headmaster could not regard this latest **escapade** (prank) as a boyish joke and expelled the young man.

　　註解　惡作劇 (名詞)

4019. The feudal lord demanded **fealty** (loyalty) of his vassals.

　　註解　忠誠 (名詞)

4020. He could not apply himself to any task and **frittered** (wasted) away his time in idle conversation.

　　註解　浪費 (動詞)

4021. He achieved his high position by **guile** (duplicity) and treachery.

　　註解　狡計，欺騙 (名詞)

4022. Because he was **indigent** (poor), he was sent to the welfare office.

　　註解　貧窮的 (形容詞)

4023. The ripe peach was **delectable** (luscious).

　　註解　美味的 (形容詞)

4024. The culprit pleaded guilty to a minor **crime** (misdemeanor) rather than facetrial for a felony.

　　註解　輕罪 (名詞，同 misdemeanour)

4025. Even a **novice** (beginner) can do good work if he follows these simple directions.

　　註解　新手 (名詞)

4026. He marveled at her **prodigious** (enormous) appetite.

　　註解　巨大的 (形容詞)

4027. Your vicious conduct in this situation is **culpable** (reprehensible).

    | 註解 | 該受譴責的 (形容詞)

4028. This chef has the knack of making most foods more **sapid** (relishable) and appealing.

    | 註解 | 有風味的 (形容詞)

4029. Fish ladders had to be built in the dams to assist the salmon returning to **spawn** (lay eggs) in their native streams.

    | 註解 | 產卵 (不定詞)

4030. We hope this radio will help overcome the **tedium** (boredom) of your stay in the hospital.

    | 註解 | 煩悶 (名詞)

4031. The water was **turbid** (muddy) after the children had waded through it.

    | 註解 | 混濁的 (形容詞)

4032. He was very **vindictive** (revengeful) and never forgave an injury.

    | 註解 | 有深仇的 (形容詞)

4033. Although he is not as yet a **doddering** (shaky) and senile old man, his ideas and opinions no longer can merit the respect we gave them years ago.

    | 註解 | 戰慄的 (形容詞)

4034. Such an idea is **germinal** (creative); I am certain that it will influence thinkers and philosphere for many generations.

    | 註解 | 原始的，創造的 (形容詞)

4035. The relatives who received little or nothing sought to **invalidate** (destroy) the will by claiming that the deceased had not been in his right mind when he had signed the document.

    | 註解 | 作廢 (不定詞)

4036. We shall have to navigate very cautiously over the reefs as we have a **neap** (lowest) tide this time of the month.

    | 註解 | 最低潮，小潮 (名詞)

4037. Walter Lippman has pointed out that moralists who do not attempt to explain the moral code they advocate are often regarded as **pharisaical** (self-righteous) and ignored.

    | 註解 | 偽善的 (形容詞)

4038. I do not attach any **stigma** (brand) to the fact that you were accused of this crime; the fact that you were acquitted clears you completely.

> 註解　烙印，標記 (名詞)

4039. This legislation is **unilateral** (one-sided) since it binds only one party in the controversy.

> 註解　片面的 (形容詞)

4040. His **acquiescent** (compliant) manner did not indicate the extent of his reluctance to join the group.

> 註解　默認的，順從的 (形容詞)

4041. I will **asseverate** (aver) my conviction that he is guilty.

> 註解　斷言 (動詞)

4042. A **carping** (querulous) critic disturbs sensitive people.

> 註解　找碴的 (形容詞)

4043. The continuation of this contract is **contingent** (conditional) on the quality of your first output.

> 註解　有條件的 (形容詞)

4044. Do not attempt to increase your stature by **decrying** (disparaging) the efforts of your opponents.

> 註解　輕視的 (形容詞)

4045. The funeral **dirge** (lament with music) stirred us to tears.

> 註解　喪曲 (名詞)

4046. In that **eerie** (weird) setting, it was easy to believe in ghosts and other supernatural beings.

> 註解　奇異的 (形容詞)

4047. He tried to **eschew** (avoid) all display of temper.

> 註解　避開 (不定詞)

4048. This is an entirely **feasible** (practical) proposal.

> 註解　可實行的 (形容詞)

4049. The **frolicsome** (prankish) puppy tried to lick the face of its master.

> 註解　嬉戲的，頑皮的 (形容詞)

4050. He is naive, simple, and **guileless** (straightforward); he cannot be guilty offraud.

> 註解　不狡滑的，正直的 (形容詞)

4051. The tribal king offered to **immolate** (sacrifice) his daughter to quiet the angry gods.

   註解 犧牲，供奉 (不定詞)

4052. Although he seemed to accept cheerfully the **indignities** (outrages) heaped upon him, he was inwardly very angry.

   註解 侮辱，傷害 (名詞)

4053. The soft **luster** (gloss) of the silk in the dim light was pleasing.

   註解 光澤 (名詞)

4054. Hamlet described his **misgivings** (doubts) to Horatio but decided to fence with Laertes despite his foreboding of evil.

   註解 焦慮 (名詞)

4055. We must trace the source of these **noxious** (harmful) gases before they asphyxiate us.

   註解 有毒的 (形容詞)

4056. Tourists are urged not to **profane** (desecrate) the sanctity of holy places by wearing improper garb.

   註解 玷污，誤用 (不定詞)

4057. "The Gold Bug" is a **splendid** (sumptuous) example of the author's use of ratiocination.

   註解 輝煌的 (形容詞)

4058. The students enjoyed the professor's **sapient** (shrewd) digressions more than his formal lectures.

   註解 有智慧的 (形容詞)

4059. Let us not be misled by such **specious** (plausible) arguments.

   註解 似是而非的 (形容詞)

4060. Do you have the **temerity** (rashness) to argue with me?

   註解 魯莽，輕率 (名詞)

4061. The habitat of the horned **viper** (poisonous snake), a particularly venomous snake, is in sandy regions like the Sahara or the Sinai peninsula.

   註解 毒蛇 (名詞)

4062. Their romance could not flourish because of the presence of her **duenna** (chaperone).

   註解 媬姆，女伴 (名詞，同 chaperon)

4063. He **inveighed** (railed) against the demagoguery of the previous speaker and urged that the audience reject his philosophy as dangerous.

註解 痛罵 (動詞)

4064. His fear of flying was more than mere nervousness; it was a real **phobia** (morbid fear).

註解 恐懼症 (名詞)

4065. In his will, he requested that after payment of debts, taxes, and funeral expenses, the **residue** (balance) be given to his wife.

註解 剩餘 (名詞)

4066. His **stilted** (inflated) rhetoric did not impress the college audience; they were immune to bombastic utterances.

註解 不自然的，誇大的 (形容詞)

4067. **Untoward** (Unfortunate) circumstances prevent me from being with you on this festive occasion.

註解 不幸的 (形容詞)

4068. His **acquittal** (release) by the jury surprised those who had thought him guilty.

註解 釋放 (名詞)

4069. He worked **assiduously** (studiously) at this task for weeks before he felt satisfied with his results.

註解 勤勉地，專心地 (副詞)

4070. Buzzards are nature's scavengers; they eat the carrion (rottenness) left behind by other predators.

註解 腐肉 (名詞)

4071. As the effects of the opiate wore away, the contortions (distortions) of the patient became more violent and demonstrated how much pain he was enduring.

註解 曲解 (名詞)

4072. If we accept your premise, your conclusions are easily **deducible** (inferable).

註解 可推論的 (形容詞)

4073. His **disavowal** (disclaiming) of his part in the conspiracy was not believed by the jury.

註解 否認 (名詞)

4074. The coin had been handled so many times that its date had been **rubbed out** (effaced).

　註解　磨掉 (動詞，完成被動式)

4075. The **fecundity** (fertility) of his mind is illustrated by the many vivid images in his poems.

　註解　豐富，生產力 (名詞)

4076. Your **perverse** (forward) behavior has alienated many of us who might have been your supporters.

　註解　荒謬的，魯莽的 (形容詞)

4077. In the **guise** (costume) of a plumber, the detective investigated the murder case.

　註解　喬裝，服裝 (名詞)

4078. In the face of these **indisputable** (incontrovertible) statements, I withdraw my complaint.

　註解　明白的 (形容詞)

4079. Let us not brood over past mistakes since they are unalterable (irrevocable).

　註解　不能改變的 (形容詞)

4080. Her large and **lustrous** (radiant) eyes gave a tough of beauty to an otherwise drab face.

　註解　光亮的 (形容詞)

4081. This agreement is **nugatory** (futile) for no court will enforce it.

　註解　無效的 (形容詞)

4082. In this **licentious** (profligate) company, he lost all sense of decency.

　註解　不守法的，浪費的 (形容詞)

4083. Do not try to **rationalize** (reason) your behavior by blaming your companions.

　註解　合理化，藉口 (不定詞)

4084. I am afraid that my parents will **reprimand** (condemn) me when I show them my report card.

　註解　斥責 (動詞)

4085. The **disdainful** (sardonic) humor of nightclub comedians who satirize or ridicule patrons in the audience strikes some people as amusing and others asrude.

　　註解　輕視的，嘲笑的 (形容詞)

4086. We were frightened by the **spectral** (ghostly) glow that filled the room.

　　註解　妖怪的 (形容詞)

4087. The **turgid** (distended) river threatened to overflow the leaves and flood the countryside.

　　註解　擴張的 (形容詞)

4088. Rip Van Winkle's wife was a veritable **virago** (shrew).

　　註解　潑婦 (名詞)

4089. His tendency to utter **acrimonious** (stinging) remarks alienated his audience.

　　註解　尖刻的 (形容詞)

4090. The Coast Guard tries to prevent traffic in contraband (smuggling) goods.

　　註解　走私的 (形容詞)

4091. The ships in the harbor were not **discernible** (perceivable) in the fog.

　　註解　可看見的 (形容詞)

4092. Those students who had access to his **esoteric** (recondite) discussions were impressed by the scope of his thinking.

　　註解　秘密的 (形容詞)

4093. Her **frowzy** (slovenly) appearance and her cheap decorations made her appear ludicrous in this group.

　　註解　懶散的 (形容詞)

4094. Scientists are constantly seeking to discover the **immutable** (unchangeable) lawsof nature.

　　註解　不變的 (形容詞)

4095. Cyranto **indited** (wrote) many letters for Christian.

　　註解　撰寫 (動詞)

4096. I will **iterate** (repeat) the warning I have previously given to you.

　　註解　重述 (動詞)

4097. Farming was easy in this **luxuriant** (ornate) soil.

　　註解　肥沃的 (形容詞)

4098. His tyrannical conduct proved to all that his nickname, King Eric the Just, was a **misnomer** (wrong name).

註解　錯誤的名字 (名詞)

4099. The nurse was a cheerful but **phlegmatic** (cool).

註解　冷靜的 (形容詞，同 phlegmatical)

4100. Seldom have I seen food and drink served in such **profusion** (copiousness).

註解　豐盛 (名詞)

4101. His **raucous** (strident) laughter irritated me.

註解　粗啞的 (形容詞)

4102. I am confident that we are ready for any **reprisals** (relatiations) the enemy may undertake.

註解　報復 (名詞)

4103. Its hunger **sated** (cloyed), the lion dozed.

註解　吃飽的 (形容詞)

4104. People shunned him because of his **splenetic** (spiteful) temper.

註解　壞脾氣的 (形容詞)

4105. At one time in our history, **temporal** (secular) rulers assumed that they had been given their thrones by divine right.

註解　世俗的 (形容詞)

4106. By bribing the **turnkey** (jailer), the prisoner arranged to have better food brought to him in his cell.

註解　獄吏，獄卒 (名詞，同 jailor，gaoler)

4107. I do not accept the premise that a man is **virile** (manly) only when he is belligerent.

註解　剛健的 (形容詞)

4108. The **animus** (antagonism) of the speaker became obvious to all when he began to indulge in sarcastic and insulting remarks.

註解　惡意，敵對 (名詞)

4109. Hamlet resented his mother's **celerity** (rapidity) in remarrying within a month after his father's death.

註解　快速 (名詞)

4110. The **dulcet** (melodious) sounds of the birds at dawn were soon drowned out by the roar of traffic passing our motel.
　　　| 註解 | 悅耳的 (形容詞)

4111. He found working on the assembly line **irksome** (tedious) because of the monotony of the operation he had to perform.
　　　| 註解 | 令人厭煩的 (形容詞)

4112. In my efforts to correct this situation I felt **nonplussed** (confounded) by the stupidity of my assistants.
　　　| 註解 | 狼狽的，困惑的 (形容詞)

4113. Steel is highly **resilient** (elastic) and therefore is used in the manufacture of springs.
　　　| 註解 | 有彈性的 (形容詞)

4114. Unless we allerviate conditions in the lowest **stratum** (layer) of our society, we may expect grumbling and revolt.
　　　| 註解 | 階層 (名詞)

4115. Because of its **ursine** (bearlike) appearance, the great panda has been identified with the bears; actually, it is closely related to the raccoon.
　　　| 註解 | 似熊的 (形容詞)

4116. While this scheme was being **gestated** (evolved) by the conspirators, they maintained complete silence about their intentions.
　　　| 註解 | 孕育，計劃 (動詞，被動進行式)

4117. The **resurgent** (reviving) nation surprised everyone its quick recovery after total defeat.
　　　| 註解 | 復活的，重振的 (形容詞)

4118. According to recent **actuarial** (calculating) tables, life expectancy is greater today than it was a century ago.
　　　| 註解 | 統計的 (形容詞)

4119. He resented the **animadversions** (remarks) of his critics, particularly becausehe realized they were true.
　　　| 註解 | 批判 (名詞)

4120. His **bilious** (cranky) temperament was apparent to all who heard him rant about his difficulties.
　　　| 註解 | 任性的，古怪的 (形容詞)

4121. We could not appreciate the beauty of the many **cascades** (waterfalls) as we were forced to make detours around each of them.

　　註解　小瀑布 (名詞)

4122. Two writers **collaborated** (cooperated) in preparing this book.

　　註解　合作 (動詞)

4123. I will not attempt to **contravene** (contradict) your argument for it does not affect the situation.

　　註解　侵犯，反駁 (不定詞)

4124. Such **defamation** (calumny) of character may result in a slander suit.

　　註解　誹謗 (名詞)

4125. His voice was high-pitched and **effeminate** (womanish).

　　註解　優柔的 (形容詞)

4126. The boxer was fooled by his oppenent's sham **blow** (feint) and dropped hisguard.

　　註解　打擊，佯攻 (名詞)

4127. This tree should **fructify** (bear fruit) in three years.

　　註解　結果實 (動詞)

4128. This arrest will **impair** (worsen) his reputation in the community.

　　註解　傷害 (動詞)

4129. The sultry weather in the tropics encourages a life of **indolence** (laziness).

　　註解　怠惰 (名詞)

4130. He was a(n) **itinerant** (nomadic)) peddler and traveled through Pennsylvaniaand Virginia selling his wares.

　　註解　巡迴的，流浪的 (形容詞)

4131. The city morgue is a **macabre** (gruesome) spot for the uninitiated.

　　註解　恐怖的 (形容詞)

4132. She accused him of being a **hater of women** (misogynist) because he had been a bachelor all his life.

　　註解　討厭女人的人 (名詞片語)

4133. We must **nurture** (educate) the young so that they will develop into good citizens.

　　註解　教育 (動詞)

4134. He prided himself on his ability to analyze a person's character by studying his **physiognomy** (face).

    註解　相貌 (名詞)

4135. The students showed their **reprobation** (disapproval) of his act by rebusing to talk with him.

    註解　拒絕 (名詞)

4136. The guests, having eaten until they were **satiated** (surfeited), now listened inattentively to the speakers.

    註解　吃飽的 (形容詞)

4137. Although there are **sporadic** (occasional) outbursts of shooting, we may report that the major rebellion has been defeated.

    註解　斷斷續續的 (形容詞)

4138. A visitor may be denied admittance to this country if he has been guilty moral **turpitude** (depravity).

    註解　污點，腐敗 (名詞)

4139. A(n) **dynamic** (energetic) government is necessary to meet the demands of a changing society.

    註解　有活力的 (形容詞)

4140. You should be able to identify this horse easily as it is the only **piebald** (mottled) horse in the race.

    註解　混色的，斑點的 (形容詞)

4141. She wore the **reticulate** (netlike) stockings so popular with teenagers at that time.

    註解　網狀的 (形容詞)

4142. He is the kind of individual who is more easily impressed by a **suave** (bland) approach than by threats or bluster.

    註解　溫和的 (形容詞)

4143. I fail to understand what **motivated** (actuated) you to reply to this letter sonastily.

    註解　激發 (動詞)

4144. Her **animated** (lively) expression indicated a keenness of intellect.

    註解　生動的 (形容詞)

4145. The **astringent** (binding) quality of the unsweetened lemon juice made swallowing difficult.

　註解　凝固的 (形容詞)

4146. Her **penitent** (contrite) tears did not influence the judge when he imposed sentence.

　註解　後悔的 (形容詞)

4147. As a result of her husband's failure to appear in court, she was granted a divorce by **default** (neglect).

　註解　缺席，不出庭 (名詞)

4148. Some of us cannot stand the way she **effervesces** (bubbles) over trifles.

　註解　興奮，大笑 (動詞)

4149. West Point cadets are proud of their **esprit de corps** (comradeship).

　註解　團體精神，友誼 (名詞，法國字)

4150. He was famous for his **germane** (felicitous) remarks and was called upon to serve as master-of-ceremonies at many a banquet.

　註解　恰當的 (形容詞)

4151. He accepted the assignment with such **gusto** (enthusiasm) that I feel he would have been satisfied with a smaller salary.

　註解　趣味，熱心 (名詞)

4152. He was **impaled** (pierced) by the spear hurled by this adversary.

　註解　刺傷 (動詞，被動式)

4153. The founders of our country had **indomitable** (unconquerable) will power.

　註解　不能征服的 (形容詞)

4154. He looked for exotic foods to stimulate his **jaded** (fatigued) appetite.

　註解　厭倦的 (形容詞)

4155. Cancer **macerated** (wasted away) his body.

　註解　折磨 (動詞)

4156. There is a striking **parallelism** (similarity) between the two ages.

　註解　相似 (名詞)

4157. The **variegated** (pied) Piper of Hamelin got his name from the multicolored clothing he wore.

　註解　雜色的 (形容詞)

4158. We kept our fires burning all night to frighten the **ravening** (rapacious) wolves.

註解　捕食的，貪婪的 (形容詞)

4159. He announced that he would **repudiate** (disavow) all debts incurred by his wife.

註解　否認 (動詞)

4160. The **satiety** (repletion) of the quests at the sumptuous feast became apparent when they refused the delicious dessert.

註解　飽足 (名詞)

4161. Such a **sportive** (playful) attitude is surprising in a person serious as you usually are.

註解　開玩笑的 (形容詞)

4162. I had to struggle to break his **tenacious** (pertinacious) hold on my arm.

註解　抓住不放的，頑強的 (形容詞)

4163. Under the **tutelage** (guardianship) of such masters of the instrument, he made rapid progress as a virtuoso.

註解　教導 (名詞)

4164. The virus is highly **virulent** (poisonous) and has made many of us ill for days.

註解　有毒的 (形容詞)

4165. In the appendix to the novel, the critic sought to **annotate** (comment) many of the more esoteric references.

註解　註解，評語 (不定詞)

4166. To the delight of his audience, he completed his task with **eclat** (brilliance) andconsummate ease.

註解　喝采 (名詞，法國字)

4167. Many service employees rely more on **gratuities** (tips) than on salaries for their livelihood.

註解　小費 (名詞)

4168. The testimonies of the witnesses provide **irrefragable** (indisputable) proof that my client is innocent; I demand that he be released at once.

註解　不可否認的 (形容詞)

4169. **Objurgations** (Rebukes) and even threats of punishment did not deter the young hoodlums.

   註解　叱責 (名詞)

4170. Although we could not understand the words of the song, we got the impression from the **plangent** (plaintive) tones of the singers that it was a lament of some kind.

   註解　哀愁的 (形容詞)

4171. "By the **rood**" (crucifix) used to be a strong oath.

   註解　對著十字架，誓言 (名詞)

4172. Your analysis is highly **subjective** (personal); you have permitted your emotions and your opinions to color your thinking.

   註解　主觀的，個人的 (形容詞)

4173. His business **acumen** (insight) helped him to succeed where others had failed.

   註解　敏銳，洞察力 (名詞)

4174. He incurred the **animosity** (animus) of the ruling class because he advocated limitations of their power.

   註解　怨恨 (名詞)

4175. That was a very **astute** (wily) observation.

   註解　狡猾的 (形容詞)

4176. The plot of the novel was too **bizarre** (odd) to be believed.

   註解　古怪的 (形容詞)

4177. A **cataclysm** (deluge) such as the French Revolution affects all countries.

   註解　劇變，大災難 (名詞)

4178. To **controvert** (contradict) your theory will require much time but it is essential that we disprove it.

   註解　否定 (不定詞)

4179. This ruse will **put to rout** (discomfit) the enemy.

   註解　擊敗 (動詞片語)

4180. The literature of the age reflected the **effete** (barren) condition of the writers; no new ideas were forthcoming.

   註解　枯竭的，不生產的 (形容詞)

4181. The **estranged** (separated) wife sought a divorce.

   註解　分開的 (形容詞)

4182. Henley writes of the "**fell** (cruel) clutch of circumstance" in his poem "Invictus."

註解　殘忍的 (形容詞)

4183. This building marks the **fruition** (fulfillment) of all our aspirations and years of hard work.

註解　成果 (名詞，同 fulfilment)

4184. In this **impasse** (deadlock), all turned to prayer as their last hope.

註解　僵局，相持不下 (名詞，法國字)

4185. Because his argument was **indubitably** (unquestionably) valid, the judge accepted it .

註解　毫無疑問地 (副詞)

4186. We tried understand the **jargon** (gibberish) of the peddlers in the market-placebut could not find any basis for comprehension.

註解　術語，胡言亂語 (名詞)

4187. I do not think he will be a good ambassador because he is not accustomed tothe **Machiavellian** (crafty) maneuverings of foreign diplomats.

註解　馬基維利的，狡猾的 (形容詞，意大利政治家)

4188. He called the unfortunate waiter a clumsy **oaf** (lout).

註解　笨蛋，鄉巴佬 (名詞)

4189. The enemy **pillaged** (sacked) the quiet village and left it in ruins.

註解　搶奪 (動詞)

4190. If the doctor's **prognosis** (prediction) is correct, the patient will be in a coma for a least twenty-four hours.

註解　診斷，預告 (名詞)

4191. She looked at the snake with **repugnance** (antipathy).

註解　嫌惡，反感 (名詞)

4192. Their clothes were **saturated** (soaked) by the rain.

註解　滲透 (動詞，被動式)

4193. He tried to pay the check with a **spurious** (bogus) ten-dollar bill.

註解　偽造的 (形容詞)

4194. I cannot accept the **dogmas** (tenets) of your faith.

註解　教條 (名詞)

4195. Before leaving for his first visit to France and England, he discussed his **planof a trip** (itinerary) with people who had been there and with his travel agent.

  註解 旅行計劃 (名詞片語)

4196. The wealthy man offered **oblations** (pious donations) so that the church might be able to provide for the needy.

  註解 捐獻 (名詞)

4197. Although a member of the political group, he took only a **theoretical** (platonic) interest in its ideals and goals.

  註解 理論的，柏拉圖式的 (形容詞，同 theoretic)

4198. In the **annals** (records) of this period, we find no mention of democratic movements.

  註解 紀年表 (名詞)

4199. Airplanes are sometimes launched from battleships by **catapults** (slingshots).

  註解 軍艦甲板上彈弓 (名詞)

4200. Tea sandwiches and cookies were offered at the **light meal** (collation).

  註解 便餐 (名詞片語)

4201. The **contumacious** (disobedient) mob shouted defiantly at the police.

  註解 頑固的 (形容詞)

4202. The children, who had made him an idol, were hurt most by his **defection** (desertion) from our cause.

  註解 過失，背棄 (名詞)

4203. The lawyer was **disconcerted** (upset) by the evidence produced by his adversary.

  註解 困惑的 (形容詞)

4204. Visitors were impressed by her **ethereal** (heavenly) beauty, her delicate charm.

  註解 天使般的 (形容詞)

4205. The entire country was in a state of **agitation** (ferment).

  註解 煽動 (名詞)

4206. **Guttural** (Throaty) sounds are produced in the throat or in the back of the tongue and palate.

  註解 咽喉的，嘶啞的 (形容詞)

4207. An **indulgent** (lenient) parent many spoil a child by creating an artificial atmosphere of leniency.

註解 縱容的 (形容詞)

4208. He gazed at the painting with **jaundiced** (yellowed) eyes.

註解 猜疑的 (形容詞)

4209. I can see through your wily **machinations** (schemes).

註解 陰謀 (名詞)

4210. Nothing he did could **mitigate** (appease) her wrath; she was unforgiving.

註解 減輕 (動詞)

4211. He was **obdurate** (callous) in his refusal to listen to our complaints.

註解 無情的，鐵石心腸的 (形容詞)

4212. His desk was cluttered with paper, pen, ink, dictionary and other **paraphernalia** (odds and ends) of the writing craft.

註解 隨身用品，零零星星的東西 (名詞)

4213. I **prognosticate** (prophesy) disaster unless we change our wasteful ways.

註解 預測 (動詞)

4214. The **realm** (kingdom) of possibilities for the new invention was endless.

註解 王國 (名詞)

4215. They played Mozart's **requiem** (dirge) at the funeral.

註解 輓歌 (名詞)

4216. Do not be misled by his **saturnine** (taciturn) countenance; he is not as gloomy as he looks.

註解 嚴肅的 (形容詞)

4217. It is easy to see how crime can breed in such a **squlid** (filthy) neighborhood.

註解 不幸的 (形容詞)

4218. The allegiance of our allies is held by rather **tenuous** (rare) ties.

註解 微薄的，罕見的 (形容詞)

4219. You must be **omnipresent** (ubiquitous) for I meet you wherever I go.

註解 無所不在的 (形容詞)

4220. The stern **visage** (appearance) of the judge indicated that he had decided to impose a severe penalty.

註解 面容，外表 (名詞)

4221. The plot of the play is **jejune** (meager) and fails to capture the interest of the audience.

註解 空洞的 (形容詞，同 meagre)

4222. Even though your argument is **plausible** (specious), I still would like to have more proof.

註解 似合理的 (形容詞)

4223. The backwoodsman looked out of place in his **rustic** (uncouth) attire.

註解 古怪的 (形容詞)

4224. I found the **valedictory** (saying farewell) address too long; leave-taking should be brief.

註解 告別的 (形容詞)

4225. He was **adamant** (hard) in his determination to punish the wrongdoer.

註解 堅定不移的 (形容詞)

4226. The enemy in its revenge tried to **annihilate** (destroy) the entire population.

註解 消滅 (不定詞)

4227. His tendency toward violence was **athwart** (across) the philosophy of the peace movement.

註解 穿越 (介詞)

4228. Despite the salesperson's **blandishments** (flatteries), the customer did not buy the outfit.

註解 甜言蜜語 (名詞)

4229. The "proud man's **contumely** (insult)" is distasteful to Hamlet.

註解 傲慢 (名詞)

4230. The death of his wife left him **disconsolate** (sad).

註解 哀傷的 (形容詞)

4231. The mob showed its irritation by hanging the judge in **effigy** (dummy).

註解 肖像 (名詞)

4232. He **ferreted** (drove) out their secret.

註解 搜出 (動詞)

4233. The people against whom he **fulminated** (thundered) were innocent of any wrongdoing.

註解 猛烈攻擊 (動詞)

4234. Although not a minister, David Belasco used to wear clerical **habiliments** (garbs).

註解 服裝 (名詞)

4235. Such **ineffable** (unutterable) joy must be experienced; it cannot be described.

註解 難以言語形容的 (形容詞)

4236. His program of folk songs included several madrigals (pastoral songs) which he sang to the accompaniment of a lute.

註解 情歌，田園歌曲 (名詞)

4237. The **mobile** (movable) blood bank operated by the Red Cross visited our neighborhood today.

註解 流動的 (形容詞)

4238. She made a(n) **obeisance** (bow) as the king and queen entered the room.

註解 鞠躬 (名詞)

4239. They **pinioned** (restrained) his arms against his body but left his legs free so that he could move about.

註解 綁住 (動詞)

4240. His **prolix** (verbose) arguments irritated the jury.

註解 嚕嚕囌囌的 (形容詞)

4241. we offer a **rebate** (discount) of ten percent to those who pay cash.

註解 折扣，退費 (名詞)

4242. The prodigal son **squandered** (waste) the family estate.

註解 浪費 (動詞)

4243. You must have an **ulterior** (unstated) motive for your behavior.

註解 未表明的 (形容詞)

4244. This is an **adhesive** (viscid) liquid.

註解 有黏性的 (形容詞)

4245. The evil of class and race hatred must be eliminated while it is still in a(n) **embryonic** (rudimentary) state; otherwise, it may grow to dangerous proportions.

註解 未發達的 (形容詞)

4246. His account of the event was a lengthy **jeremiad** (lament), unrelieved by any light moments.

註解 悲痛 (名詞)

4247. He enjoyed the attentions showered upon him while he was a valetudinarian and insisted that they be continued long after his **recovery** (restoration) fromhis illness.

　　　| 註解 |　復原 (名詞)

4248. In time of war, many **atrocities** (brutal deeds) are committed by invading armies.

　　　| 註解 |　暴行，不人道的行為 (名詞)

4249. The people in the room were shocked by his blasphemous (impious) language.

　　　| 註解 |　污辱神明的，邪惡的 (形容詞)

4250. He was treated for **contusions** (bruises) and abrasions.

　　　| 註解 |　撞傷，瘀傷 (名詞)

4251. The hoodlums **profaned** (defiled) the church with their scurrilous writing.

　　　| 註解 |　玷污 (動詞)

4252. He tried to unite the **discordant** (inharmonious) factions.

　　　| 註解 |　不調和的 (形容詞)

4253. Greenhouse gardeners are concerned with the coinciding of the plants, **efforescent** (flowering) period with certain holidays.

　　　| 註解 |　開花的 (形容詞)

4254. To every one's surprise, the speech was laudatory (eulogistic) rather than critical in tone.

　　　| 註解 |　讚賞的 (形容詞)

4255. He felt that the **fervent** (ardent) praise was excessive and somewhat undeserved.

　　　| 註解 |　熱烈的 (形容詞)

4256. His **fulsome** (repulsive) praise of the dictator annoyed his listeners.

　　　| 註解 |　過度稱讚的，討厭的 (形容詞)

4257. The English teacher criticized his story because of its **hackneyed** (trite) plot.

　　　| 註解 |　陳舊的 (形容詞)

4258. He was proud of his **impeccable** (irreproachable) manners.

　　　| 註解 |　純潔的，無可責難的 (形容詞)

4259. The constant turmoil in the office proved that he was an inept (incompetent) administrator.

   註解　不合適的 (形容詞)

4260. The canoe was tossed about in the **whirlpool** (maelstrom).

   註解　漩渦 (名詞)

4261. The tapeworm is an example of the kind of **parasite** (sycophant) that may infest the human body.

   註解　寄生蟲 (名詞)

4262. In the opera La Boheme, we get a picture of the promiscuous (haphazard) life led by the young artists of Paris.

   註解　雜亂的，隨便的 (形容詞)

4263. Donkeys are reputed to be the most **recalcitrant** (rebellious) of animals.

   註解　反抗的 (形容詞)

4264. Our faculty includes many world-famous **savants** (scholars).

   註解　著名學者 (名詞)

4265. The **stagnant** (motionless) water was a breeding ground for disease.

   註解　不流動的 (形容詞)

4266. Since they have ignored our **ultimatum** (warning), our only recourse is to declare war.

   註解　最後通牒，哀的美敦書 (名詞)

4267. Melted tar is a **gluey** (viscous) substance.

   註解　膠狀的，黏黏的 (形容詞)

4268. His **prophetic** (apocalyptic) remarks were dismissed by his audience as wild surmises.

   註解　預言的，啟示的 (形容詞)

4269. Mohammed began his **hegira** (flight) when he was 53 years old.

   註解　逃亡 (名詞，同 hejira)

4270. At this critical **juncture** (crisis), let us think carefully before determining the course we shall follow.

   註解　時刻 (名詞)

4271. His essays were, for the main part, **polemics** (controversies) in support of the party's policy.

   註解　爭論 (名詞)

4272. The food was brought in on silver **salvers** (trays) by the waiters.

註解 盤子 (名詞)

4273. The parents of the eloped couple tried to annul (invalidate) the marriage.

註解 取消 (不定詞)

4274. Polis victims need physiotherapy to prevent the atrophy (degeneration) of affected limbs.

註解 虛脫，退化 (名詞)

4275. I regard your remarks as **blatant** (clamorous) and ill-mannered.

註解 喧鬧的 (形容詞)

4276. Some drugs act as laxatives when taken in small doses but act as **purgatives** (cathartics) when taken in much larger doses.

註解 瀉藥，清腸胃藥 (名詞)

4277. Radio City Music Hall has a **colossal** (huge) stage.

註解 巨大的 (形容詞)

4278. Because much needed legislation had to be enacted, the governor ordered the legislature to **convene** (assemble) in special session by January 15.

4279. The universe is composed of **discrete** (separate) bodies.

註解 個別的 (形容詞)

4280. He had the **temerity** (effrontery) to insult the guest.

註解 魯莽，無恥 (名詞)

4281. As his case was transferred from one **functionary** (official) to another, he began to despair of ever reaching a settlement.

註解 公務員，機關 (名詞)

4282. After his long illness, he was pale and **haggard** (gaunt).

註解 憔悴的 (形容詞)

4283. Now that he was wealthy, he gladly contributed to funds to assist the **impecunious** (destitute) and the disabled.

註解 貧窮的 (形容詞)

4284. After listening to the please for clemency, the judge was **inexorable** (implacable) and gave the convicted man the maximum punishment allowed by law.

註解 無情的 (形容詞)

4285. The philanthropist was most **magnanimous** (generous).

註解 度量大的 (形容詞)

4286. Although his story is based on a **modicum** (small quantity) of truth, most of the events he describes are fictitious.

　　註解　少量 (名詞)

4287. The **pious** (devout) parents gave their children a religious upbringing.

　　註解　虔誠的 (形容詞)

4288. They erected a lighthouse on the **promontory** (headland) to warn approaching ships of their nearness to the shore.

　　註解　海岬 (名詞)

4289. Unless you **repudiate** (recant) your confession, you will be punished severely.

　　註解　取消，否決 (動詞)

4290. Because of public resentment, the king had to **rescind** (cancel) his order.

　　註解　撤銷 (不定詞)

4291. I envy his **savoir faire** (sophistication); he always knows exactly what to do and say.

　　註解　急智 (名詞，法國字)

4292. His conduct during the funeral ceremony was **sedate** (staid) and solemn.

　　註解　安詳的 (形容詞)

4293. She took **umbrage** (resentment) at his remarks.

　　註解　不快，憤恨 (名詞)

4294. He was given to **visionary** (fanciful) schemes which never materialized.

　　註解　空想的 (形容詞)

4295. He was more a student of **jurisprudence** (science) than a practitioner of the law.

　　註解　法律哲學 (名詞)

4296. The crowd became **obstreperous** (boisterous) and shouted their disapproval of the proposals made by the speaker.

　　註解　吵鬧的 (形容詞)

4297. This **addle** (muddled) headed plan is so preposterous that it does not deserve any consideration.

　　註解　混亂的 (形容詞)

4298. A bird that cannot fly is an **anomaly** (irregularity).

　　註解　反常，非常規 (名詞)

4299. By withdrawing their forces, the generals hoped to **attenuate** (weaken) the enemy lines.

註解 消弱 (不定詞)

4300. He was extremely **catholic** (liberal) in his reading tastes.

註解 普遍的，充分的 (形容詞)

4301. After the recent outbreak of fires in private homes, the fire commissioner ordered that all **combustible** (inflammable) materials be kept in safe containers.

註解 易燃的 (形容詞)

4302. The lawyer is **conversant** (familiar) with all the evidence.

註解 熟悉的 (形容詞)

4303. His life was saved when his cigarette case **deflected** (swerved) the bullet.

註解 偏離 (動詞)

4304. Use your **discretion** (prudence) in this matter.

註解 謹慎 (名詞)

4305. The **effulgent** (radiant) rays of the rising sun lit the sky.

註解 光輝的 (形容詞)

4306. We must remember that none of us is infallible (unerring).

註解 絕不會錯的，正確的 (形容詞)

4307. She always discarded all garments which were no longer **modish** (fashionable).

註解 流行的 (形容詞)

4308. Do not **obfuscate** (confuse) the issues by dragging in irrelevant arguments.

註解 錯亂 (動詞)

4309. I am not a **pariah** (social outcaste) to be shunned and ostracized.

註解 賤民，無賴漢 (名詞)

4310. The **piquant** (stimulating) sauce added to our enjoyment of the meal.

註解 開胃的，刺激的 (形容詞)

4311. She was **prone** (prostrate) to sudden fits of anger.

註解 容易的，無法抵抗的 (形容詞)

4312. Let us **recapitulate** (summarize) what has been said thus far before going ahead.

註解 簡述，摘要 (動詞)

4313. The **abrogation** (rescission) of the unpopular law was urged by all political parties.

> 註解　廢止 (名詞)

4314. I doubt that he has the **stamina** (strength) to run the full distance of the marathon race.

> 註解　體力 (名詞)

4315. We have been able to explore the terrene (terrestrial) regions much more thoroughly than the aquatic or celestial regions.

> 註解　陸地的 (形容詞)

4316. We were surprised by the **unanimity** (unison) with which our proposals were accepted by the different groups.

> 註解　全體一致 (名詞)

4317. Fraud will **mar** (vitiate) the contract.

> 註解　損毀 (動詞)

4318. I find your remarks **apropos** (properly) of the present situation timely and pertinent.

> 註解　適當地 (副詞)

4319. The long-winded orator soon had his audience in a **comatose** (lethargic) state.

> 註解　昏睡的 (形容詞)

4320. The cavalry rushed into the melee and **hewed** (hacked) the enemy with their swords.

> 註解　砍殺 (動詞)

4321. Comparison will be easier if you place **side by side** (juxtapose) the two objects.

> 註解　並排 (動詞片語)

4322. It will take time for the **Occident** (West) to understand the ways and customs of the Orient.

> 註解　西方國家，歐美國家 (名詞)

4323. The display of the **sarcophagus** (stone coffin) in the art museum impresses meas a morbid exhibition.

> 註解　石棺 (名詞)

4324. Your attempt to **superimpose** (impose) another agency in this field will merely increase the bureaucratic nature of our government.

　　註解　添加 (不定詞)

4325. The **feud** (vendetta) continued for several generations despite all attempts by authorities to end the killings.

　　註解　宿仇，血仇 (名詞)

4326. The critic's **caustic** (burning) remarks angered the hapless actors who were the subjects of his sarcasm.

　　註解　刻薄的 (形容詞)

4327. I would rather have **comely** (agreeable) wife than a rich one.

　　註解　合適的 (形容詞)

4328. During the transit strike, commuters used various kinds of **conveyances** (vehicles).

　　註解　交通工具 (名詞)

4329. The lawyers sought to examine the books of the **defunct** (dead) corporation.

　　註解　死亡的 (形容詞)

4330. They were annoyed and bored by his discursive (digressing) remarks.

　　註解　推論的 (形容詞)

4331. For a brief moment, the entire skyline was bathed in an orange-red hue in the **evanescent** (vanishing) rays of the sunset.

　　註解　短暫的，易消失的 (形容詞)

4332. When his finger began to **fester** (suppurate), the doctor lanced it and removed the splinter which had caused the pus to form.

　　註解　化膿 (不定詞)

4333. The story of his embezzlement of the funds created a **frenzy** (furor) on the Stock Exchange.

　　註解　狂熱 (名詞)

4334. In those **halcyon** (tranquil) days, people were not worried about sneak attacks and bombings.

　　註解　太平的 (形容詞)

4335. We could see by his brazen attitude that he was **impenitent** (obdurate).

　　註解　無悔悟的 (形容詞)

4336. Jesse James was an **infamous** (ill-famed) outlaw.
　　　註解　無恥的 (形容詞)

4337. Do not take my **jocular** (waggish) remarks seriously.
　　　註解　滑稽的 (形容詞)

4338. In their stories of the trial, the reporters ridiculed the **magniloquent** (pompous) speeches of the defense attorney.
　　　註解　誇張的 (形容詞)

4339. I first learned of his death when I read the **obituary** (death notice) column in the newspaper.
　　　註解　訃聞 (名詞)

4340. All this legal **parlance** (idiom) confuses me; I need an interpreter.
　　　註解　用語，術語 (名詞)

4341. She showed her **resentment** (pique) by her refusal to appear with the other contestants at the end of the contest.
　　　註解　憤怒 (名詞)

4342. I am sure disease must **propagate** (multiply) in such unsanitary and crowded areas.
　　　註解　傳播 (動詞)

4343. The **recession** (retreat) of the troops from the combat area was completed in an orderly manner.
　　　註解　撤退 (名詞)

4344. His **resonant** (echoing) voice was particularly pleasing.
　　　註解　回聲的 (形容詞)

4345. I admire his **terse** (pithy) style of writing.
　　　註解　簡潔的 (形容詞)

4346. His anger is **unassuaged** (unsatisfied) by your apology.
　　　註解　不滿的 (形容詞)

4347. Such **vitriolic** (corrosive) criticism is uncalled for.
　　　註解　尖酸刻薄的 (形容詞)

4348. The Brooklyn Bridge was the archetype (prototype) of the many spans that now connect Manhattan with Long Island and New Jersey.
　　　註解　原型 (名詞)

4349. I cannot express the **odium** (repugnance) I feel at your heinous actions.
　　　註解　厭惡 (名詞)

4350. The most objectionable feature of these formal banquets is the **after dinner** (postprandial) speech.

　　註解　宴後的 (形容詞)

4351. His tale of **supernal** (celestial) beings was skeptically received.

　　註解　天上的，神聖的 (形容詞)

4352. He repeated the message **word for word** (verbatim).

　　註解　逐字地 (副詞)

4353. He was **expert at** (adept at) the fine art of irritating people.

　　註解　擅長於 (形容詞)

4354. We shall have to overcome the antagonism (hostility) of the natives before our plans for settling this area can succeed.

　　註解　敵對 (名詞)

4355. His outstanding **attribute** (quality) was his kindness.

　　註解　特質 (名詞)

4356. The extent of the **blighted** (destroyed) areas could be seen only when viewed from the air.

　　註解　毀壞的 (形容詞)

4357. The roast turkey and other comestibles (edibles), the wines, and the excellent service made this Thanksgiving dinner particularly memorable.

　　註解　食物 (名詞)

4358. The **festive** (convivial) celebrators of the victory sang their college songs.

　　註解　歡樂的 (形容詞)

4359. He felt that he would debase himself if he **deigned** (condescended) to answer his critics.

　　註解　屈就 (動詞)

4360. You make enemies of all you despise (disdain).

　　註解　輕視 (動詞)

4361. Her **effusive** (gushing) manner of greeting her friends finally began to irritate them.

　　註解　感情豐富的 (形容詞)

4362. Your **evasive** (eluding) answers convinced the judge that you were withholding important evidence.

　　註解　迴避的 (形容詞)

4363. The opponents of the political party in power organized a **fusion** (coalition) of disgruntled groups and became important element in the election.
註解 結合 (名詞)

4364. He was laid to rest in hallowed (consecrated) ground.
註解 神聖的 (形容詞)

4365. His **domineering** (imperious) manner indicated that he had long been accustomed to assuming command.
註解 專制的 (形容詞)

4366. Sants Claus is always vivacious and jocund (merry).
註解 高興的 (形容詞)

4367. It is difficult to comprehend the magnitude (greatness) his crime.
註解 輕重量 (名詞)

4368. There is a slight **moiety** (half) of the savage in her personality which is noteasily perceived by those who do not know her well.
註解 一半，二分之一 (名詞)

4369. I am afraid he will **objurgate** (reproach) us publicly for this offense.
註解 責備 (動詞)

4370. The peace **parley** (conference) has not produced the anticipated truce.
註解 談判，會議 (名詞)

4371. He spent many happy hours in his **piscatorial** (piscatory) activities.
註解 釣魚的 (形容詞)

4372. I dislike your **propensity** (penchant) to belittle every contribution he makes to our organization.
註解 傾向 (名詞)

4373. Although he had been the **recipient** (receiver) of many favors, he was not grateful to his benefactor.
註解 受惠者 (名詞)

4374. The judge granted the condemned man a **respite** (reprieve) to enable his attorneys to file an appeal.
註解 緩刑 (名詞)

4375. Let us not widen the **schism** (division) by further bickering.
註解 派系 (名詞)

4376. He is so thorough that he analyzes **tertiary** (third) causes where other writers are content with primary and secondary reasons.

註解 第三的 (形容詞)

4377. He is so **unassuming** (modest) that some people fail to realize how great a man he really is.

註解 謙遜的 (形容詞)

4378. He became more **vituperative** (abusive) as he realized that we were not going to grant him his wish.

註解 辱罵的 (形容詞)

4379. You cannot keep your **complicity** (participation) in this affair secret very long; you would be wise to admit your involvement immediately.

註解 共謀，參與 (名詞)

4380. The scientific advances of the twentieth century have enabled man to invade the **empyreal** (fiery) realm of the eagle.

註解 天空的 (形容詞)

4381. Having been **hoodwinked** (deluded) once by the fast-talking salesman, he was extremely cautious when he went to purchase a used car.

註解 欺騙 (動詞，完成被動式)

4382. In America, we discard as offal (garbage) that which could feed families in less fortunate parts of the world.

註解 垃圾 (名詞)

4383. The recent drought in the Middle Atlantic States has emphasized the need for extensive research in ways of making sea water **potable** (drinkable).

註解 飲用的 (形容詞)

4384. I will **cleave** (adhere) to this opinion until proof that I am wrong is presented.

註解 分開，堅持 (動詞)

4385. The **antediluvian** (antiquated) customs had apparently not changed for thousands of years.

註解 古老的 (形容詞)

4386. They decided to wage a war of **attrition** (abrasion) rather than to rely on anall-out attack.

註解 消耗 (名詞)

4387. As described by Chaucer, the cavalcade (parade) of Canterbury pilgrims was a motley group.

註解 一隊人馬 (名詞)

4388. A spirit of **comity** (civility) should exist among nations.

註解 禮儀 (名詞)

4389. Congress was **convoked** (convened) at the outbreak of the emergency.

註解 召集 (動詞，被動式)

4390. If you **delete** (erase) this paragraph, the composition will have more appeal.

註解 刪除 (動詞)

4391. When he tried to answer the questions, he **evinced** (displayed) his ignorance of the subject matter.

註解 表明 (動詞)

4392. The neglected wound became **fetid** (malodorous).

註解 有惡臭的 (形容詞)

4393. Several in the audience were deceived by his **fustian** (bombastic) style; they mistook pomposity for erudition.

註解 浮誇的 (形容詞)

4394. I think you were frightened by a **delusion** (hallucination) which you created in your own mind.

註解 幻想 (名詞)

4395. This new material is **impermeable** (impervious) to liquids.

註解 不透水的 (形容詞)

4396. In the twentieth century, physicists have made their greatest discoveries about the characteristics of **infinitesimal** (minute) objects like the atom and its parts.

註解 極小的 (形容詞)

4397. There was great **jubilation** (rejoicing) when the armistice was announced.

註解 歡呼 (名詞)

4398. The hospital could not take care of all who had been wounded or **mutilat**ed (maimed) in the railroad accident.

註解 殘廢的 (形容詞)

4399. We tried to **mollify** (soothe) the hysterical child by promising her many gifts.

    註解   安慰 (不定詞)

4400. The sergeant ordered the men to march "**Oblique** (standing) Right."

    註解   傾斜的 (形容詞)

4401. We enjoyed the clever **travesties** (parodies) of popular songs which the chorussang.

    註解   滑稽的模仿 (名詞)

4402. I enjoy reading his essays because they are always compact and **meaty** (concise).

    註解   有內容的，簡要的 (形容詞)

4403. The natives offered sacrifices to **propitiate** (appease) the gods.

    註解   取悅 (不定詞)

4404. The two nations signed a(n) **reciprocal** (interacting) trade agreement.

    註解   互惠的 (形容詞)

4405. The toreador wore a **resplendent** (lustrous) costume.

    註解   華麗的 (形容詞)

4406. You have not produced a **scintilla** (least bit) of evidence to support your argument.

    註解   一點點 (名詞)

4407. He thought of college as a place where one drank beer from **steins** (beer mugs) and sang songs of lost lambs.

    註解   啤酒杯 (名詞)

4408. My advice is to avoid discussing this problem with him today as he is rather **testy** (tetchy).

    註解   暴躁的 (形容詞)

4409. He had a sudden fit of **unbridled** (violent) rage.

    註解   沒約束的，激烈的 (形容詞)

4410. She had always been **animated** (vivacious) and sparkling.

    註解   愉快的 (形容詞)

4411. He was sickened by the **encomiums** (laudations) and panegyrics expressed byspeakers who had previously been among the first to vilify the man they were now honoring.

    註解   讚頌 (名詞)

4412. The crowd listened to his **exhortative** (hortatory) statements with ever growing excitement; finally they rushed from the hall to carry out his suggestions.

註解　勸告的 (形容詞，同 hortative)

4413. His voice has a **lachrymose** (tearful) quality which is more appropriate at a funeral than a class reunion.

註解　令人落淚的 (形容詞)

4414. The angler found a **supple** (pliant) limb and used it as a fishing rod.

註解　柔軟的 (形容詞)

4415. I do not like the rides in the amusement park because they have a **giddy** (vertiginous) effect on me.

註解　頭暈的 (形容詞)

4416. Excess **fatty** (adipose) tissue should be avoided by middle-aged people.

註解　肥胖 (名詞)

4417. The gorilla is the strongest of the **anthropoid** (manlike) animals.

註解　似人類的 (形容詞)

4418. You have taken an **atypical** (irregular) case.

註解　非典型的 (形容詞，同 atypic)

4419. His walking stick served him as a **bludgeon** (club) on many occasions.

註解　短棒 (名詞)

4420. I respect your sensible criticisms, but I dislike the way you **cavil** (carp) about unimportant details.

註解　苛責，挑剔 (動詞)

4421. He had **copious** (plentiful) reasons for rejecting the proposal.

註解　眾多的 (形容詞)

4422. Workers in nuclear research must avoid the **deleterious** (harmful) effects of radioactive substances.

註解　有害的 (形容詞)

4423. Your **untidy** (disheveled) appearance will hurt your chances in this interview.

註解　不整潔的 (形容詞)

4424. We found his **egotism** (vanity) unwarranted and irritating.

註解　自大 (名詞)

4425. He **evoked** (called up) much criticism by his hostile manner.

　註解　引起 (動詞)

4426. Like a(n) **gadfly** (animal-biting fly), he irritated all the guests at the hotel; within forty-eight hours, everyone regarded him as an annoying busybody.

　註解　牛虻 (名詞)

4427. The minority party agreed not to hamper (obstruct) the efforts of the leaders to secure a lasting peace.

　註解　阻礙 (不定詞)

4428. I regard your remarks as **insolent** (impertinent) and resent them.

　註解　粗野的 (形容詞)

4429. His greatest **infirmity** (weakness) was lack of willpower.

　註解　弱點 (名詞)

4430. I believe that this plan is not **judicious** (discreet); it is too risky.

　註解　明智的 (形容詞)

4431. The witch uttered **maledictions** (curses) against her captors.

　註解　詛咒 (名詞)

4432. . His moral decadence was marked by his obliquity (perversity) from the ways of integrity and honesty.

　註解　不道德，荒謬 (名詞)

4433. He could not live on the small **wage** (pittance) he received as a pension and had to look for an additional.

　註解　薪俸 (名詞)

4434. I think it is advisable that we wait for a more **propitious** (favorable) occasion to announce our plans.

　註解　有利的 (形容詞)

4435. If they attack us, we shall be compelled to **reciprocate** (repay) and bomb their territory.

　註解　回報 (不定詞)

4436. He offered to make **indemnification** (restitution) for the window broken by hisson.

　註解　賠償 (名詞)

4437. I enjoy her dinner parties because the food is excellent and the conversation **scintillates** (sparkles).

註解　才智橫溢，發出光芒 (動詞)

4438. You have the **uncanny** (mysterious) knack of reading my innermost thoughts.

註解　奇怪的 (形容詞)

4439. The crowd grew **vociferous** (clamorous) in its anger and threatened to take the law into its own hands.

註解　嘈雜的 (形容詞)

4440. Until the heavy rains of the past spring, this **gully** (arroyo) had been a dry bed.

註解　溝渠 (名詞)

4441. Your presence at the scene of the dispute **compromises** (adjusts) our claim to neutrality in this matter.

註解　調和 (動詞)

4442. In this painting we see a Triton blowing on his **conch** (large seashell).

註解　貝殼 (名詞)

4443. Although she is now a boisterous **girl** (hoyden), I am sure she will outgrow her tomboyish ways and quiet down.

註解　喧鬧的女孩 (名詞)

4444. His friends tried to overcome the **lassitude** (languor) into which he had fallen by tacking him to parties and to the theater.

註解　疲倦 (名詞)

4445. On Christmas Eve, Santa Claus is **omnipresent** (ubiquitous).

註解　到處都在的 (形容詞)

4446. The surgeon refused to lance the abscess until it **suppurated** (maturated).

註解　化膿 (動詞)

4447. His **adjuration** (solemn urging) to tell the truth did not change the witnesses'testimony.

註解　發誓 (名詞)

4448. His **audacity** (boldness) in this critical moment encouraged.

註解　膽識 (名詞)

4449. The gloomy skies and the sulphurous odors from the mineral springs seemed to **bode** (foreshadow) evil to those who settled in the area.
   | 註解 | 預兆 (不定詞)

4450. I intend to **cede** (transfer) this property to the city.
   | 註解 | 割讓 (不定詞)

4451. Because she refused to give him any answer to his proposal of marriage, he called her a **flirt** (coquette).
   | 註解 | 調情者 (名詞)

4452. He is a powerful storyteller, but he is weakest in his **delineation** (portrayal) of character.
   | 註解 | 描繪，描寫 (名詞)

4453. Although he was young, his remarks indicated that he was **disingenuous** (sophisticated).
   | 註解 | 不坦白的，老練的 (形容詞)

4454. He was a(n) **egregious** (shocking) liar.
   | 註解 | 過份的，極壞的 (形容詞)

4455. The primitive conditions of the period were symbolized by the porcelain **ewer** (female goat) and basin in the bedroom.
   | 註解 | 母羊 (名詞)

4456. The prisoner was **fettered** (shackled) to the wall.
   | 註解 | 加腳鐐，加手銬 (動詞，被動式)

4457. When he attempted to land the sailfish, he was so nervous that he dropped the **gaff** (hook) into the sea.
   | 註解 | 大魚鉤 (名詞)

4458. We are impressed by his **imperturbability** (calmness) in this critical moment and are calmed by it.
   | 註解 | 鎮定 (名詞)

4459. After the balloons were **inflated** (enlarged), they were distributed among the children.
   | 註解 | 脹大 (動詞，被動式)

4460. The opposition claimed that his trip to Europe was merely a political **junket** (excursion).
   | 註解 | 考察，旅行 (名詞)

4461. We must try to bring these **malefactors** (criminals) to justice.

註解　罪犯 (名詞)

4462. The City of Pompeil was destroyed by volcanic ash rather than by **molten** (melted) lava flowing from Mount Vesuvius.

註解　熔化的 (形容詞)

4463. We must quiet the **restive** (unmanageable) animals.

註解　倔強的，難駕馭的 (形容詞)

4464. The farm boy felt out of place in the school attended by the **scions** (offsprings) of the wealthy and noble families.

註解　子孫，後代 (名詞)

4465. He found the loan shark's demands **unscrupulous** (unconscionable) and impossible to meet.

註解　無遠慮的，不合理的 (形容詞)

4466. Slacks became the **vogue** (mode) on many college campuses.

註解　時尚 (名詞)

4467. Many have sought to fathom the **enigmatic** (obscure) smile of the Mona Lisa.

註解　不可思議的，不明的 (形容詞)

4468. The ascent of the **hummock** (small hill) is not difficult and the view from the hilltop is ample reward for the effort.

註解　小山丘 (名詞)

4469. Because of the prisoner's record, the district attorney refused to reduce the charge from grand **lareny** (theft) to petit larceny.

註解　竊盜 (名詞)

4470. The emperor was spared the **onus** (burden) of signing the surrender papers; instead, he relegated the assignment to his generals.

註解　負擔，責任 (名詞)

4471. The police quickly found the distributors of the **bogus** (counterfeit) twenty-dollar bills.

註解　偽造的 (形容詞)

4472. The only **disinterested** (unprejudiced) person in the room was the judge.

註解　公正的 (形容詞)

4473. The colonies rebelled against the **exactions** (extortions) of the mother country.

> 註解   榨取，勒索 (名詞)

4474. Our ambitious venture ended in a **fiasco** (total tailure).

> 註解   完全失敗 (名詞)

4475. He could not **gainsay** (deny) the truth of the report.

> 註解   否認 (動詞)

4476. This **hapless** (unfortunate) creature had never known a moment's pleasure.

> 註解   不幸的 (形容詞)

4477. You cannot change their habits for their minds are **impervious** (impenetrable) to reasoning.

> 註解   專橫的，不可理解的 (形容詞)

4478. We must thwart his **malevolent** (vindictive) schemes.

> 註解   惡意的 (形容詞)

4479. I resent the **obloquy** (infamy) that you are casting upon my reputation.

> 註解   不名譽的行為 (名詞)

4480. He read many **recondite** (abstruse) books in order to obtain the material for his scholarly thesis.

> 註解   深奧的 (形容詞)

4481. The lifeguard tried to **resuscitate** (revive) the drowned child by applying artificial respiration.

> 註解   使甦醒 (不定詞)

4482. They feared the plague and regarded it as a deadly **scourge** (lash).

> 註解   災難，打擊 (名詞)

4483. I do not want to **brand** (stigmatize) this young offender for life by sending him to prison.

> 註解   烙印，責難 (不定詞)

4484. These springs are famous for their **therapeutic** (curative) qualities.

> 註解   治療的 (形容詞，同 therapeutical)

4485. Ethyl chloride is very **mercurial** (volatile) liquid.

> 註解   多變的，揮發性的 (形容詞)

4486. The manner in which the United States was able to **assimilate** (absorb) the hordes of immigrants during the nineteenth and the early part of the twentieth centuries will always be a source of pride.

　註解　吸收 (不定詞)

4487. Water was brought to the army in the desert by an improvised **conduit** (aqueduct) from the adjoining mountain.

　註解　水管，溝渠 (名詞)

4488. He accumulated his small fortune by diligence and **husbandry** (frugality).

　註解　節儉 (名詞)

4489. His **praiseworthy** (laudable) deeds will be remembered by all whom he aided.

　註解　值得讚美的 (形容詞)

4490. He was not severely cut; the flying glass had merely **scarified** (scratched) him.

　註解　劃傷 (動詞，完成式)

4491. He thrived on the **adulation** (flattery) of his henchmen.

　註解　奉承 (名詞)

4492. His extreme **antipathy** (aversion) to dispute caused him to avoid argumentative discussions with his friends.

　註解　反感，憎惡 (名詞)

4493. He interpreted the departure of the birds as a **prophecy** (augury) of evil.

　註解　預言，徵兆 (名詞)

4494. He vowed to remain **celibate** (unmarried).

　註解　獨身的 (形容詞)

4495. After sleeping in small roadside cabins, they found their hotel suite **commodious** (roomy).

　註解　寬敞的 (形容詞)

4496. He was not a churchgoer; he was interested only in **corporeal** (bodily) matters.

　註解　具體的，物體的 (形容詞)

4497. His remarks were so **disjointed** (disconnected) that we could not follow his reasoning.

　註解　雜亂的，不連貫的 (形容詞)

4498. He could not repress as **ejaculation** (exclamation) of surprise when he heard the news.

> 註解　失聲，呼喊 (名詞)

4499. He had been Chancellor of the **Exchequer** (Treasury) before his promotion to the high office he now holds.

> 註解　國庫 (名詞)

4500. I cannot accept government by **fiat** (command); I feel that I must be consulted.

> 註解　任命 (名詞)

4501. In his lengthy **noisy speech** (harangue), the principal berated the offenders.

> 註解　高談闊論 (名詞)

4502. We tried to curb his **rash** (impetuous) behavior because we felt that in his haste he might offend some people.

> 註解　輕率的 (形容詞)

4503. I find your behavior **obnoxious** (offensive); please amend your ways.

> 註解　令人生厭的 (形容詞)

4504. His **stingy** (parsimonious) nature did not permit him to enjoy any luxuries.

> 註解　小氣的 (形容詞)

4505. The dove has a **plaintive** (mournful) and melancholy call.

> 註解　哀傷的 (形容詞)

4506. If you encounter any enemy soldiers during your **reconnaissance** (reconnoitering), capture them for questioning.

> 註解　偵察 (名詞)

4507. I can recommend him for a position of responsibility for I have found him avery **conscientious** (scrupulous) young man.

> 註解　盡責的，審慎的 (形容詞)

4508. He performed his daily **stint** (supply) cheerfully and willingly.

> 註解　供應量 (名詞)

4509. Uriah Heep disguised his nefarious actions by **unctuous** (bland) protestations of his "ability."

> 註解　溫柔的 (形容詞)

4510. This scheme is a snare and a delusion (hallucination).

   註解　幻想 (名詞)

4511. She felt no **elation** (exaltation) at finding the purse.

   註解　得意揚揚 (名詞)

4512. He discovered she was **fickle** (faithless).

   註解　不專心的 (形容詞)

4513. I think your machine **encroaches** (infringes) on my patent.

   註解　侵害 (動詞)

4514. She waited at the subway **kiosk** (summerhouse).

   註解　涼亭 (名詞)

4515. This is a **malignant** (virulent) disease; we may have to use drastic measures tostop its spread.

   註解　惡性的，毒性的 (形容詞)

4516. Nothing is more disgusting to me than the obsequious (sycophantic) demeanor of the people who wait upon you.

   註解　卑躬的，奉承的 (形容詞)

4517. As a judge, not only must I be unbiased, but I must also avoid any evidence of **partiality** (inclination) when I award the prize.

   註解　偏袒的 (名詞)

4518. The pupil did not need to spend much time in study as he had a **retentive** (holding) mind.

   註解　記性好的 (形容詞)

4519. The captured soldier was held in **thrall** (slave) by the conquering army.

   註解　奴隸 (名詞)

4520. He was a **voluble** (glib) speaker, always ready to talk.

   註解　健談的 (形容詞)

4521. I will end all your **conjectures** (surmises); I admit I am guilty as charged.

   註解　推測 (名詞)

4522. His argument was so **convoluted** (intricate) that few of us could follow it intelligently.

   註解　錯綜複雜的 (形容詞)

4523. The evils that **ensued** (followed) were the direct result of the miscalculations of the leaders.

   註解　後果，跟隨 (動詞)

4524. This salesman is guilty of **hyperbole** (exaggeration) in describing his product; it is wise to discount his claims.

註解 誇張 (名詞)

4525. In his youth he led a life of **lechery** (lustfulness) and debauchery; he did not mend his ways until middle age.

註解 好色 (名詞)

4526. The chaplain delivered his sermon from a hastily improvised **lectern** (readingdesk).

註解 讀經臺 (名詞)

4527. He refused to defend himself against the slander and **opprobrium** (vilification) hurled against him by the newspapers; he preferred to rely on his record.

註解 不名譽的事，中傷 (名詞)

4528. The President cannot levy taxes; that is the **prerogative** (privilege) of the legislative branch of government.

註解 特權 (名詞)

4529. His superficial scientific treaties were filled with **sciolisms** (quackeries) and outmoded data.

註解 一知半解，欺騙行為 (名詞)

4530. He was denounced as a **wastrel** (profligate) who had dissipated his inheritance.

註解 遊手好閒的人 (名詞)

4531. The **adumbration** (foreshadowing) of the future in science fiction is often extremely fantastic.

註解 輪廓，預示 (名詞)

4532. This tyranny was the **antithesis** (contrast) of all that he had hoped for, and he fought it with all his strength.

註解 對照 (名詞)

4533. His **austere** (stern) demeanor prevented us from engaging in our usual frivolous activities.

註解 嚴格的 (形容詞)

4534. Unless we find a witness to **corroborate** (confirm) your evidence, it will not stand up in court.

註解 確認 (不定詞)

4535. Do not **disparage** (belittle) anyone's contribution; these little gifts add up tolarge sums.

註解 輕視 (動詞)

4536. The essay on the lost crew was **elegiacal** (mournful) in mood.

註解 悲哀的 (形容詞，同 elegiac)

4537. Although this book purports to be a biography of George Washington, many of the incidents are **fictitious** (imaginary).

註解 假想的 (形容詞)

4538. Watching children **gamboling** (skipping) in the park is a pleasant.

註解 歡跳 (動名詞)

4539. The crocus is an early **harbinger** (forerunner) of spring.

註解 先驅 (名詞)

4540. We must regard your blasphemy as an act of impiety (irreverence).

註解 不敬 (名詞)

4541. These remarks indicate that you are ingenuous (naive) and unaware of life'sharsher realities.

註解 坦白的 (形容詞)

4542. He always helped both his **kith** (familiar friends) and kin.

註解 親友 (名詞，kith and kin 必須同時使用)

4543. Although extremely wealthy, he was regarded as a(n) **parvenu** (upstart) by the aristocratic members of society.

註解 暴發戶 (名詞)

4544. The theatrical company reprinted the **plauditory** (applauding) comments of the critics in its advertisement.

註解 稱讚的 (形容詞)

4545. I do not like this author because he is so unimaginative and **prosaic** (commonplace).

註解 平淡的 (形容詞)

4546. The religious people ostracized the **recreant** (coward) who had abandoned their faith.

註解 不忠實的 (形容詞)

4547. Because of the **reticence** (uncommunicativeness) of the key witness, the caseagainst the defendant collapsed.

註解 沉默 (名詞)

4548. Your **indecent** (scurrilous) remarks are especially offensive because they are untrue.

> 註解 　不適當的，下流的 (形容詞)

4549. When he died, many poets wrote threnodies (dirges) about his passing.

> 註解 　輓歌 (名詞，同 threnodes)

4550. When they **unearthed** (dug up) the city, the archeologists found many relics ofan ancient civilization.

> 註解 　挖掘 (動詞)

4551. Stories of Bohemian life in Paris are full of tales of artists, starving or freezing in their **ateliers** (workshops).

> 註解 　工作室 (名詞)

4552. The **hyperborean** (arctic) blasts brought snow and ice to the countryside.

> 註解 　北極地區的 (形容詞)

4553. Although many critics hailed his Fifth Symphony as his major work, he did not regard it as his major **opus** (work).

> 註解 　作品 (名詞)

4554. Your ignoring their pathetic condition is tantamount (equal) to murder.

> 註解 　同等的 (形容詞)

4555. He found this **adventitious** (accidental) meeting with his friend extremely fortunate.

> 註解 　意外的 (形容詞)

4556. He felt **apathetic** (indifferent) about the conditions he had observed and did not care to fight against them.

> 註解 　不重要的 (形容詞)

4557. The **austerity** (severity) and dignity of the court were maintained by the new justices.

> 註解 　嚴肅 (名詞)

4558. Her **exemplary** (outstanding) behavior was praised at commencement.

> 註解 　可為模範的 (形容詞)

4559. A dog's **fidelity** (loyalty) to its owner is one of the reason why that animal is a favorite household pet.

> 註解 　忠誠 (名詞)

4560. An inveterate **gamester** (gambler), he was willing to wager on the outcome of any event, even one which involved the behavior of insects.
   註解　賭棍 (名詞)

4561. The congregation was offended by his irreverent (impious) remarks.
   註解　不敬的 (形容詞)

4562. Our tariff policy is a **moot** (debatable) subject.
   註解　可討論的 (形容詞)

4563. His speeches were aimed at the **vulgar** (plebeian) minds and emotions; they disgusted the more refined.
   註解　粗俗的，平民的 (形容詞)

4564. In earlier days, the church **proscribed** (ostracized) dancing and cardplaying.
   註解　禁止，排斥 (動詞)

4565. Loud and angry **recriminations** (countercharges) were her answer to his accusations.
   註解　反唇相譏，反擊 (名詞)

4566. The queen's **retinue** (attendants) followed her down the aisle.
   註解　侍從 (名詞)

4567. The sailors decided to **scuttle** (sink) their vessel rather than surrender it to the enemy.
   註解　弄沉 (不定詞)

4568. I am afraid that this imaginative poetry will not appeal to such a **stolid** (impassive) person.
   註解　不易動感情的 (形容詞)

4569. There is a(n) **unearthly** (weird) atmosphere in his work which amazes the casual observer.
   註解　不可思議的 (形容詞)

4570. The wolf is a **voracious** (ravenous) animal.
   註解　貪食的 (形容詞)

4571. Many medieval paintings depict saintly characters with **aureoles** (halos) around their heads.
   註解　光環 (名詞)

4572. I have no authority to **hypothecate** (mortgage) this property as security for the loan.

註解 抵押 (不定詞)

4573. They made the **welkin** (sky) ring with their shouts.

註解 天空 (名詞)

4574. At the height of the battle, the casualties were so numerous that the victims **weltered** (wallowed) in their blood while waiting for medical attention.

註解 湧出 (動詞)

4575. **Adverse** (Hostile) circumstances compelled him to close his business.

註解 不利的 (形容詞)

4576. He discovered a small **aperture** (hole) in the wall, through which the insects had entered the room.

註解 孔洞 (名詞)

4577. There was a **complacent** (self-satisfied) look on his face as he examined his paintings.

註解 自得意滿的 (形容詞)

4578. He felt that he could **demean** (humiliate) himself if he replied to the scurrilous letter.

註解 降低，屈辱 (動詞)

4579. He argued that the project was an elusory (elusive) one and would bring disappointment to all.

註解 難懂的 (形容詞)

4580. The evangelist will **exhort** (urge) all sinners in his audience to reform.

註解 勸告 (動詞)

4581. That incident is a(n) **figment** (invention) of your imagination.

註解 虛構 (名詞)

4582. We cannot condone such **knavery** (rascality) in public officials.

註解 惡行 (名詞)

4583. In these stories of **pastoral** (rural) life, we find an understanding of the daily tasks of country folk.

註解 鄉村的 (形容詞)

4584. The union leader was given **plenary** (full) power to negotiate a new contract with the employers.

　　　註解　完全的 (形容詞)

4585. He dropped his libel suit after the newspaper published a **retraction** (withdrawal) of its statement.

　　　註解　撤回 (名詞)

4586. The **sebaceous** (oily) glans secrete oil to the hair follicles.

　　　註解　脂肪的 (形容詞)

4587. The criminal tried to **throttle** (strangle) the old man.

　　　註解　勒死 (不定詞)

4588. My answer to your proposal is an **unequivocal** (obvious) and absolute "NO."

　　　註解　明白的 (形容詞)

4589. Such behavior is **idiosyncratic** (private); it is as easily identifiable as a signature.

　　　註解　特質的 (形容詞)

4590. The hospital was in such a filthy state that we were afraid that many of the patients would suffer from **septic** (putrid) poisoning.

　　　註解　敗血的，腐爛的 (形容詞)

4591. Identification by fingerprints is based on the difference in shape and number of the **whorls** (rings) on the fingers.

　　　註解　環紋 (名詞)

4592. We must learn to meet **adversity** (poverty) gracefully.

　　　註解　災難，貧困 (名詞)

4593. She distributed gifts in a **bountiful** (generous) and gracious manner.

　　　註解　慷慨的 (形容詞)

4594. Many automatic drying machines remove excess moisture from clothing by **centrifugal** (radiating) force.

　　　註解　離心力的 (形容詞)

4595. The courtier obeyed the king's orders in a(n) complaisant (obliging) manner.

　　　註解　順從的 (形容詞)

4596. The funeral **cortege** (procession) proceeded slowly down the avenue.

　　　註解　儀仗，行列 (名詞，法國字)

4597. The **dispersion** (scattering) of this group throughout the world may be explained by their expulsion from their homeland.

　註解　散佈 (名詞)

4598. The boys **filched** (stole) apples from the fruit stand.

　註解　偷取 (動詞)

4599. The mammoth (gigantic) corporations of the twentieth century are a mixed blessing.

　註解　巨大的 (形容詞)

4600. Actors feared the critic's **mordant** (stinging) pen.

　註解　尖酸的 (形容詞)

4601. Because he was so **blunt** (obtuse), he could not follow the teacher's reasoning and asked foolish questions.

　註解　遲鈍的 (形容詞)

4602. He was renowned for his **rectitude** (uprightness) and integrity.

　註解　誠實 (名詞)

4603. The evangelist maintained that an angry Deity would exact **retribution** (vengeance) from the sinners.

　註解　報應 (名詞)

4604. He felt that everyone was trying to **thwart** (frustrate) his plans.

　註解　反對 (不定詞)

4605. She approached the guillotine with unfaltering (steadfast) steps.

　註解　堅決的 (形容詞)

4606. I am safely **vouchsafe** (guarantee) you a fair return on your investment.

　註解　擔保 (動詞)

4607. In Hindu mythology, the **avatar** (incarnation) of Vishnu is thoroughly detailed.

　註解　神明下凡 (名詞)

4608. His wit is the kind that **scintillates** (coruscates) and startles all his listeners.

　註解　閃光 (動詞)

4609. This mirage is an illusion; let us not be fooled by its **illusive** (deceiving) effect.

　註解　虛幻的 (形容詞)

4610. As a young boy, he was **lissome** (agile) and graceful; he gave promise of developing into a fine athlete.

  註解　敏捷的 (形容詞)

4611. The **sequacious** (ductile) members of Parliament were only too willing to do the bidding of their leader.

  註解　盲從的 (形容詞)

4612. It was not the aristocrat but the yeoman (middle-class farmer) who determined the nation's polocies.

  註解　自耕農，小地主 (名詞)

4613. The abolitionists **pleaded for** (advocated) freedom for the slaves.

  註解　提倡 (動詞)

4614. **Cosmic** (vast) rays derive their name from the fact that they bombard the earth's atmosphere from outer space.

  註解　宇宙的，浩大的 (形容詞)

4615. Upon the **demise** (death) of the dictator, a bitter dispute about succession topower developed.

  註解　死亡 (名詞)

4616. A strong odor of sulplur emanated (originated) from the spring.

  註解　發散，產生 (動詞)

4617. The **mores** (customs) of Mexico are those of Spain with some modifications.

  註解　關稅 (名詞)

4618. She offered a(n) **plethora** (excess) of reasons for her shortcomings.

  註解　過多 (名詞)

4619. The commanded "At EASE" does not permit you to take a **recumbent** (reclining) position.

  註解　休息的，斜躺的 (形容詞)

4620. The dog was intelligent and quickly learned to retrieve (recover) the game killed by the hunter.

  註解　恢復 (不定詞)

4621. The church leaders decided not to interfere in secular (worldly) matters.

  註解　世俗的 (形容詞)

4622. Why are we **vying** (contending) with each other for his favors?

  註解　競爭的 (形容詞)

4623. He was the kind of individual who would **hoodwink** (cozen) his friends in a cheap card game but remain eminently ethical in all his business dealings.
   > 註解 欺騙 (動詞)

4624. As the instigator of this heinous murder, he is as much **imbrued** (drenched) inblood as the actual assassin.
   > 註解 污染的 (形容詞)

4625. Man has always hurled **projectiles** (missiles) at his enemy whether in the form of stones or of highly explosive shells.
   > 註解 拋射物 (名詞)

4626. The captain maintained that he ran a **taut** (tight) ship.
   > 註解 拉緊的 (形容詞)

4627. Because of his **aesthetic** (artistic) nature, he was emotionally disturbed by ugly things.
   > 註解 愛美的 (形容詞)

4628. His nonchalance and **aplomb** (poise) in times of trouble always encouraged his followers.
   > 註解 沉著 (名詞)

4629. The medical examiner ordered an **autopsy** (postmortem) to determine the cause of death.
   > 註解 驗屍 (名詞)

4630. He was disliked because his manner was always full of **braggadocio** (boasting).
   > 註解 自誇 (名詞)

4631. He was **compliant** (yielding) and ready to conform to the pattern set by his friends.
   > 註解 順從的 (形容詞)

4632. One of the mayor aims of the air force was the complete **demolition** (destruction) of all means of transportation by bombing of rail lines and terminals.
   > 註解 破壞 (名詞)

4633. At first, the attempts of the Abolitionists to **emancipate** (set free) the slaves were unpopular in New England as well as in the South.
   > 註解 解放 (不定詞)

4634. Grass grew there, a(n) **exiguous** (small) outcropping among the rocks.

　　　註解　微小的 (形容詞)

4635. It is not until we reach the **finale** (conclusion) of this play that we can understand the author's message.

　　　註解　結局 (名詞)

4636. She wore a **garish** (gaudy) rhinestone necklace.

　　　註解　俗麗的 (形容詞)

4637. I resent his **haughtiness** (arrogance) because he is no better than we are.

　　　註解　驕傲 (名詞)

4638. I think it is **impolitic** (inexpedient) to raise this issue at the present time because the public is too angry.

　　　註解　不智的 (形容詞)

4639. She felt that they were **inimical** (unfriendly) and were hoping for her downfall.

　　　註解　不友善的 (形容詞)

4640. Tom and Betty were lost in the labyrinth (maze) of secret caves.

　　　註解　迷宮 (名詞)

4641. The doctors called the family to the beside of the **moribunded** (near death) patient.

　　　註解　將死的 (形容詞)

4642. The **occult** (mysterious) rites of the organization were revealed only to members.

　　　註解　神秘的 (形容詞)

4643. Before hanging wallpaper, it is advisable to drop a **plumb** (vertical) line from the ceiling as a guide.

　　　註解　垂直的 (形容詞)

4644. We must run this state dinner according to **protocol** (diplomatic etiquette) if weare to avoid offending any of our guests.

　　　註解　外交禮節 (名詞)

4645. The doctors were worried because the patient did not **recuperate** (recover) asrapidly as they had expected.

　　　註解　恢復 (動詞)

4646. The parents were worried because they felt their son was too quiet and **sedate** (grave).

註解　嚴肅的 (形容詞)

4647. She scolded him in a strident (creaking) voice.

註解　尖銳的 (形容詞)

4648. I believe we may best describe his **credo** (creed) by saying that it approximates the Golden Rule.

註解　信條 (名詞)

4649. The medicine man **eviscerated** (disembowel) the animal and offered the entrails to the angry gods.

註解　取出，切腹取腸 (動詞)

4650. This latest arrest will **exacerbate** (embitter) the already existing discontent of the people and enrage them.

註解　激怒 (動詞)

4651. For the two weeks before the examination, the student **immured** (imprison) himself in his room and concentrated upon his studies.

註解　幽禁 (動詞)

4652. The ash is so fine that it is **imperceptible** (impalpable) to the touch but it can be seen as a fine layer covering the window ledge.

註解　微小的，無法感觸到的 (形容詞)

4653. He exasperated the reporters by his lubricity (slipperiness); they could not pin him down to a definite answer.

註解　狡猾 (名詞)

4654. Many of us find English **orthography** (correct spelling) difficult to master because so many of our words are not written phonetically.

註解　正確拼字 (名詞)

4655. His **overweening** (presumptuous) pride in his accomplishments was not justified.

註解　自負的 (形容詞)

4656. In these days of automatic weapons, it is suicidal for troops to charge in **serried**(crowed) ranks against the foe.

註解　密集的 (形容詞)

4657. Until their destruction by fire in 83 B.C., the **sibylline** (oracular) books were often consulted by the Romans.

註解　神秘的 (形容詞)

4658. Although the critics deplored his use of mixed metaphors, he continued to write in **similitudes** (similarities).

註解　類似 (名詞)

4659. "Joyful happiness" is an illustration of **tautology** (pleonasm).

註解　重複語，冗言 (名詞)

4660. His **apocryphal** (sham) tears misled no one.

註解　虛偽的 (形容詞)

4661. To prepare for the emergency, they built an auxiliary (helper) power station.

註解　輔助的 (形容詞)

4662. The **bravado** (swagger) of the young criminal disappeared when he was confronted by the victims of his brutal attack.

註解　作威者 (名詞)

4663. Mathematics problems sometimes require much **cerebration** (thought).

註解　思考 (名詞)

4664. The Spanish Inquisition devised many demoniac (fiendish) means of torture.

註解　凶惡的 (形容詞，同 demoniacal)

4665. People avoided discussing contemporary problems with him because of his **disputatious** (argumentative) manner.

註解　好爭論的 (形容詞)

4666. His handwriting was **embellished** (adorned) with flourishes.

註解　修飾 (動詞，被動式)

4667. The **exodus** (departure) from the hot and stuffy city was particularly noticeable on Friday evenings.

註解　離開 (名詞)

4668. He hoped to **garner** (store up) the world's literature in one library.

註解　收藏 (不定詞)

4669. His snobbishness is obvious to all who witness his **hauteur** (haughtiness) when he talks to those whom he considers his social inferiors.

註解　傲慢 (名詞)

4670. I feel that you have not grasped the full **import** (significance) of the message sent to us by the enemy.

註解 重要性 (名詞)

4671. I cannot approve of the **iniquitous** (wicked) methods you used to gain your present position.

註解 不公平的 (形容詞)

4672. Her body was **lacerated** (mangled) in the automobile crash.

註解 裂傷的 (形容詞)

4673. His evil intentions were **manifest** (understandable) and yet we could not stop him.

註解 明白的 (形容詞)

4674. When we first meet Hamlet, we find him **morose** (sullen) and depressed.

註解 陰沉的 (形容詞)

4675. Do not **protract** (prolong) this phone conversation as I expect an important business call within the next few minutes.

註解 延長 (動詞)

4676. I think these regulations are too stringent (rigid).

註解 苛刻的 (形容詞)

4677. Long before he had finished his tirade (harangue) we were sufficiently aware of the seriousness of our misconduct.

註解 長篇演說 (名詞)

4678. Apply this **unguent** (ointment) to the sore muscles before retiring.

註解 軟膏 (名詞)

4679. Although he was reputed to be a crotchety (whimsical) old gentleman, I foundhis ideas substantially sound and sensible.

註解 古怪的 (形容詞)

4680. His **affiliation** (associating) with the political party was of short duration for he soon disagreed with his collegues.

註解 聯盟，關係 (名詞)

4681. Her **brazen** (insolent) contempt for authority angered the officials.

註解 無禮的 (形容詞)

4682. The judge was especially severe in his sentencing because he felt that the criminal had shown no **compunction** (remorse) for his heious crime.

註解 懊悔 (名詞)

4683. To **demur** (delay) at this time will only worsen the already serious situation; now is the time for action.

   註解 猶豫 (不定詞)

4684. The bank teller confessed his **embezzlement** (stealing) of the funds.

   註解 侵吞 (名詞)

4685. I am sure this letter will exonerate (exculpate) you.

   註解 免罪 (動詞)

4686. The old lady was **finicky** (fussy) about her food.

   註解 苛求的 (形容詞，同 finical)

4687. The **mortician** (undertaker) prepared the corpse for burial.

   註解 殯葬業者 (名詞)

4688. I find the task of punishing you most **odious** (hateful).

   註解 討厭的 (形容詞)

4689. The audience applauded as the **podium** (pedestal).

   註解 十全十美 (名詞)

4690. I am not afraid of a severe winter because I have stored a large quantity of **provender** (fodder) for the cattle.

   註解 牧草 (名詞)

4691. Even though it is February, the air is **redolent** (fragrant) of spring.

   註解 芳香的 (形容詞)

4692. In his **stupor** (daze), the addict was unaware of the events taking place around him.

   註解 昏迷 (名詞)

4693. **Titanic** (Gigantic) waves beat against the shore during the hurricane.

   註解 巨大的 (形容詞)

4694. Suckling asked, "why so pale and wan (pallid), fond lover?"

   註解 蒼白的 (形容詞)

4695. Let us be serious; this is not a ludicrous (laughable) issue.

   註解 可笑的 (形容詞)

4696. Mountain climbing at this time of year is temerarious (rash) and foolhardy.

   註解 不顧一切的，輕率的 (形容詞)

4697. He felt a(n) **affinity** (kinship) with all who suffered; their pains were his pains.

   註解 | 密切關係 (名詞)

4698. He was **averse** (reluctant) to revealing the sources of his information.

   註解 | 不願意的 (形容詞)

4699. He failed to **compute** (calculate) the interest.

   註解 | 計算 (不定詞)

4700. She was (coy) and reserved.

   註解 | 端莊的，害羞的 (形容詞)

4701. The man who married a dumb wife asked the doctor to make him deaf because of his wife's **garrulity** (talkativeness) after her cure.

   註解 | 嘮叨，多嘴 (名詞)

4702. To **imprecate** (curse) Hitler's atrocities is not enough; we must insure against any future practice of genocide.

   註解 | 詛咒 (不定詞)

4703. The duck was followed by his lackeys (footmen).

   註解 | 跟班 (名詞)

4704. She was so **mortified** (humiliated) by her blunder that she ran to her room intears.

   註解 | 受到羞辱的 (形容詞)

4705. Her **poignant** (piercing) grief left her pale and weak.

   註解 | 刺骨的，強烈的 (形容詞)

4706. The neighboring countries tried not to offend the Russians because they could be **redoubtable** (formidable) foes.

   註解 | 勇敢的 (形容詞)

4707. The nation was **seething** (boiling) with discontent as the noblemen continued their arrogant ways.

   註解 | 激昂的 (形容詞)

4708. The detective was **stymied** (stumped) by the contradictory evidence in the robbery investigation.

   註解 | 完全阻礙的 (形容詞)

4709. In his usual **maladroit** (bungling) way, he managed to upset the cart and spill the food.

   註解 | 笨拙的 (形容詞)

4710. It is extremely difficult to overcome the **tenacity** (persistency) of a habit such as smoking.

註解　固執 (名詞)

4711. In the **apothecaries'** (druggists') weight, twelve ounces equal one pound.

註解　藥劑師 (名詞)

4712. They found a **breach** (fissure) in the enemy's fortifications and penetrated their lines.

註解　裂縫 (名詞)

4713. He could understand the **covert** (implied) threat in the letter.

註解　暗示的 (形容詞)

4714. He became **embroiled** (entangled) in the heated discussion when he tried to arbitrate the dispute.

註解　牽連的 (形容詞)

4715. The mountain climbers secured footholds in tiny **fissures** (crevices) in the rock.

註解　裂縫 (名詞)

4716. Until the development of the airplane as a military weapon, the fort was considered **impregnable** (invulnerable).

註解　不能攻破的 (形容詞)

4717. The sounding of the alarm frightened the **marauders** (raiders).

註解　盜匪 (名詞)

4718. The poor test papers indicate that the members of this class have a **paucity** (scarcity) of intelligence.

註解　少量，缺少 (名詞)

4719. I am ready to accept your proposal with the **proviso** (stipulation) that you meet your obligations within the next two weeks.

註解　但書，附文，約定 (名詞)

4720. Do you mean to tell me that I can get no **redress** (remedy) for my injuries?

註解　補償 (名詞)

4721. The entire valley **reverberated** (echoed) with the sound of the church bells.

註解　回聲 (動詞)

4722. He is particularly good in roles that require **suavity** (urbanity) and sophistication.

   註解　柔和，文雅 (名詞)

4723. His **wanton** (unchaste) pride costs him many friends.

   註解　放縱的 (形容詞)

4724. I cannot undrestand your **tergiversation** (evasion); I was certain that you were devoted to our cause.

   註解　搪塞，藉口 (名詞)

4725. **Brevity** (Conciseness) is essential when you send a telegram or cablegram; you are charged for every word.

   註解　簡短 (名詞)

4726. Sometimes his flippant and **chaffing** (bantering) remarks annoy us.

   註解　開玩笑的，嘲弄的 (形容詞)

4727. The child was **covetous** (avaricious) by nature and wanted to take the toys belong to his classmates.

   註解　貪心的 (形容詞)

4728. The critic **emended** (amended) the book by selecting the passages which he thought most appropriate to the text.

   註解　修正 (動詞)

4729. Henry James was an American **expatriate** (exile) who settled in England.

   註解　被驅逐的人 (名詞)

4730. After several **spasmodic** (fitful) attempts, he decided to postpone the start of the project until he felt more energetic.

   註解　間斷的 (形容詞)

4731. I resent he **innuendos** (insinuations) in your statement more than the statement itself.

   註解　影射 (名詞)

4732. The sailor had been taught not to be **laggard** (sluggish) in carrying out orders.

   註解　落伍的，緩慢的 (形容詞)

4733. This simple **motif** (theme) runs throughout the entire score.

   註解　主題 (名詞)

4734. Browning informs us that the Duck resented the bough of cherries some **officious** (meddlesome) fool brought to the Duchess.

   註解　管閒事的 (形容詞)

4735. Only a **poltroon** (coward) would so betray his comrades at such a dangerous time.

   註解　膽小鬼 (名詞)

4736. your composition is **redundant** (repetitious); you can easily reduce its length.

   註解　反複的 (形容詞)

4737. He was awakened from his **reverie** (daydream) by the teacher's questions.

   註解　幻想 (名詞，同 revery)

4738. Although this book has a **semblance** (guise) of wisdom and scholarship, a careful examination will reveal many errors and omissions.

   註解　類似，外表 (名詞)

4739. The captain treated his **subalterns** (subordinates) as though they were children rather than commissioned officers.

   註解　僚屬 (名詞)

4740. The beggar was dirty and **unkempt** (disheveled).

   註解　蓬亂的 (形容詞)

4741. The **glorification** (apotheosis) of a Roman emperor was designed to insure his eternal greatness.

   註解　讚美 (名詞)

4742. His refusal to go with us filled us with **vexation** (chagrin).

   註解　苦惱 (名詞)

4743. She tried to **conciliate** (pacify) me with a gift.

   註解　安慰 (不定詞)

4744. We must wait until we **deplete** (exhaust) our present inventory before we order replacements.

   註解　用盡，消耗 (動詞)

4745. His sedentary life had left him with **flaccid** (flabby) muscles.

   註解　軟弱的 (形容詞)

4746. Hitler's **heinous** (atrocious) crimes will never be forgotten.

   註解　極惡的，殘忍的 (形容詞)

4747. He was constantly being warned to mend his **improvident** (thriftless) ways and begin to "save for a rainy day."

> 註解　無遠見的，不節儉的 (形容詞)

4748. She had an **inordinate** (unrestrained) fondness for candy.

> 註解　無節制的 (形容詞)

4749. The **maritime** (nautical) provinces depend on the sea for their wealth.

> 註解　靠近海的 (形容詞)

4750. The captain had gathered a **motley** (parti-colored) crew to sail the vessel.

> 註解　雜色的 (形容詞)

4751. His crime of **peculating** (embezzling) public funds entrusted to his care is especially damnable.

> 註解　侵吞 (動名詞)

4752. The room **reeked** (emitted) with stale tobacco smoke.

> 註解　充滿，發出 (動詞)

4753. He was avoided by all who feared that he would **revile** (vilify) and abuse them if they displeased him.

> 註解　辱罵 (動詞)

4754. It is not our aim to **subjugate** (conquer) our foe; we are interested only in establishing peaceful relations.

> 註解　征服 (不定詞)

4755. She knows she can **wheedle** (cajole) almost anything she wants from her father.

> 註解　甜言蜜語 (動詞)

4756. He stared, **agape** (openmounthed), at the many strange animals in the zoo.

> 註解　發呆的 (形容詞)

4757. Hamlet was uncertain about the identity the **apparition** (phantom) that had appeared and spoken to him.

> 註解　幽靈出現 (名詞)

4758. In a small room adjoining the cathedral, many ornately decorated **chalices** (goblets) made by the most famous European goldsmiths were on display.

> 註解　高腳酒杯 (名詞)

4759. She was **coy** (coquettish) in her answers to his offer.

> 註解　害羞的 (形容詞)

4760. The young man quickly **dissipated** (squandered) his inheritance.

> 註解　浪費 (動詞)

4761. The Romans used to **flagellate** (flogged) criminals with a whip that had three knotted strands.

> 註解　鞭打 (不定詞)

4762. This restaurant is famous and popular because of the **geniality** (kindliness) of the proprietor who tries to make everyone happy.

> 註解　誠懇 (名詞)

4763. They enjoyed their swim in the calm **lagoon** (lake).

> 註解　小湖 (名詞，同 lagune)

4764. The patent medicine man was a **mountebank** (charlatan).

> 註解　江湖郎中，騙子 (名詞)

4765. Many people in this country who admired dictatorships underwent a **revulsion**(reaction) when they realized what Hitler and Mussolini were trying to do.

> 註解　劇變 (名詞)

4766. I cannot understand what caused him to drop his **sensual** (carnal) way of life and become so ascetic.

> 註解　肉體上的 (形容詞)

4767. We must strive to **sublimate** (refine) these desires and emotions into worthwhile activities.

> 註解　昇華，精練 (不定詞)

4768. The only way to curb this **unruly** (disobedient) mob is to use tear gas.

> 註解　難控制的 (形容詞)

4769. The odors from the kitchen are **whetting** (sharppening) my appetite; I will be ravenous by the time the meal is served.

> 註解　刺激的 (形容詞)

4770. It took weeks to assort the agglomeration (heap) of miscellaneous items he had collected on his trip.

> 註解　一堆，大量 (名詞)

4771. The **crabbed** (peevish) old man was avoided by the children beacuse he scolded them when they made noise.

> 註解　好抱怨的 (形容詞)

TOEFL

4772. The encouraging cheers of the crowd lifted the team's **flagging** (drooping) spirits.

　註解　消沉的 (形容詞)

4773. I cannot **impugn** (gainsay) your honesty without evidence.

　註解　指責，否定 (動詞)

4774. I fall to understand the reason for your outlandish behavior; your motives are **inscrutable** (incomprehensible).

　註解　不可思議的 (形容詞)

4775. The **laity** (layman) does not always understand the clergy's problems.

　註解　門外漢 (名詞)

4776. The severity with which he was **pommeled** (beat 或 beaten) was indicated by the bruises he displayed on his head and face.

　註解　毆打 (動詞，被動式)

4777. After reading so many redundant speeches, I find his **aphoristic** (sententious) style particulary pleasing.

　註解　格言的，警語的 (形容詞)

4778. We must learn to recognize **sublime** (exalted) truths.

　註解　高尚的 (形容詞)

4779. Your levity is **unseemly** (indecent) at this time.

　註解　不適宜的 (形容詞)

4780. Peter Pan is a **whimsical** (quaint) play.

　註解　古怪的 (形容詞)

4781. He was **aghast** (horrified) at the news of the speaker who had insulted his host.

　註解　恐怖的 (形容詞)

4782. **Albeit** (Although) fair, she was not sought after.

　註解　雖然 (連接詞，同 Nevertheless)

4783. The **agility** (nimbleness) of the acrobat amazed and thrilled the audience.

　註解　敏捷 (名詞)

4784. The **aggregate** (sum) wealth of this country is staggering to the imagination.

　註解　總數 (名詞)

4785. He was amazed when the witches hailed him with his correct **appellation** (title).

　　註解　稱呼 (名詞)

4786. The police will **apprehend** (dread) the culprit and convict him before long.

　　註解　覺察 (動詞)

4787. He held his head **awry** (distorted), giving the impression that he had caught cold in his neck during the night.

　　註解　歪斜的 (形容詞)

4788. A **balmy** (fragrant) breeze refreshed us after the sultry blast.

　　註解　溫和的 (形容詞)

4789. His **baneful** (ruinous) influence was peared by all.

　　註解　毀滅的 (形容詞)

4790. His frequent use of cliches made his essay seem **banal** (hackeyed).

　　註解　平凡的 (形容詞)

4791. When the warden learned that several inmates were planning to escape, hetook steps to **balk** (foil) their attempt.

　　註解　阻止 (不定詞)

4792. She was forced to change her telephone number because she was **badgered** (pestered) by obscene phone calls.

　　註解　困擾 (動詞，被動式)

4793. She was offended by his **brusque** (blunt) reply.

　　註解　粗率的 (形容詞，同 brusk)

4794. In some states, it is illegal to dissect **cadavers** (corpses).

　　註解　屍體 (名詞)

4795. Some people seem to enjoy the **cacophony** (discord) of an orchestra that is tuning up.

　　註解　不調和的聲音 (名詞)

4796. The soldiers remembered the **buxom** (plump) nurse who had always been so pleasant to them.

　　註解　豐滿的 (形容詞)

4797. The meadow was the scene of **bucolic** (pastoral) gaiety.

　　註解　鄉村的 (形容詞，同 bucolical)

4798. Your deceitful tactice in this case are indications of **chicanery** (trickery).

    註解　奸計 (名詞)

4799. Dismayed by his **boorish** (churlish) manners at the party, the girls vowed never to invite him again.

    註解　粗野的 (形容詞)

4800. Do not place any **credence** (belief) in his promises.

    註解　相信 (名詞)

4801. We were surprised at his reaction to the failure of his project; instead of being **crestfallen** (dispirited), he was busily engaged in planning new activities.

    註解　沮喪的 (形容詞)

4802. The toothless **crone** (hag) frightened us when she smiled.

    註解　老巫婆 (名詞)

4803. The mountain climbers found footholds in the tiny **fissures** (crevices) in the mountainside.

    註解　裂縫 (名詞)

4804. The **depravity** (corruption) of his behavior shocked all.

    註解　墮落 (名詞)

4805. He was mentally **deranged** (insane).

    註解　精神錯亂的 (形容詞)

4806. They greeted his proposal with derision (ridicule) and refused to consider itseriously.

    註解　嘲笑 (名詞)

4807. A tour of this smokehouse will give you an idea of how the pioneers used to **desiccate** (dry up) food in order to preserve it.

    註解　弄乾 (不定詞)

4808. If you do not yield, I am afraid the enemy will **despoil** (plunder) the buildings.

    註解　掠奪 (動詞)

4809. To spit in the classroom is **despicable** (abject).

    註解　卑劣的 (形容詞)

4810. The soldiers **desecrated** (profaned) the temple.

    註解　污辱 (動詞)

4811. The **derelict** (abandoned) craft was a menace to navigation.

註解　廢棄的 (形容詞)

4812. After the **depredations** (plunderings) of the invaders, the people were penniless.

註解　毀滅，破壞 (名詞)

4813. Your **deprecatory** (disapproving) criticism has offended the author.

註解　不贊成的 (形容詞)

4814. Some contemporary musicians deliberately use **dissonance** (discord) to achieve certain effects.

註解　不協調 (名詞)

4815. The **distraught** (upset) parents searched the ravine for their lost child.

註解　憂心的 (形容詞)

4816. We could hear **divers** (differing) opinions of his ability.

註解　不同的 (形容詞)

4817. There are **diverse** (various) ways of approaching this problem.

註解　種種的 (形容詞)

4818. A farmer cannot neglect his **diurnal** (daily) tasks at any time; cows, for example, must be milked regularly.

註解　每日的 (形容詞)

4819. The spokes of the wheel **diverge** (vary) from the hub.

註解　脫出 (動詞)

4820. Because of his concentration on the problem, the professor often appeared **absentminded** (distrait) and unconcerned about routine.

註解　茫然的 (形容詞)

4821. He was **endued** (endowed) with a lion's courage.

註解　賦予，天賦 (動詞，被動式)

4822. This editorial will **engender** (cause) racial intolerance unless it is denounced.

註解　產生 (動詞)

4823. Despite all attempts to decipher the code, it remained an **enigma** (puzzle).

註解　謎題 (名詞)

4824. We shall have to **re-energize** (invigorate) our activities by getting new members to carry on.

註解　鼓舞 (不定詞)

4825. Some people **encumber** (burden) themselves with too much luggage when they take short trips.

註解　妨害，負荷 (動詞)

4826. Despite the teacher's scoldings and **expostulations** (remonstrances), the class remained unruly.

註解　告誡 (名詞)

4827. We must **extirpate** (root up) and destroy this monstrous philosophy.

註解　根除 (動詞)

4828. He found that he could not **extricate** (disentangle) himself from the trap.

註解　解脫 (動詞)

4829. Do not be fooled by **extrinsic** (external) causes. We must look for the intrinsic reason.

註解　外在的 (形容詞)

4830. If you behave, I will **expunge** (remove) this notation from your record.

註解　移除 (動詞)

4831. It is easier for us to **mitigate** (extenuate) our own shortcomings than those of others.

註解　緩和 (不定詞)

4832. The headstrong youth **mocked** (flouted) all authority; he refused to be curbed.

註解　嘲弄 (動詞)

4833. Her cheeks, **flecked** (spotted) with tears, were testimony to the hours of weeping.

註解　斑點 (動詞)

4834. He has an uncamny **flair** (talent) for discovering new artists before the public has become aware of their existence.

註解　本領，天才 (名詞)

4835. Modern architecture has discarded the **ornate** (flamboyant) trimming on buildings and emphasizes simplicity of line.

註解　華麗不實的 (形容詞)

4836. His complexion was even more **florid** (ruddy) than usual because of his anger.

註解　鮮紅的 (形容詞)

4837. Meteorologists watch the **fluctuations** (waverings) of the barometer in order to predict the weather.

    註解　波動 (名詞)

4838. The bodies of the highwaymen were **left** dangling from the **gibbet** (gallows) asa warning to other would be transgressors.

    註解　絞架 (名詞)

4839. The lawyer objected that the testimony **being** offered was not **germane** (pertinent) to the case at hand.

    註解　恰當的，有關係的 (形容詞)

4840. Her family was proud of its **gentility** (**refinement**).

    註解　文雅，高貴 (名詞)

4841. We are looking for a man with a(n) **genteel** (elegant) appearance who can inspire confidence by his cultivated manner.

    註解　有教養的，高雅的 (形容詞)

4842. Operatic performers are trained to make **exaggerated gesticulations** (gestures) because of the large auditoriums in which they appear.

    註解　做手勢，表情 (名詞)

4843. The snow began to fall in the **gloaming** (twilight) and continued all through thenight.

    註解　黃昏 (名詞)

4844. There was a **hiatus** (gap) of **twenty** years in the life of Rip van Winkle.

    註解　脫漏，中斷 (名詞)

4845. He was a **hirsute** (hairy) **individual** with a heavy black beard.

    註解　多毛的 (形容詞)

4846. **Homespun** (Domestic) wit like **homespun** cloth was often coarse and plain.

    註解　手織的，樸素的 (形容詞)

4847. His speeches were always **homilies** (**sermons**), advising his listeners to repent and reform.

    註解　講道，說教 (名詞)

4848. In **heterogeneous** (dissimilar) groupings, we have an unassorted grouping, while in homogeneous groupings we have **people** or things which have common traits.

    註解　不同種類的 (形容詞)

4849. Bears prepare for their long **hibernal** (wintry) sleep by overeating.

> 註解 寒冬的 (形容詞)

4850. He was proud of his **histrionic** (theatrical) ability and wanted to play the role of Hamlet.

> 註解 演劇的 (形容詞)

4851. By **inadvertence** (oversight), he omitted two questions on the examination.

> 註解 粗心 (名詞)

4852. He became **inarticulate** (speechless) with rage and uttered sounds without meaning.

> 註解 說不清楚的 (形容詞)

4853. The warden will **incarcerate** (imprison) the felon.

> 註解 監禁 (動詞)

4854. Your attitude is so fiendish that you must be a devil **incarnate** (personified).

> 註解 化身的 (形容詞)

4855. During the winter, **many** people were **incapacitated** (disabled) by respiratory ailments.

> 註解 不適於的 (形容詞)

4856. She was asked to **identify** the still and **inanimate** (lifeless) body.

> 註解 無生命的 (形容詞)

4857. The Declaration of Independence mentions the **nontransferable** (inalienable) rights that all of us possess.

> 註解 不可剝奪的 (形容詞)

4858. What are you trying to **insinuate** (imply) by that remarks?

> 註解 暗示 (不定詞)

4859. He refused to join us in a midnight cup of **coffee** because he claimed it gave him **wakefulness** (insomnia).

> 註解 不能入睡，失眠 (名詞)

4860. We will not discuss reforms until the **rebellious** (insurgent) troops have returned to their homes.

> 註解 反叛的 (形容詞)

4861. He was a man of great **integrity** (**purity**).

> 註解 正直 (名詞)

4862. In the face of **insurmountable** (**insuperable**) difficulties they maintained their courage and will to resist.
註解　不能克服的 (形容詞)

4863. I am afraid that this statement **will instigate** (provoke) a revolt.
註解　煽動 (動詞)

4864. When rumors of his **bankruptcy** (**insolvency**) reached his creditors, they began to press him for payment of the money dure them.
註解　破產 (名詞)

4865. The fifth column is **treacherous** (insidious) because it works secretly within our territory for our defent.
註解　叛逆的，陰險的 (形容詞)

4866. They sat quietly before the **flickering** (lambent) glow of the fireplace.
註解　閃耀的 (形容詞)

4867. This article **ridicules** (lampoons) the pretensions of some movie moguls.
註解　訕笑 (動詞)

4868. The hot, tropical weather created a feeling of languor (lassitude) and encouraged drowsiness.
註解　倦怠 (名詞)

4869. Many **lesions** (injuries) are the result of disease.
註解　傷害 (名詞)

4870. The stuffy room made him **drowsy** (lethargic).
註解　昏昏欲睡的 (形容詞)

4871. Such **levity** (lightness) is improper on this serious occasion.
註解　輕率 (名詞)

4872. He is a **lecherous** (unchaste) and wicked old man.
註解　好色的 (形容詞)

4873. The running water will **lave** (wash) away all stains.
註解　洗淨 (動詞)

4874. The power of a grain of wheat to grow into a plant remains **latent** (dormant) if it is not planted.
註解　潛在的，休眠的 (形容詞)

4875. The **lascivious** (lustful) books were confiscated and destroyed.
註解　淫亂的 (形容詞)

4876. Her siege of illness left her **sluggish** (languid) and pallid.

> 註解　呆滯的 (形容詞)

4877. Many animals display **maternal** (motherly) instincts only while their offspring are young and helpless.

> 註解　母親般的 (形容詞)

4878. The cast around the **matrix** (mold) was cracked.

> 註解　母體 (名詞)

4879. He felt his marriage was suffering because of his **meddlesome** (interfering) mother-in-law.

> 註解　愛管閒事的 (形容詞)

4880. We were disappointed because he gave a rather **mediocre** (ordinary) performance in this role.

> 註解　平凡的 (形容詞)

4881. The band played a **medley** (mixture) of Gershwin tunes.

> 註解　混合曲 (名詞)

4882. Italian is a **mellifluous** (smooth) language.

> 註解　流暢的 (形容詞)

4883. Let us **commemorate** (memorialize) his great contribution by dedicating this library in his honor.

> 註解　紀念 (動詞)

4884. From the moment we left the ship, we were surrounded by **mendicants** (beggars) and peddlers.

> 註解　乞丐 (名詞)

4885. We must **masticate** (chew) our food carefully and slowly in order to avoid stomach disorders.

> 註解　咀嚼，咬爛 (動詞)

4886. She reached her decision only after much **meditation** (reflection).

> 註解　沉思 (名詞)

4887. The captain tried to ascertain the cause of the **melee** (fight) which had broken out among the crew members.

> 註解　混戰 (名詞)

4888. Take this book as a **memento** (token) of your visit.

> 註解　紀念品 (名詞)

4889. For a moment he **mused** (pondered) about the beauty of the scene, but his thoughts soon changed as he recalled his own personal problems.

註解 沉思 (動詞)

4890. The attic was dark and **musty** (stale).

註解 發霉的 (形容詞)

4891. The **gloom** (murkiness) and fog of the waterfront in that evening depressed me.

註解 幽暗 (名詞)

4892. His opinions were **fickle** (mutable) and easily influenced by anyone who had any powers of persuasion.

註解 多變的 (形容詞)

4893. The torturer threatened to **maim** (mutilate) his victim.

註解 使殘廢 (不定詞)

4894. The captain had to use force to quiet his **unruly** (mutinous) crew.

註解 不守法的，背叛的 (形容詞)

4895. The monarch regarded himself as **omnipotent** (all-powerful) and responsible to no one for his acts.

註解 全能者 (名詞)

4896. I do not pretend to be **all-knowing** (omniscient), but I am positive about this item.

註解 全知的 (形容詞)

4897. The Ancient Mariner admired the **iridescent** (opalescent) sheen on the water.

註解 彩虹色的 (形容詞)

4898. I find your conduct so **opprobrious** (disgraceful) that I must exclude you from classes.

註解 可恥的 (形容詞)

4899. You have come at an **opportune** (timely) moment for I need a new secretary.

註解 及時的 (形容詞)

4900. I want something **opaque** (dark) placed in this window so that no one will be able to watch me.

註解 昏暗的，不透光的 (形容詞)

4901. He asked for an assistant because his work load was **burdensome**
(onerous).

> 註解　沉重的 (形容詞)

4902. What you say is **bookish** (pedantic) and reveals an unfamiliarity with the
realities of life.

> 註解　拘泥的，引經據典的 (形容詞)

4903. After reading these stodgy philosophers, I find his **transparent** (pellucid)
style very enjoyable.

> 註解　顯明的 (形容詞)

4904. He had a strong **penchant** (liking) for sculpture.

> 註解　愛好 (名詞)

4905. The **suspended** (pendent) rock hid the entrance to the cave.

> 註解　懸掛的 (形容詞)

4906. He was damned to eternal **damnation** (perdition).

> 註解　詛咒，全敗 (名詞)

4907. These plants are hardy **perennials** (lastings) and will bloom for many
years.

> 註解　終年不斷的 (形容詞)

4908. He overlooked many weaknesses when he inspected the factory in his
perfunctory (superficial) manner.

> 註解　草率的，表面的 (形容詞)

4909. He was a **parsimonious** (penurious) man, averse to spending money even
for the necessities of life.

> 註解　小氣的 (形容詞)

4910. When he realized the enormity of his crime, he became remorseful and
repentant (penitent).

> 註解　後悔的 (形容詞)

4911. The excited students dashed **pell-mell** (disorderly) into the stadium to
celebrate the victory.

> 註解　雜亂地 (副詞，同 pellmell)

4912. The king did not know what these omens might **presage** (portend) and
asked his soothsayers to interpret them.

> 註解　預兆 (名詞)

4913. I regard our present difficulties and dissatisfactions as **ominous** (portentous) omens of future disaster.

   註解 惡兆的 (形容詞)

4914. The **monarch** (potentate) spent more time at Monte Carlo than he did at home with his people.

   註解 帝王，君主 (名詞)

4915. I think this stock is a **precarious** (risky) investment and advise against its purchase.

   註解 危險的 (形容詞)

4916. The little girl **babbled** (prattled) endlessly about her dolls.

   註解 兒童語 (動詞)

4917. The board of directors decided that the plan was **practicable** (feasible) and agreed to undertake the project.

   註解 可實行的 (形容詞)

4918. He offered a **medley** (potpourri) of folk songs from many lands.

   註解 混合曲 (名詞)

4919. This juvenile delinquent is a(n) **potential** (inactive) murderer.

   註解 潛在的，可能的 (形容詞)

4920. The overweight gentleman wore suits in special sizes for **stout** (portly) figures.

   註解 肥胖的 (形容詞)

4921. It is difficult to delve into the **psyche** (soul) of a human being.

   註解 靈魂 (名詞)

4922. His **puerile** (childish) pranks sometimes offended his serious-minded friends.

   註解 稚氣的 (形容詞)

4923. We must keep his friendship for he will make a **puissant** (potent) ally.

   註解 有權勢的 (形容詞)

4924. He asked for **punitive** (punishing) measures against the offender.

   註解 處罰的 (形容詞，同 punitory)

4925. As **caterer** (purveyor) of rare wines and viands, he traveled through France and Italy every year in search of new products to sell.

   註解 供應糧食者，辦宴會者 (名詞)

4926. The sociological implications of these inventions are beyond the **purview** (scope) of this book.

> 註解   範圍，本文 (名詞)

4927. If the **purport** (intention) of your speech was to arouse the rabble, you succeeded admirably.

> 註解   主旨，意義 (名詞)

4928. Our **puny** (tiny) efforts to stop the flood were futile.

> 註解   很小的 (形容詞)

4929. As a child he was **combative** (pugnacious) and fought with everyone.

> 註解   好鬥的 (形容詞)

4930. I do not envy the judges who have to select this year's Miss America from this collection of female **comeliness** (pulchitrude).

> 註解   漂亮 (名詞)

4931. We could see the blood vessels in his temple **throb** (pulsate) as he became more angry.

> 註解   跳動 (名詞)

4932. The **caustic** (pungent) aroma of the smoke made me cough.

> 註解   腐蝕性的，刺鼻性的 (形容詞)

4933. We admired the **refulgent** (radiant) moon and watched it for a while.

> 註解   光亮的 (形容詞)

4934. He has a **regal** (royal) manner.

> 註解   忠誠的 (形容詞)

4935. I shall **reiterate** (repeat) this message until all have understood it.

> 註解   重複 (動詞)

4936. Let me know what you have spent and I will **reimburse** (repay) you.

> 註解   補償 (動詞)

4937. John **regaled** (entertained) us with tales of his adventures in Africa.

> 註解   分享，招待 (動詞)

4938. The **refractory** (unmanageable) horse was eliminated from the race.

> 註解   倔強的，未馴服的 (形容詞)

4939. He sang a **wanton** (ribald) song which offended many of us.

> 註解   胡亂的，下流的 (形容詞)

4940. In the face of the many rumors of scandal, which are **rife** (current) at the moment, it is best to remain silent.

> 註解　充斥的，眾多的 (形容詞)

4941. Many settlers could not stand the **severities** (rigors) of the New England winter.

> 註解　酷烈，嚴寒 (名詞)

4942. His remarks were so **ludicrous** (risible) that the audience howled with laughter.

> 註解　可笑的 (形容詞)

4943. The **rococo** (ornate) style in furniture and architecture, marked by scrollwork and excessive decoration, flourished during the middle of the eighteenth centry.

> 註解　洛可可式的，過度修飾的 (形容詞，歐洲流行)

4944. I am afraid you will have to alter your **roseate** (optimistic) views in the light of the distressing news that has just arrived.

> 註解　樂觀的 (形容詞)

4945. The candidate for the football team had a **robust** (vigorous) physique.

> 註解　強壯的 (形容詞)

4946. The plane was lost in the stormy sky until the pilot saw the city through a **rift** (break) in the clouds.

> 註解　裂縫 (名詞)

4947. Annabel Lee was buried in the sepulcher (tomb) by the sea.

> 註解　墳墓 (名詞，同 sepulchre)

4948. The **severance** (partition) of church and state is a basic principle of our government.

> 註解　分離 (名詞)

4949. By the time the police arrived, the room was a **slaughterhouse** (shambles).

> 註解　屠宰場 (名詞，同 slaughter house)

4950. We are often misled by **slogans** (shibboleths).

> 註解　標語，口號 (名詞)

4951. You will never get the public to buy such **sham** (shoddy) material.

> 註解　假的，冒充貨的 (形容詞)

4952. The criminal's ankles were **shackled** (fettered) to prevent his escape.

> 註解　腳鐐 (動詞，被動式)

4953. Uriah Heep was a very **cringing** (servile) individual.

> 註解　奉承的 (形容詞)

4954. The **placidity** (serenity) of the sleepy town was shattered by a tremendous explosion.

> 註解　平靜 (名詞)

4955. Although he had hoped for a long time to **segregate** (sequester) himself in a small community, he never was able to drop his busy round of activities in thecity.

> 註解　隔離 (不定詞)

4956. I heard of this **sub rosa** (privately) and I cannot tell you about it.

> 註解　秘密地 (副詞，拉丁語)

4957. I intend to **substantiate** (verify) my statement by producing of witnesses.

> 註解　證明 (不定詞)

4958. The **nicety** (subtlety) of his remarks was unnoticed by most of his audience.

> 註解　精細 (名詞，同 subtilty，subtitity)

4959. His remarks are always **succinct** (terse) and pointed.

> 註解　簡明的 (形容詞)

4960. He felt that it was beneath his dignity to **sully** (tarnish) his hands in such menial labor.

> 註解　污染 (不定詞)

4961. I cannot recall when I have had such a **sumptuous** (lavish) feast.

> 註解　奢侈的 (形容詞)

4962. My suspicions were aroused when I read **sundry** (several) items in the newspapers about your behavior.

> 註解　種種的，多樣的 (形容詞)

4963. In his **summation** (summary), the lawyer emphasized the testimony given by the two witnesses.

> 註解　總結 (名詞)

4964. We shall be ever grateful for the **succor** (assistance) your country gave us when we were in need.

> 註解　救助 (名詞，同 succour)

4965. As soon as we realized that you had won our support by a **pretense** (subterfuge), we withdrew our endorsement of your candidacy.

> 註解　藉口 (名詞，同 pretence)

4966. The king granted William Penn a **tract** (pamphlet) of land in the New World.

> 註解　區域，冊子 (名詞)

4967. You will find the children in this school very **docile** (tractable) and willing to learn.

> 註解　聽話的，溫順的 (形容詞)

4968. I am happy that my reputation is **unsullied** (untarnished).

> 註解　清白的 (形容詞)

4969. He was the **unwitting** (unintentional) tool of the swindlers.

> 註解　非故意的 (形容詞)

4970. His **fluctuation** (vacillation) when confronted with a problem annoyed all of us who had to wait until he made his decision.

> 註解　徘徊，猶疑不決 (名詞)

4971. She followed every **caprice** (vagary) of fashion.

> 註解　善變，奇怪行為 (名詞)

4972. He delivered an uninspired and **insipid** (vapid) address.

> 註解　乏味的 (形容詞)

4973. We are **vanguard** (forerunner) of a tremendous army that is following us.

> 註解　先驅 (名詞)

4974. The courtier was **urbane** (suave) and sophisticated.

> 註解　文雅的 (形容詞)

4975. I find your theory **untenable** (unsupportable) and must reject it.

> 註解　難獲支持的 (形容詞)

4976. By her **gracious** (winsome) manner, she made herself liked by everyone who met her.

> 註解　親切的，迷人的 (形容詞)

4977. I am afraid he will **wreak** (inflict) his wrath on the innocent as well as the guilty.

> 註解　發洩 (動詞)

4978. It must be a horrible experience to see a ghost; it is even more horrible to see the **wraith** (ghost) of a person we know to be alive.

註解 生魂 (名詞)

4979. As was his **wont** (custom), he jogged two miles every morning before going towork.

註解 習慣 (名詞)

4980. Merlin amazed the knights with his **sorcery** (wizardry).

註解 巫術 (名詞)

4981. Such **idiotic** (witless) and fatuous statements will create the impression that you are an ignorant individual.

註解 極笨的 (形容詞)

4982. He is as **wily** (artful) as a fox in avoiding trouble.

註解 狡詐的 (形容詞)

4983. After a **hectic** (too busy) year in the city, George was glad enough to return to the peace and quiet of the country.

註解 火紅的，興奮的 (形容詞)

4984. The loud, **raucous** (harsh) laughter of the troop irritated the lieutenant.

註解 粗啞的 (形容詞)

4985. Eventually, the criminal **expiated** (paid the penalty for) this murder and many other crimes on the gallows.

註解 補償，贖罪 (動詞)

4986. Despite the awesome **fecundity** (fruitfulness) of certain species of fish, the balance of nature limits the population.

註解 生殖力 (名詞)

4987. To the rest of us, the outlook just then seemed more ominous than **propitious** (favorable).

註解 有利的 (形容詞)

4988. **Subterranean** (Underground) temperatures are frequently higher than those above the surface of the earth.

註解 地下的 (形容詞，同 subterraneous)

4989. Because the official could not attend the meeting herself, she had send a **surrogate** (substitute), or deputy.

註解 代理人 (名詞)

4990. If the leaders felt any **compunction** (twinge of guilt) about planning and carrying out unprovoked attacks on neighboring countries, they showed no sign of it.

   註解　懊悔 (名詞)

4991. The treatment seemed to be worsening the skin condition rather than **ameliorating** (improving) it.

   註解　改善 (現在分詞)

4992. Watch for **concomitants** (accompaniments) of a severe head cold such as a feeling of tiredness and aches in the joints and muscles.

   註解　相伴物 (名詞)

4993. **Disparaging** (Belittling) remarks that belittle the faculty have no place in aschool campaign.

   註解　輕視的 (形容詞)

4994. To everyone's surprise, Rosa did not object to the plan; instead she **acquiesced**(agreed) at once.

   註解　默許 (動詞)

4995. The series of thefts called for **drastic** (extreme) action, for example, installingan alarm system and putting iron bars on all the windows.

   註解　徹底的 (形容詞)

4996. A law should not be **immutable** (unchangeable); rather, it should be changedwhen the times and the people demand it.

   註解　不變的 (形容詞)

4997. Michael looked at the dead roach on the shelf without trying to conceal his **repugnance** (disgust) or distaste.

   註解　嫌惡 (名詞)

4998. The overpowering odor of roses spread from room to room, **permeating** (spreading through) the whole house.

   註解　擴散 (現在分詞)

4999. Occasionally one of Judy's friends would **impose** (take advantage of) on her generosity.

   註解　利用 (動詞)

5000. It was like Harry never to think of the **orthodox** (conventional) solution to a problem.

   註解　傳統的 (形容詞)

國家圖書館出版品預行編目資料

TOEFL 托福字彙. 中冊／李英松著. --初版.--
新北市：李昭儀，2021.9
　　面；　公分
ISBN 978-957-43-9141-7（平裝）

1. 托福考試 2. 詞彙

805.1894　　　　　　　　　110012612

TOEFL托福字彙. 中冊

作　　者　李英松
校　　對　李英松、李昭儀
發 行 人　李英松
出　　版　李昭儀
　　　　　E-mail：lambtyger@gmail.com
　　　　　郵政劃撥：李昭儀
　　　　　郵政劃撥帳號：0002566 0047109
設計編印　白象文化事業有限公司
　　　　　專案主編：水邊　　經紀人：洪怡欣
代理經銷　白象文化事業有限公司
　　　　　412台中市大里區科技路1號8樓之2（台中軟體園區）
　　　　　出版專線：（04）2496-5995　　傳真：（04）2496-9901
　　　　　401台中市東區和平街228巷44號（經銷部）
　　　　　購書專線：（04）2220-8589　　傳真：（04）2220-8505
印　　刷　普羅文化股份有限公司
初版一刷　2021 年 9 月
定　　價　400 元

白象文化
www.ElephantWhite.com.tw

印書小舖
PressStore出版總統

出版・經銷・宣傳・設計
f 自費出版的領導者　購書 白象文化生活館